BETWEEN

THE

VEIL

THE THINGS UNSEEN

WRITTEN BY

DANIEL HOLDINGS

EDITED BY
LINDA LEMIEUX

COVER BY
JD HOPWOOD

TABLE OF CONTENTS

Dedication

Acknowledgements

Preface

Quote

Internet References

About The Author

For Pop,
Now On The Other Side Of The Veil,
But Missed

Acknowledgements

To my biggest critics and my greatest supporters, my wife Vickie, and my daughter Sarrah, I could not do what I do, nor be the man that I am, without these two wonderful women in my life. I love you two!

A heartfelt thank you to my Pop, Vickie's Dad, who became my own father over the thirty plus years that I knew him. Although he's gone, his lessons and wisdom keeps on giving.

A very warm thank you to my editor, Linda Lemieux, whose keen insight and attention to detail have made this book so much better than it would have been without her.

In the same vain, thank you to JD Hopwood who's brutal honesty and creative gifting helped craft a fitting cover for the words contained herein.

Thank you to my friend Larry Taylor who allowed me to loosely portray him as a character in this novel. Although this author has taken creative liberties, much of the Larry Taylor storyline is a combination of stories and conversations with Larry himself!

Watchman Steve Quayle was, and is, a wealth of information in the development of this book. His tireless efforts on warning people have been instrumental in preparing those who will listen for those things that are coming upon the earth. I appreciate his friendship and support.

The term "The Great Deception" is not my own, but borrowed with permission from L.A. Marzulli's series The Nephilim Trilogy and specifically the book, The Unholy Deception. LA has had a great deal of influence in my work and my life and his persistence in teaching people about the supernatural is tireless. He was the first Watchman that I ever spoke to when I was waking up and I so much appreciate his friendship and insight.

A warm thank you to Doug Hagmann of the Hagmann & Hagmann Report for his endorsement of this book and his support. He and Joe are on the frontlines and I am grateful for these men of courage.

Thanks to my friend "Big Brain" Stan Deyo for the idea about the Tower of Babal and Nimrod and for other technical issues. I've learned so much from this man and his wife Holly. Thank you both!

Thank you to my Hermano, Alvaro Mora and his daughter Stephanie for allowing me to make them characters in the novel. Thank you also to Dave Duckett whom I've roughly based the Goose character on.

Although I have neither met nor spoke to Tom Horn, I am so grateful for his and Cris Putnam's in depth work on ExoVaticana. In addition, much of my insight about transhumanism was gleaned from Tom's lectures and writings.

No one could do what I do without support. That friendship and encouragement comes in many different ways. The list of people who have helped with this project is way too long to put here - But you know who you are! Thank you!!!

To my faithful readers – Thank you for deeming my work worthy of your time and imagination.

Last, but certainly not least, I am most grateful for the God who inspires, directs, teaches and provides. He is the Author and Finisher of my faith and I am forevermore changed by the things that He has helped me to understand. I hope that those supernatural insights change you too.

PREFACE

Between The Veil (BTV) is a cacophony of information, much of it true, woven into a story that is designed to change your paradigm. Some of it will challenge you; some of it will entertain you and some of it may frustrate you. Nonetheless, contained herein are nuggets of pure gold that you will find if you take the time to mine them.

Although I walk with the Creator of the Universe, this book is not designed to be religious. That said, it would be impossible to speak about extra-dimensional realities and not acknowledge the God who created them.

I believe that everything in scripture is true. Yet, there are things that we simply cannot understand - This side of The Veil. However, with the clearer understanding of science, specifically physics, I believe that the unseen world, the one that lay in dimensions adjoining to our own, will be easier to fathom – If we have the courage to look. Consequently, in a break from the "pop culture" way that the Bible and its tenets are portrayed in the mainstream, this novel is designed specifically to help you see things… differently.

The hyperlink Internet references have been painstakingly sought out to illustrate this fictional story. They are not exhaustive, but designed to encourage you to look deeper into those issues. But be careful, not all of them are good things.

My strong suggestion is that you read through the story once and resist the temptation to follow each and every link. Then, after you finish BTV, go back through it and freely jump around. In approaching the story this way, you'll be able to follow it without getting lost.

Lastly, I would be remiss if I failed to mention the days in which we are living. Many of the issues represented in BTV are real and perhaps frightening to people. However, unless we know what is truly going on in the world, we will not be able to prepare ourselves, or our families, for those things coming upon the earth.

You cannot get much of this information in mainstream media or even at your local church. While BTV is classified as fictional entertainment, it is this author's hope that you will find it helpful in understanding a world on fire.

I hope that you enjoy your journey through the things unseen as you walk…

Between the Veil…

DANIEL HOLDINGS

IN ORDER TO MORE FULLY UNDERSTAND THIS
REALITY, WE MUST TAKE INTO ACCOUNT OTHER
DIMENSIONS OF A BROADER REALITY.

John Archibald Wheeler
Physicist

BETWEEN

THE

VEIL

PROLOGUE

<u>SINAR – 3500 BC</u>

T he howling wind tore angrily at his crimson-red cape, whipping and tugging at it like two jackals fighting over the dead carcass of a fresh kill.

Nimrod was the greatest leader and king that the world had ever seen. He was a head taller than any of his people, and had never lost a battle. To prove this immortality, both to himself and the so-called Most High, he stood in broad-shouldered defiance, arms out and balancing himself at the current apex of this monument, the largest Tower to ever be built, daring this God to knock him off.

That which made him great was a secret known to only a handful of people. When the first man, Adam, had realized his nakedness in the Garden of Eden, God fashioned clothing for His creation to cover himself.

It was thought that these garments had magical qualities and as a consequence, they had been handed down to each succeeding generation. Preserved even through the Great Flood by Noah on the Ark, they finally ended up in the hands of Nimrod.

At the age of twenty, he became the first one in all of the generations since Adam to actually put the garments on. The results had been immediate. He became stronger, faster, wiser and more cunning than any other mortal being.

Commotion from the platform below caught his attention. He squinted downward just in time to see a group of jeering men shooting arrows at the setting sun.

A common practice, his people's attitude toward the God of Heaven mirrored his own. Like Nimrod, his people thought more of themselves than mere servants of an entity which they could not see or touch.

He took in the sight of the wide Tower under his feet.

Already hundreds of cubits tall, this would not be the highest point of the Tower. They would continue to add to its height until it reached into the very heavens of The Most High, El Elyon, and then… they would slay Him.

Nimrod commanded his people to build the Tower using brick instead of stone and tar instead of mud, layer upon layer. Each level became self-sustaining and was used to fabricate more materials so that the structure could be built even taller.

It was already the height of a mountain, far taller than any man made structure. His people thought of him as a wise and powerful leader, able to accomplish anything he'd set his hand to. And why shouldn't they?

He was king over all the people of the earth and his kingdom was unified because everyone on earth spoke the same language. This ability to communicate enabled the people to have common goals – his goals.

He'd gathered together all the leaders of his kingdom, Phut, Mitzraim, Cush and Canaan, along with their families, to plan the greatest project of his adventurous life.

His mind drifted back to the conversation. The group sat transfixed and awestruck at his brilliance as he painted a verbal picture of a grand city to dwarf all other cities. In the center of that great city would be a Tower larger than any mountain. Such a mammoth Tower would bring his people fame, he told them, and the world would talk about their accomplishment.

They agreed and set right to work.

However, unbeknownst to his people, this plan was not his own. The Others had inspired and instructed him on how to build the great Tower and its surrounding city. They also told him of the special powers that the

Tower would possess.

[1]They spoke of a road system in the heavens with which one could travel to distant places, even beyond the visible world. They told stories of how they moved in and out, between the seen and unseen, between heaven and earth itself. They talked of how this gave them power to wield their will over mankind.

The Others called the gates to these invisible roads "portals" and said that they were located in the high places. They said that many of these portals occurred naturally, but that they also had the knowledge to create them. Most of these gates were in the sky which was why the Tower had to be so tall.

He didn't fully understand their knowledge, but it didn't matter. He saw what they could do and that was enough. Once he had these portals for himself, nothing would stop him.

The Tower was far from complete despite the fact that they'd been working on it for dozens of years. Already far taller than any other man-made structure, building materials were brought up on a daily basis. However, the transporters of those materials started out weeks in advance in order to reach the top.

The swarms of willing and enthusiastic workers carried bricks, wood and other exotic material up the winding road to the various places that needed to be finished. Some workers were tasked with the finishing work, while others continued to build the main structure taller.

Yet Nimrod could not have known that the One True God would see the evil in his heart and would put a stop to his madness.

Construction on The Tower of Babel would be stopped and Nimrod's people scattered. No longer would they all be able to speak the same language and as a consequence of their previous exploits, war and death followed them.

Still, in spite of the confusion brought by El Elyon... the portals remain.

- PART I -
NEW REALITIES

ONE

His bare feet slid across warm, dark, dingy glass.

Bryce Cooper listened hard but he didn't hear anything – no people, no animals, no birds or even bugs. This place was as barren of life as the empty landscape around him.

It's not just barren, Cooper thought. *It's like all the life that was here was sucked out of this place.*

The scarred, flat plane looked to be scorched black in many places.

Cooper wrinkled his nose. *What is that smell?*

A pungent odor pervaded the air, like a million match books snuffed out, leaving only the sulfury stench remaining.

"What is this place?" Bryce asked his silent Companion. "Was it destroyed in the past, or will it be in the future?"

The Companion waved his hand in a sweeping motion, "This place was destroyed while you were away. It is what the prophet warned about millennia ago."

Cooper twisted his mouth tightly, "I've read what the prophets said, but I don't remember this."

"When the bomb fell, all of this city's inhabitants were killed."

"Bombs?" the physicist asked, slowly understanding.

"Yes. The force was so powerful that it laid waste to every structure, every tree and every hill. Its fire was so intense that it turned the sand that you are walking on to smooth, blackened glass."

The revelation made Bryce want to look up into his Companion's face, but he couldn't. It wasn't just reverence that didn't allow him to look in the Companion's face, but also some invisible weight that the physicist felt at being in His presence. A holiness and a majesty accompanied this man that was clad in a simple white robe and sandals.

Who am I that I should even be talking to Him, Cooper wondered to himself? *I don't have to look at Him to hear the pain in his voice. All of these people, those lives... gone.*

"The radiation caused by those bombs will remain for centuries," Bryce's Host said, "No one will ever live here again."

A verse out of the Book of Isaiah flashed through Cooper's photographic memory. He looked off at the miles of wasteland before him and felt tears begin to puddle in his eyes as he pulled Isaiah 17:1-3 from the pages of his mind. He read aloud:

> *"The burden of Damascus. Behold, Damascus is taken away from being a city, and it shall be a ruinous heap. The cities of Aroer are forsaken: they shall be for flocks, which shall lie down, and none shall make them afraid. The fortress also shall cease from Ephraim, and the kingdom from Damascus, and the remnant of Syria: they shall be as the glory of the children of Israel, saith the Lord of hosts."*

"We..." Bryce stammered at the realization, "we... we're in... we're in Damascus?" He looked around again as a tear rolled down his cheek. "At least, what was Damascus."

"Yes, Bryce. You are correct. What was warned of by the Prophet has now come to pass."

Bryce bit his lip, "All those people..."

Slowly Cooper's head rose until he met the Companion's gaze. His breath caught in his throat and he wanted to look away, but he willed himself to gaze into his host's eyes.

This was the fullest view that the Montanan had of the One who stood before him. His eyes were like fire and his hair was white as snow.

"So," Cooper asked, "This is it then? It's started?"

A deep sorrow that the Companion carried with him was etched on his face, "Time is at an end," He said, "I did not want this, but I warned that when you see all of these things, My coming would be soon. Those things that I've allowed you to be part of, all of these things that you've seen and heard even before you knew Me, are ushering in the time of the end.

"More will happen before history's conclusion. Many will suffer, but these things must occur. You have been chosen to bring about some of these events. You will not be able to stop them, but you must warn everyone who will listen and you must do all I have told you to."

Bryce considered the glass under his bare feet. *Who am I that He should choose me? What can I do?*

Cooper still had the Garments on and wasn't wearing shoes. The Garments were a reconstructed version of the Jewish High Priest's garments from Solomon's Temple and made of fine linen, gold and precious gems.

Before the Reset, and back when he was the Team Leader at the Large Hadron Collider, or LHC, in Geneva, he'd made the Garments for use in his ATLAS 7 experiment. ATLAS stood for "A Toroidal LHC Apparatus" and the seven denoted the seventh time that the experiment had run.

In an effort to disguise the fact that he simply duplicated the Garments, he called them the Harmonic Particle Refractor, or simply the Refractor. Bryce used the Garments to accentuate the harmonic frequencies of particles in order to make them easier to track in the experiment. To his surprise, he found that they had interdimensional properties that had now come into play, which explained the reason for his wearing them this day.

After the Reset, he removed the sensors that were incorporated in the Garments, and stored them behind glass. The priests of The Temple Reconstruction Movement called him last week and asked if they could borrow them.

How the priests knew about the Garments, and why they wanted to use them, surprised Bryce and he determined to hand-deliver them to Israel.

In Solomon's Temple, as directed by the Torah, the Holy of Holies is where the Ark of the Covenant was kept. This small room was separated from the rest of the Temple by a Veil, or curtain. Once a year, the High Priest was instructed to enter into the Holy of Holies, beyond the Veil, to represent the Hebrew nation's needs before God.

In modern-day Jerusalem, a historic Third Temple had been constructed on The Temple Mount, complete with the original Ark of the Covenant, which had been recovered intact, only weeks ago.

The new Temple's priests wanted to use Cooper's Garments to enter the Holy of Holies. However, when Bryce got to Jerusalem, the Temple priests told him that they were convinced that it was he, Cooper, who was supposed to enter into the Holy of Holies with the Garments.

Cooper didn't understand this request. Bryce was Jewish and a descendent of the first High Priest, Aaron. Although it would have been an honor to represent the Jewish people before the Ark, he wasn't a practicing Jew. To complicate matters, the physicist had come to believe in Yeshua as the Messiah. That made Cooper a Christian.

Still, they insisted that he had to go. Apparently an angel had appeared to them and thoroughly convinced them.

As they requested, he went before the recovered Ark of the Covenant and when be placed the Urimm and Thumimm together, he disappeared and ended up here, in Damascus.

Still considering the ground, Cooper looked at his host's feet. They were very tanned, almost like bronze. He also saw the scars there, not exactly on his feet, but where the foot met the ankle.

You must have been in agony, Bryce thought.

He swallowed hard, "But who am I Lord? I didn't even believe in you until a couple of years ago. I don't deserve Your trust."

His Companion knew his thoughts and placed a reassuring hand on Bryce's shoulder. Cooper felt a tingling shock at His touch as warmth flowed from the top of his head to the tips of his toes. Never before had Bryce felt the kind of unconditional love as he did at that moment.

"Look at Me, Bryce."

The Companion's voice was gentle, but Cooper felt its power… its life. The physicist could hardly stand, but he pulled his head up to look into His eyes.

"It is enough that you believe now. I have chosen you. You will be able to do this. I will help you. Do you remember the vision you had when you fell off your horse?"

The Montanan's eyes narrowed at the memory, "Yes… yes I do."

Lazy Hoof – Three Days Ago

Shooting stars of color sprayed in all directions like celebratory Independence Day festivities. The colors faded into hot, white sprigs that diminished and melted into his peripheral view.

He was floating in the air above the outskirts of Geneva, Switzerland. He could see the snowcapped Alps glistening under the sun. A cool breeze blew, but he wasn't cold. The day was clear and crisp and the sky was a vibrant blue.

Hovering at a couple thousand feet, he had a clear field of view of the CERN facility and the surrounding farmlands. CERN's name was taken from a now-defunct acronym of a previous French agency which was currently known as the European Organization for Nuclear Research.

Buried under those farmlands at almost six-hundred feet below ground was the [2]LHC. The world's most powerful particle accelerator with its seventeen-mile, circular beam tunnel was commonly referred to in pop-culture as an "atom-smasher".

Cooper knew the area well and he mused about his former life as he floated, unaided in the sky. Activity on the ground caught his attention and he willed himself to go lower for a better look.

From this vantage point, he saw small specks moving in and out of the main CERN building, L1. Although, they looked no bigger than pixels on a screen, he knew them to be people.

A blur of movement caught his eye as the LHC's entire seventeen-mile beam tunnel began to rotate counterclockwise.

As it spun, the natural colors of white, brown and green began to smudge and bleed together, making everything in this vortex blend into a dull gray color.

Then it struck him: *It's a portal opening from the power of the accelerator deep below the surface.*

From the center of the swirling vortex, black vapor spat in erratic squirts. The blackness continued until it became an increasing ooze of a tar-like substance. Like a spigot that had been turned on all the way, the dark substance rushed as a torrent, blotting out all other colors below.

The blackness jelled and become a thick, black membrane.

Movement in the corner of his eye caught Cooper's attention. He looked up just in time to see a white light streaking down to earth.

Is that a falling star? No, not a meteor… more like lightning. Lightning in the middle of the day?

It was headed for the exact center of the churning black membrane.

Not knowing exactly what to expect with the collision, Bryce was surprised that it made no sound as it struck and was instantly absorbed, leaving no trace.

Well, that was unimpressive.

He spoke too soon. The lightning strike appeared to cause the blackness to grow exponentially. Faster and faster it stretched in all directions and then the black circle began to climb.

Uh oh!

As the spectacle arose, Cooper realized that it was not a liquid or solid mass, but the joining of individual giant beings who were midnight-black in color and too numerous to count. Soon the grotesque creatures rose to the same height in the sky that he was and now he could clearly see them for what they were.

Soot-covered, the black-winged creatures looked like gargoyles with massive muscles bulging from humanoid bodies. Their eyes were blood-red and rage and anger were etched deeply into their contorted faces.

Cooper knew exactly who and what they were, because he had seen their type before.

"Can this get any worse?" Bryce muttered.

With an unexpected, sudden violence, he was jerked from that place to find himself floating in space, in front of a massive ball of fire.

It was the sun and it was hot.

Intellectually he knew that he couldn't get burned. After all, he reasoned, I'm in outer space with no oxygen or space suit. Yet, somehow that didn't really make him feel any better.

Gazing beyond the spastically flaming orange and yellow ball, he could see billions of stars in the distance. His attention was brought back to the sun's violent eruptions of molten plasma.

Like flaming fingers moving over the surface of the sun in a rhythmic display, the glowing feelers danced and shifted in a choreographed ballet over the sun's surface.

"That's beautiful."

As Bryce watched in awe, beauty was replaced by something else.

Speckles began to form on the orange and yellow burning plasma ball. Those little deformities grew into holes, or more accurately, dents of darkness all over the sun.

The dents spread even further until they gave the sun a rough, honeycombed, sphere-like appearance rather than its normal, round solid mass.

I've never seen sunspots like that.

The metamorphosis continued as the untouched plasma between some of the dark dents began to fester, twist and stretch into long, stringy lines that, while still attached at both ends, flipped and vibrated wildly as the colors swapped between red, orange and yellow.

One by one, these plasma filaments multiplied all over the solar disk, connecting long strings of fire that flipped and twisted between the original dark dents.

What in the world?

By the time that the filaments were done connecting, before him stood a giant, round, molten, ball in space that resembled more of a flaming, spherical spider web than the earth's sun.

At the web's completion, the filaments began to destabilize as they snapped and whipped hot, red and orange string fibers off the sun and hurled them into space. Gaining momentum, spitting fire leaped out as plasma projectile after projectile was flung in every direction.

Absorbed by the scene in front of him, he watched as a flare ripped off of the sun from a particularly active region, just below the sun's equator. Cooper turned and followed the helium and hydrogen missile with his eyes for a while as it shot out into space.

Crack!

From his side and slightly behind him, Cooper jerked his head back to the front just in time to see a fiery finger aimed right for him.

He darted to the side and heard a SWOOSH and felt heat as the solar bolt zipped past him.

"That was close!"

Before him, the flare's fire spread out and expanded as it headed... directly for earth.

"No!"

Cooper reared up and bolted.

He overtook the CME and reached earth's atmosphere long before the strike. Bryce couldn't help but take in the beauty of the planet as he hovered in the air, "More than just a spinning globe in history class," he said, taking in the blue sphere's majesty.

Checking behind him, he saw that the flare was still a long way off.

As he spun forward again, it surprised him that the rotating black membrane had grown significantly. Although it hadn't yet covered the whole earth, he did see other smaller spinning black circles, sprouting up across the globe.

Those can't be coming from particle accelerators, he thought. There's not that many. What could generate pools of blackness like that? No... not just blackness, darkness... evil. It won't be long until the whole earth's covered.

Another sight that stunned him; the earth, still tilted on its axis, began to wobble and shake violently, like a drunkard stumbling.

Plumes and pillars of gray and black smoke belched up into the Earth's atmosphere. The puffs were replaced by billowing fire that rolled up into the sky.

The earth's crust is destabilizing.

The ground shook and shifted violently as the core of the earth became super-heated and started to expand. Severe volcanic activity and mega earthquakes began to rip the planet apart.

"No! Please!"

Mesmerized by the horrific scene, Cooper was caught off guard as a huge wall of water welled up in the area of the Alaskan Aleutian Islands. It rolled and kept building before it reached the Pacific coast of North America. The tsunami wiped out everything in its path.

"Oh God..." he moaned in horror.

He floated closer to the ground. He was a few hundred feet up in the air and could see war and death break out on every continent. There was widespread looting and people were killing each other.

He saw civilians killing the military and the military killing civilians. He saw militaries under the same flag killing and fighting amongst themselves. In every part of the world, countries were at war and death was consuming the planet.

"No…"

Suddenly pillars of red exploded in various countries throughout the earth. From those pillars rose huge mushroom clouds.

He closed his eyes, "NO! STOP!"

When he opened them again, he saw that the darkness that originated from the LHC had now enveloped the whole Earth.

He watched as the last mushroom cloud towered above South Korea, and then it disappeared under the ubiquitous darkness that now wrapped the whole Earth.

A roar from behind him caused him to jerk to the side automatically.

[3]The CME almost sideswiped him. As it hit, the fire scorched the earth like a blow torch.

He was crying now, tears freely flowing down his cheeks.

A piercing ringing in his ears tore him away from the scene and Cooper became aware that the back of his head felt like it was on fire.

Then he opened his eyes.

Damascus, Syria - Present Day

Unconsciously, the owner of the Lazy Hoof Ranch in Missoula, Montana, Dr. Bryce Obadiah Cooper, rubbed his backside at the memory.

The vision, or dream, or hallucination occurred while he was in the middle of trying to break one of his Quarter Horses on the ranch. He was bucked off the horse in the middle of a corral and landed on his butt, hitting his head.

At the time, Cooper thought that the fall had knocked him out, but his ranch manager, Danny Mendez and his best friend, Mac, had rushed to his side the instant he was bucked off. They told him that he never lost consciousness, but the vision felt like it lasted a very long time. Now he stood with the Companion as he recounted the vivid lingering memory.

Much had happened over the last few days, giving validity to those things he'd seen. There had been earthquakes and tsunamis. Wars had sprouted overnight. Nuclear bombs had been dropped. And a spiritual darkness had descended over the entire world.

Recalling a part of the vision, in more of a statement than a question, Cooper said, "Lord, that darkness… it started at the LHC."

Knowing his thoughts, sadness filled his Companion's face, "That is correct. However, much more will happen. These things are necessary. You will be used to implement some of those things. You cannot stop what is coming. But you will be used to bring about the fulfillment of what the prophets warned about for centuries. Now, you must go on your journey. The one who has been with you all along, will help when needed."

"My journey, Lord?"

"Yes. You have several appointments that you must keep. Only you can accomplish them on my behalf."

"Appointments?" Bryce asked in surprise. "Where… how will I get there?"

For the first time, his Companion smiled warmly, "Between the Veil, all things are possible."

TWO

If Dr. Bryce Obadiah Cooper was anything, it was pragmatic. He'd won the Nobel Prize a few years ago for his Dimensional Theory. He'd published many scientific papers in various physics disciplines and was considered the preeminent voice in the science world.

At 5'11", broad-shouldered and fit, he worked out regularly and possessed enough informal training by his Uncle Joe in the martial art of Aikido to easily be classified as a second-degree black belt.

From the rurals of Montana, his wavy, sandy brown hair, hazel eyes and cleft chin indicated a hodgepodge of genetic soup. Down the line, his mother heralded from Jewish ancestors who came over to the New World with Christopher Columbus. To add to the mix, Bryce's great grandfather, on his father's side, was a Blackfoot Indian called Wolf Eyes.

Because of that distant Native American heritage, Bryce maintained an ever-present tan. His gene pool also bespoke to his sure dexterity in the outdoors, even temperament and conservative mindset.

Nevertheless, the brilliant physicist had seen many strange things in the last few years that defied "normal" explanation. He'd come to accept many unusual phenomena that were not readily explained by science.

Dark, filtered light showed through the glass ceiling and danced off the shiny metallic-looking walls and floor.

"Where are we?" Cooper asked Gabe.

"Just off the Yemen coast. Under the Gulf of Aden."

"I, I don't understand," Bryce blinked rapidly, "Unnnddderrrr the Gulf of Aden? We're underwater?"

"Yes," Gabe pointed through a wall of windows, "This is a portal. [4]A stargate, if you will."

"A stargate? You mean like on television?"

Gabe's eyebrows raised in amusement, "Not quite like on television. Watch."

A huge circle on the bottom of the sea began to glow faintly, becoming brighter until it lit up the entire seabed. A metallic edge slowly pushed through the ocean floor. It rose inch by inch until a disk-shaped object filled the illuminated circle.

Bryce's mouth gaped open in disbelief as a UFO the size of a suburban house emerged from the gate. When it was fully through, it moved slowly away from the circle until it was out of sight. Only then did the light go dark.

Cooper was dumbstruck and stared out the window for a long time in silence. Gabe let him process what he'd just observed. Finally he turned back to his Companion, and said, "Well... that's something you don't see every day."

"That is something that most humans wouldn't believe if they saw it," Gabe added.

"You got that right. So that's a stargate?"

"That's a stargate."

"And let me guess, those aren't the Fallen?"

Gabe shook his head, "Not the Fallen, but you are half right."

"The Nephilim then?"

"That's right. Their genetically modified life forms anyway."

"Genetically modified... come on. Give me a break. What are you talking about?"

"You will see. Come, follow me."

The illuminated being and the physicist walked into the light.

BELOW GROUND, RAF LAKENHEATH, UK – PRESENT DAY

"Come on!!! Wake up!," Bryce said, as he slapped and shook the pale face of the man strapped to the operating table. Finally the man stirred.

"Wha... what's going on?" he stammered in a weak, raspy voice. "Who are you?"

Cooper looked over his shoulder at Gabe, who was standing by the door. In his human appearance, the young man with the melodious voice was not anywhere near his true height.

He looked like a big stocky kid in his twenties with long blond hair, combed straight back, piercing blue eyes and a barrel chest. "We must hurry," Gabe said, "They will be coming back soon to finish what they started. We are present in their dimension. They will see us."

"Right," Bryce said, as he unstrapped the patient.

The patient was Percival Charles Williamson, an up-and-coming geneticist who arrived for his current assignment three years ago. From the start, this job had ominous warnings, but the young Brit saw it as a necessary stepping stone to his career.

Above Ground, RAF Lakenheath, UK – Three Years Ago

Like many Ministry of Defense positions, the rigorous security and psychological testing could have easily put off any young researcher. But Percy, as his friends called him, understood that, if he could get past the security scrutinization of government projects, he could position himself in the ideal situation. He learned that lesson from his cousin, Digby Williamson.

Although Digby was in a different scientific discipline, physics, through his hard work and perseverance, Percy saw him appointed as the personal research assistant to the Director, one Dr. Grover McNabb, at the Large Hadron Collider in Geneva, Switzerland.

The way that Digby related the story, Dr. McNabb had hired him on the spot at the recommendation of the world-renowned Dr. Bryce Cooper. Digby made it clear that he'd never met Dr. Cooper, but with such a strong recommendation, Dr. McNabb was persuaded.

Digby surmised that the recommendation had come because of his reputation for hard work. He told Percy, "If I didn't push through all of the red tape, I wouldn't have gotten to work at the LHC. If I didn't work at the LHC... well, you know."

What Percy "knew" was that his cousin Digby had obtained a position at Diamond Light Source, the UK's version of the LHC and because of that CERN work experience, Digby was now the project's youngest Team Leader ever.

Percy figured if that strategy worked for his cousin, it could work for him, so he pressed forward. He needed that determination because his new job was strange from the beginning.

He was told to report to R.A.F. Lakenheath in the fens of Suffolk, England. Lakenheath was only British in name. It had been the home of the 48th Air Wing of the United States Air Force for many years. As such, he assumed that he would be working with the Americans.

The strange part was the fact that the US Air Force flew their F-15 Strike Eagle out of that location, along with various other aircraft. As far as Percy knew, it was not a genetics research facility, nor did they even have a laboratory on base. Still, he knew better than to ask too many questions. So he pressed forward into the unknown.

His first few visits to the base were not unusual. The American SPs, Security Police, fingerprinted, screened, interviewed and evaluated his background very carefully. After six months, he was told that he had passed the security screening and that's when things got strange.

One day, with suitcase in hand, he was driven by Humvee across the flightline to a totally empty, hardened, aircraft hanger on the outskirts of the base property. With their dirty brown curved appearance, the hardened shelter was an exact match to all of the other hardened hangers on the base and looked like an oversized brown igloo. They were relics of the Cold War, built in the early 80's to protect the aircraft inside from a Soviet Union nuclear blast.

Are they going to fly me somewhere? Percy remembered thinking.

The lumbering, jeep-like vehicle rolled up to the hanger and stopped with a squeak of its brakes, but Percy immediately noticed that the hanger's giant steel hanger doors were closed.

"Here we be," the young, pimpled-faced, twenty-year-old, two-striped airman said with a southern accent. "You're supposed to go through there," he pointed to a regular entrance door that was built into the hanger's sliding blast doors,

"Alright. And then what?" Percy asked, taking out his handkerchief and dabbing the accumulated perspiration on his brow. It wasn't warm, but clearly the Brit was uncomfortable.

The airman shrugged, "Don't know. I'm just the driver." He hopped out and removed Percy's rolling suitcase from the back.

"Are you going to wait for me?" Percy asked, "It doesn't look like anyone is home."

The driver chuckled, "Air Force don't make mistakes. If they told you to come here, here is where you're supposed to be. I'm sure you'll be fine."

Percy swallowed hard, "Alright, thanks for the ride."

With that, the airman waved, put the Humvee in gear and sped off, leaving a cloud of diesel exhaust in his wake.

Percy extended the telescoping handle on his luggage as he turned to stare at the silent shelter.

What have I got myself into?

"Too late to turn back now, mate," he said as he walked to the door, turned the knob and pushed it open. Its steel hinges complained with a loud groan as it swung wide revealing… nothing.

A black expanse of emptiness filled his view. He couldn't see any people. There was no equipment. It didn't even smell of the oil and jet fuel, the typical odors of an airplane hangar.

"This must be a mistake," he said, and then he heard, "…*must be a mistake… mistake… mistake"* as his echo replied from the darkness.

"Blimey," he cursed, as he looked over his shoulder again. At this corner of the expansive airbase, it was far from civilization and would be a long walk back. Plus, his driver had to call the control tower for permission to cross the runway. Percy couldn't very well walk across the runway without clearance. If he tried, he was sure that security would rush out and stop him at gunpoint.

No, I have to find a phone and have them pick me up.

He took a deep breath and walked over the threshold.

Stepping inside a few paces, the darkness enveloped him.

"Crikey!"

"Crikey, crikey, crikey…" the cavern mumbled back to him.

Now what?

What is it that the Americans say? Am I being punked?

He sighed and rubbed the back of his neck.

I better find a phone or it will be a long walk back.

Leaving the door open as his only source of light, he stepped further into the void.

He started with alarm when he heard in rapid succession, "Humm-click, humm-click, humm-click," and the hanger's halogen overhead lights came on.

"Bloody He… Must be on a motion sensor…"

"Sensor, sensor, sensor…" the empty space continued to reply, but it wasn't nearly as unsettling with the lights on.

"Hello?!" he called.

"Hello… hello… hello"

That's strange… not only is it empty, it looks brand new!

There were no jet fuel stains on the cement and no smudges or grease marks anywhere. The hangar air was stuffy, but it was absent of any smell related to a jet.

He noted that the asphalt outside was just as faded and sun-beaten as everywhere else on the flightline and the curved cement roof and walls on the outside of the hanger, were the same worn, dull brown as the rest of the hangars.

The outside of this place looks to have been here a long time… but the inside? The inside hasn't been touched.

"This makes no sense…"

*"Makes no sense… no sense… no sense…"*the hanger echoed.

He grunted. *This is getting old.*

Dragging his wheeled luggage behind him, he inspected the wall of the hanger, looking for a phone.

Walking along the wall, he'd covered about half of the hanger when he said, "This has to be a mistake…"

No sooner had the words dripped from his mouth, did he hear from behind him what sounded like the grinding of cement, or a rock, sliding against itself.

Percy snapped his head around and blinked his eyes in disbelief.

At the very center of the hanger, a dark haired, bespectacled, middle-aged woman in a white lab coat stood and said, "No, make no mistake about it - this is no mistake. Dr. Williamson?"

"Ye… yes," Percy croaked.

"Please follow me." A stairwell was hidden under the slab of concrete in the center of the hanger.

That was the last time he saw the light of day.

His parents were gone and he had no siblings. No one missed him. Although like his cousin, he was a distant relative to the Queen, his only real family was Digby.

Growing up together, they could have been identical twins. Both had red hair with a receding hairline, although Percy's hair was more auburn than Digg's orange-red. They were also the same build and had a pale complexion and both wore round-framed glasses.

BELOW GROUND, RAF LAKENHEATH, UK – PRESENT DAY

The formally bound Brit looked at Dr. Cooper, "Who… who are you?"

Working quickly on the last of his straps, the fit, sandy haired man in the toga said, "I'm a friend of your cousin Digby, and we're here to get you out. But first we need a tour."

"A what? [5]Of here?! But… but they'll find us! Mr. Ahhhh… who are you again?"

"The name's Bryce Cooper and that's my frien…"

Percy's eyes grew large, "Bryce Cooper? As in Dr. Bryce Cooper? The one that Digby talks about?!"

"Guilty, I guess," the physicist said, "but we can talk about it late…"

"They are coming!" Gabe said urgently, from his lookout spot by the door.

Helping Percy to his feet, Cooper said, "Let's go! This way!"

THREE

The inside of the vast airplane was filled with artificial light. Protective shades were drawn on every window, including the cockpit, in order to protect the occupants from the radiation swirling around in the ionosphere.

Circumventing the neutron filled mushroom clouds had been a challenge. With so many direct hits upon the United States, flying would have been impossible had he not known where... and when the bombs would fall.

The airplane shook violently as the pilots fought an updraft of turbulence. In spite of the rough ride, it was good to get outside. The man had spent the last five days cooped up in the vast, man-made caverns under the [6]Denver International Airport. With its apocalyptic murals painted by Leo Tanguma, gargoyle statues perched on pillars and masonic symbols throughout, one would think that interment in the place would be uncomfortable. Nothing could have been further from the truth.

The airport was simply a cover for a subterranean city and highway system that stretched across the country and perhaps the world. The living quarters were opulent because The Group and their families may have to call them home for a long time.

A knock at the airplane cabin's door pulled the Man's attention from the book he was reading.

"Come," he commanded.

25

Silently, one of his chief advisors slid through the small room's door, "Sir, just a brief update. In spite of the detours and turbulence, we are well within our time schedule. We should arrive by the appointed hour. Is there anything I can get you?"

The Man looked back down at the book in his hand. He'd read it dozens of times, but now, more than ever, it was especially important. He was quiet for a moment and then said, "No, I'm fine," and then as an afterthought asked, "They were careful not to hit the oil fields, weren't they?"

The aide, a fifty-year-old, thin, black man of medium height and impeccably dressed, leaned against a chair, "Yes, sir, or else we couldn't have flown this way. We are," he made quote marks with his fingers, "threading the needle, the pilot said."

The oil fields in question were in North Dakota where an oil boom had been in effect since the late 2000s. Technological improvements to fracking, or hydraulic fracturing, enabled the cost-effective extraction of oil and natural gas from the Bakken Shale Deposit.

This method changed the "Badlands" forever and eventually aided the United States in becoming the [7]largest oil producer in the world, surpassing Saudi Arabia. The Man With The Book knew that the potential of future energy production kept America's enemies from bombing the area; they wanted the oil resources for themselves.

He dismissed the thin man with, "Let me know when we get close."

"Yes sir," the aide nodded and slid out.

The Man had a finger between the pages marking his spot, but flipped it over to look at the cover. The tattered sleeve read, "A Post American World."

His reading choice had caused quite a stir with the public. For some reason, people actually cared what someone like him did in his free time. Not long ago, a paparazzi [8]snapped a picture of him with this book under his arm and set the internet on fire. Conspiracy theorists wondered how he could actually think so little of America that he would read about its demise.

Yet, he was a realist. He knew that the world couldn't keep going the way it was, and that it was time for a New World Order.

"Order out of chaos," he murmured.

Before there's any order... there's a whole lot more chaos ahead.

BELOW GROUND, RAF LAKENHEATH, UK – PRESENT DAY

Percy stood weakly by Cooper's side. In spite of everything that Bryce had seen, he was still shocked by the sight in front of him.

It looked like a mammoth cave which was so large that he couldn't see the ceiling or walls. What Cooper did see was row upon row of stainless steel tables, hundreds of them filling the room.

"My God..." he said.

On top of each table, "alien Gray" bodies lay motionless.

"What is this place?" Cooper stared at the spectacle before him.

Percy's wrists were red and raw from where his bindings had dug into his flesh. He rubbed them and said, "We... we make them. That is, we clone them here. These are still in suspended animation, unactivated. I've never been in this room before and I had no idea that there were so many. The program must be much more widespread than even I imagined."

"Program?" Bryce asked as he glanced over at Gabe who nodded.

"Yes," Percy nodded. "Our genetic research program. That's what we were doing down here: genetics. We were told we were working on transhumanism. You know, making homosapien 2.0?"

Bryce nodded.

"But some things didn't quite add up so I started investigating. I stumbled across these... how do you Americans call them, 'critters', in the process of my search. It would seem that the creatures people suppose come from outer space are actually biologically engineered life forms developed in laboratories."

"Laboratories? You mean to tell me that there is more than one of these places?" the physicist asked.

"There are whispers, but yes," Percy offered, "it sounds like there are facilities like this all over the planet. Some are above ground, but most are rooted deep underground like this one to avoid detection from prying eyes." The Brit paused, his eyes scanning the vast sight, "I just had no idea there were so many."

"What you are looking at is part of the deception that is even now being revealed to the world," Gabe added.

Cooper looked at him, "I don't understand."

"These creatures are made by the Others. They will arrive as saviors. Remember, the Bible says that many christs will come before the real one?"

"Yeah... but..." Bryce fell silent.

"But this isn't what you thought it was referring to?"

"No, it isn't."

"These beings," Gabe said with lifted arms, "are manufactured. They are simply a depository for the real beings that live inside them."

Bryce pinched the bridge of his nose with a strained look on his face, "Gabe, please. You're not making any sense. What do you mean? Like... containers? I thought the

Nephilim were their own beings? Now you're talking about something going inside of these..."

"Grays" Gabe offered.

"Grays, then... Are you talking about something like... like a spirit?"

The shiny being placed His hand on his shoulder, "Bryce, you are a really smart human."

"But..." Cooper added.

"But you are still trying to understand the other side of the Veil from your world's perspective. You must accept that there are things for which science has no explanation."

"That doesn't mean that there isn't an explanation then. It just means that our 3D science hasn't caught up to it yet," Bryce quipped.

"See, you are already understanding."

Bryce looked over his shoulder, brow furrowed, at the hundreds, perhaps thousands, of Grays that lay dormant on the tables.

"The Great Deception is about to begin," Gabe said, "Time is at an end. We have much to do. Come, we must go."

"Wha... what about me?" Percy asked. "You're not going to leave me here?"

"No, we will take you to a place of safety," Gabe offered.

"And not too soon, either," Bryce said, pointing to the nearest Gray on the table closest to them. It's three-fingered hand began to move.

"They're waking up."

LARGE HADRON COLLIDER, GENEVA, SWITZERLAND – PRESENT DAY

The substantial man with the oblong head stood fixated on the large screens on the wall of the LHC's Control Room. With a sneer on his face, he admired his handiwork.

"Not too much longer now, laddies," he said in his thick brogue.

The sixty-seven year old Scotsman was originally from Edinburgh. As a youth growing up, his obtrusively large skull was once covered with a full head of long flaming red hair, a perfect match for the man's infamous temper.

His tyrannical management style, and his imposing 7'2", 325 lbs. stature intimidated most coworkers. Add to that his well-known, angry tirades and the majority of the staff avoided the imposing giant like the plague.

It was, as he often mused to himself, a genetic trait that mankind could not understand.

No matter, everything is about to change anyway. No longer will I have to hide who I really am, nor will I have to put up with their insolence.

Abbot was intimately familiar with each piece of equipment associated with the world's largest machine, the LHC. At one time, he was the admired Director of the facility. That was until his primary advocate with CERN, Alberto Francisco Giovanni, unexpectedly disappeared.

He shook his head at the memory: How could he have disappeared? Disappear is a relative term... he could disappear at will, but someone in the family, my side or the Fallen would know where he was. That meant that Giovanni must have tangled with those ignorant, short-sided, do-gooders of the other side. They might be mindless, simpletons, but they could be formidable.

Abbot still fumed at the consequences of the Italian's vanishing act.

Shortly after, it was discovered that the Italian sat on both the Board for CERN and the hyper-secret military project [10]HAARP (High Frequency Active Auroral Research Program) in Gakona, Alaska.

That scant act of double-dipping on two, highly secure projects constituted, in the CERN Board's minds, a serious conflict of interest. They quickly distanced themselves from the missing, formally most-favored Board Member.

To Abbot's detriment, anyone who was associated with Giovanni was also immediately suspect. Thus, the Scot was unceremoniously tossed out on his ear, not even allowed to clean out his desk.

But now, his inner voice thundered, now who is in control?! *Who is it that will unleash retribution on all mankind?*

The Group and the Others had implemented the last stages of the Plan. Highly placed members of the Others, including Abbot, were in key positions of power in the political, social, business and science realms.

That power enabled The Group to force UN troops to seize control of the LHC and dismiss all of the scientists and technicians. Abbot was once again securely in charge of the facility. Only this time, it operated under a much different mandate.

As Director, he never actually ran any of the LHC's previous experiments. He was more of a figurehead and politician for the project. He took great pains to hide the super-intellect that he genetically possessed. Rather, he bid his time and let the likes of Dr. Bryce Cooper do the necessary modifications to the collider in order to achieve a near speed-of-light collision.

Interestingly, Cooper unexpectedly quit just after Abbot's dismissal. His lacky, Dr. Grover Washington McNabb, became the new Director. The arrogant black man and his pencil-neck assistant Digby Williamson completed the improvements according to Cooper's specifications.

When the UN troops cleared out the human riffraff a few days ago, with minor adjustments and the installation of the Tachyon Injector, Abbot was able to boost the collision past the speed-of-light.

However, it is curious, the brooding Director thought, *Cooper could have easily had McNabb make these adjustments. To do so would have taken the beam particles to speeds faster than anything*

31

on earth; that is, anything that was built by humans. Why didn't Cooper push the envelope? It was almost like he purposefully had McNabb and his team minimize the improvements to avoid the speed-of-light.

"Director?" a voice behind him broke his reverie.

Abbot cleared his throat and turned around, "Yes? What is it?" he snapped.

"The modifications are almost ready for your final inspection," the scientist said without looking into Abbot's eyes.

"So why are you wasting my time and telling me this now?" the Director demanded. "Shouldn't you be finishing the changes and then let me know?!"

"I... ah..." the much shorter, bald man stammered, "I just thought I'd keep you apprised of our... progress."

"Look at me!" Abbot demanded.

Slowly the glistening head of the frightened man rose as he begrudgingly made eye contact with the now irate giant.

"Instead of kissing up to me, you would impress me more by finishing the improvements quickly so we can get on with the next phase of the pla... ah, experiment," he growled. "Now get back to work! I don't want to talk to you again until the changes are complete!!!"

The scientist stumbled backwards like he'd been pushed by the tyrant's mere words, "Yes, sir... I'm sorry, sir... I'll..." the evacuating technician didn't even finish his sentence as he ran for the door.

Abbot was breathing heavily. These fits of anger were coming more often and with them the metamorphosis into his ancient form. Slowly he steadied his heartbeat and felt his blood pressure lower.

No doubt the scientist saw my eyes turn red. It's no wonder that he beat a hasty retreat.

He turned back to the large screen monitors on the wall, "Soon, cousins, soon."

FOUR

S itting on the bed with his trembling hands in his lap, Mac grabbed onto his right hand with his left and squeezed so hard that it caused his brown African-American skin to nearly turn white.

The fifty-something, Philadelphia-born, Dr. Grover Washington McNabb, or Mac for short, had seen many horrific sights on the streets as he grew up, a poor black kid in the projects. At 6'6" and 290 lbs. there were few things that intimidated him. Nonetheless, he'd seen enough violence and drugs in the neighborhood to convince him that higher education and sports was a better route than the city's dead-end life.

In his youth, he'd won a full basketball scholarship to college. Although Mac was offered a chance to play pro-ball, he leaned on his aptitude in academics and found himself on the fast track for a Ph.D. at MIT. While at MIT, the up-and-coming astrophysicist met a young Bryce Cooper, who was twelve years his junior.

Bryce was a boy genius: serious, shy, quiet and reserved. With a perfect GPA at the age of thirteen, Cooper graduated with honors from the University of Montana in Missoula. He then headed to California to attend Stanford and finished his Masters degree in record time. From there he went straight to Massachusetts to attend MIT by the time he was fifteen.

Everyone else in the Ph.D. program was at least fifteen years older than Bryce. Mac was a jovial counterbalance to Bryce's shy demeanor; the older man took the Montanan under his wing.

The two hit it off immediately as their personalities played off one another easily and although Bryce academically excelled, they were equals when it came to their own disciplines.

Mac was the starry-eyed astrophysicist gazing out to the heavens, trying to piece together information applicable to the human existence, while Bryce was the serious particle physicist with a bent toward dimensional theory.

Even though their careers had taken different paths, when Bryce was handpicked for the LHC experiment by CERN a few years ago, he insisted that CERN also employ the smartest astrophysicist he knew, Mac, to come along so they could work together.

And work together they did, until… Four years ago, Bryce unexpectedly resigned from his duties at the LHC for personal reasons. Though shocked and dismayed at his departure, Mac saw that his friend had had some sort of life-changing, paradigm shift. Where Bryce was always haunted by his past and working himself into an early grave, he abruptly came to grips with his roots, embracing the ranch lifestyle and his family.

All of that seemed so far away right now. The display of violence a few days ago had shaken Mac to his core.

JERUSALEM, ISRAEL – THREE DAYS AGO

Mac stood, stretched and meandered over to the safe house kitchen for another cup of coffee. The astrophysicist walked past the front door where Diggs and Ivy, his ex-sister-in-law, were pleading their case with the Mossad agent guarding the front door.

All three of the scientists, Mac, Diggs and Ivy, had been in a near-fatal, plane crash with the Professor, Dr. Alvaro Mora, the day before. While the three air travelers in the safe house had escaped nearly unscathed, Mora had been harpooned by a piece of the aircraft's airframe and was on life-support. Mac also wanted to visit the Professor but he didn't think ganging up on the poor guard, Janne, would do any good. The poor guy was just doing his job.

An urgent banging on the front door caused Ivy and Diggs to jump.

"Over there! Now!" Janne said, pointing as he drew his Jericho Baby Eagle sidearm from its holster and held it to his side, pointing down.

The banging became more persistent.

Janne looked through the peephole. It was the outside guard, Ari, and his eyes were wide.

"Let me in!" Ari screamed, "Please! I have to come in!"

Ari told Janne when they arrived on shift that his stomach was doing flip-flops and he had to keep running to the bathroom. Something he ate, he said. Because there was no one to replace him, he came to work anyway. Janne figured that Ari's stomach was giving him fits and that was his reason for his urgency.

"Vsdr! Vsdr! (Alright! Alright!)," Janne said with a dismissive wave. He undid the deadbolt and door lock, "I told you not to..."

Before Janne even turned the handle, the door burst open and knocked him down. His unsecured, steel-black pistol slid across the room.

Janne had hit the back of his head on the ground when he fell back. He was lying on his back and lifted his head. His vision was blurry and he felt like he was going to black out.

Two grayish hands, three times the size of a normal man, clenched both sides of Ari's head as he tried to gurgle a warning.

Then, the outside guard's eyes rolled back as his nose and mouth oozed blood.

Janne croaked out, "Ari..."

The giant hands jerked Ari's head to the right in a 180-degree turn.

Janne heard his partner's neck snap.

Ari's limp, lifeless body was hurled through the air toward the kitchen.

A nine-foot tall beast with pasty gray skin, bulging muscles and rags for clothes stood drooling in the threshold with predator eyes. It shifted its weight back and forth in a manic display.

"Adoni!" Janne screamed.

Janne's Mossad training kicked in. He reached for his spare gun in his ankle holster.

The monster closed the distance in a fraction of a second.

It lifted Janne off the ground by the guard's shirt collar and punched him square in the face with its massive fist. The otherworldly hand traveled all the way through Janne's head with the sick thud of a melon falling on the ground. The balled fist squirted out the other side of the guard's head in a cloud of blood, bone and brain matter.

Ivy screamed in terror.

The creature tilted its head at the sound of the scream. It dropped Janne's body in a crumpled heap on the floor and shifted its gaze in the direction of the scream.

Ivy was on the other side of the room, frozen in fear.

The creature's solid, black eyes locked on Ivy. She screamed again.

Rage twisted the beast's face, as it slowly crept toward her, its long fangs dripping drool.

"Noooo!!!" she screamed as the monster's face came only inches from hers. She smelled putrid, hot breath as the creature panted like an animal.

She was about to scream again, but something stopped her.

Her forehead knitted in confusion and her eyes scanned the monster's tattered human clothes, its tussled, sandy, blond hair and she noticed the way it moved.

They were all familiar, even down to its mannerisms.

"It can't be!"

Seeing the recognition in her eyes, the beast took a step back and spoke for the first time. In a mocking tone, it snarled, "Honey, I told you we needed to think this through. I told you that you shouldn't go around telling people the things you saw in your lab…"

It was her husband's voice.

She stammered, "How… what…" and she shut her mouth tight at a loss for words.

The beast let out a booming cackled, "Cat got your tongue dear? I warned you… You were the one they were trying to kill on the plane. Of course they couldn't let you talk. You could have ruined their whole Plan. But you didn't die on that plane like you were supposed to. Now…" it laughed again, "now I get to kill you!"

It was the voice of her husband, Xavier. He was alive. He was a Nephilim.

JERUSALEM, ISRAEL – PRESENT DAY

"A Nephilim? All these years... And I didn't know it?" Mac whispered as his hands began to shake again. He grabbed his left hand forcefully, trying to get it to stop.

How can I ever get that scene out of my mind?

When it was all over, the two Mossad agents were dead, Ivy's neck was nearly twisted off her shoulders and Diggs, cornered by the otherworldly beast, would have been the next to die.

How in the world did I ever get over there?

It was still a mystery. One second he was in the kitchen, mouth open and watching the scene develop like a horror movie. The next...

Okay... I was in the kitchen. That I remember. Then I saw that thing come in and kill the two guards. It was so fast... it moved to the other side of the room, so I couldn't see from the kitchen. Then I heard what the monster said to Ivy. It was X! How could it be X? Then there was that sickening snap... God, Ivy... I'm sorry... I'm so, so sorry...

He started tearing up again.

Then I heard Diggs scream...

"This doesn't make any sense!" he said aloud, frustrated.

The next thing I know, I'm on the monster's back. Where did that knife come from? I don't remember grabbing a knife, much less leaving the kitchen!

BETWEEN THE VEIL, JERUSALEM – PRESENT DAY

"That's... that's doctor McNabb?" Percy asked.

Bryce glanced at Gabe who was standing off to the side, and then back to Percy, "Yup, that's Mac."

"Is he okay? He looks... confused."

"Well," Cooper said in a matter-of-fact tone, "he has a right to be confused." After a moment, he said, "Yeah, he'll

37

be okay. He's just in shock."

Percy was quiet for a moment and followed up with, ""That's good, Dr. Cooper, but what was he talking about?"

Percy didn't actually hear Mac talking. Rather, he heard his thoughts. Percy looked around the room again in disbelief. "I don't understand any of this either," he said.

Cooper, Gabe and Percy were in the same room as Mac, yet they weren't actually occupying the same space or time as him. Percy felt the floor under his feet and he saw the furniture and the walls. But if he tried hard, he could actually see through the walls. It was all like a dream.

The things that Percy had seen up until now were mind-boggling. Dr. Cooper tried to explain to him that they were between dimensions.

Between dimensions, Percy wondered?

Bryce thought back to just after he visited Damascus... or what would be considered three days ago to Mac.

You're right buddy, Cooper thought to Mac, *that's exactly what happened. Only problem is, you couldn't see what I did. And for some reason, Gabe said you weren't supposed to know how you got the knife and stopped the creature.*

— —

Cooper found himself in the safe house with his friends, but they were frozen in time like store mannequins set to a pose. Gabe was with him.

When Bryce arrived at that time and space, he found chaos... and if he didn't act, Cooper knew his friends were going to die. It took all of a split second to decide what he was going to do.

Mac was frozen in place. Bryce opened several drawers until he found a long knife with a curved 9" blade and a stout handle whose tip had a sharp split. One side of the knife was serrated and the other was as sharp as Cooper had ever seen a knife be. He guessed that it was for grilling, because it was in the same place as barbecue utensils.

"This'll do!" he said, flipping and spinning it a couple of times before grabbing Mac's hand and wrapping his friend's fingers around the handle.

Gabe was not one to show emotion, but Cooper had the distinct impression that he wasn't happy. Bryce assumed that it was something to do with the physicist interrupting occurring events.

The Montanan didn't care. He had to do something to save his friends.

Looking at the stoic being, Cooper asked Gabe, "Are ya going to help me, or are ya just going to stand there?"

Gabe had been told to help Bryce by the Companion in Damascus, so begrudgingly and without a word, the illuminated giant walked over to the frozen Mac and easily lifted him off the ground.

"There," Bryce pointed to the beast on the other side of the room, "on its back."

The gleaming winged giant effortlessly carried the 6'6" 290 lbs. Mac across the room and placed him high on the Nephilim's back. Then he stretched Mac's legs around the front of the monster and locked his ankles together. At the same time Gabe made sure that Mac's left arm was wrapped around the left arm of the giant and he stepped back and nodded at Cooper.

"Good... that's good," Bryce said with satisfaction.

Cooper took Mac's knifed hand and tried to raise it high over the back of the monster's neck. He hopped once, then twice and then finally a third time. Then he stopped jumping and blew out a frustrated sigh.

He was too short and couldn't get the knife at the right angle. Nor was he nearly high enough, because the Nephilim was at least nine feet tall in its current form. With Mac on its back, Cooper was at least six feet short. No amount of jumping was going to get him close.

He clenched his jaw. He hated to ask Gabe, but he needed him, "A little help here?"

Gabe bowed his head slightly and stepped forward. He raised Mac's arm and angled the knife just right, just above the Nephilim's neck.

"Is this what you had in mind?" he asked his human friend.

"Perfect!" Bryce answered and asked, "When will they re-animate?"

"As soon as we leave."

With that task done, Bryce blew out a heavy breath. Then his eyes drifted down to the lifeless body of Ivy. His shoulders drooped and his face downturned. He kneeled beside her.

"I know what you are thinking, Dr. Cooper. It is not possible. It is one thing to save your two remaining friends, but it was her time."

Bryce ran his hand through his hair and scratched his head, "I know, I know. I just hate to see her..." he stopped and got to his feet.

Ivy's head was twisted completely around so it appeared that her terrified eyes were looking behind her.

"I only wish we could have gotten here sooner," Cooper said solemnly.

"It wasn't meant to be, Dr. Cooper. Now come, there is much to do.

――――――――――――――――――――――――

That was before, but the whole experience was still fresh in Cooper's mind. Although he was able to intervene for Mac and Diggs, the action still felt hollow because he couldn't help Ivy.

"Is he going to be okay?" Percy asked, and then added,

40

"and how is my cousin?"

This brought a smile to Cooper's face, and he wrinkled his nose, "Diggs? He's fine. I've never known anybody as resilient as him. And yes, Mac will be okay too. It'll just take some time."

"And what about me?" Percy asked.

Bryce traded a look with Gabe, "Well, that's the thing. We're going to leave you here."

"Here?" Percy asked.

"Yeah, I figured you'd want to catch up with your cousin. But I can do that only on one condition," Cooper said, pointing at the younger man.

"What condition?"

"You have seen some things," Bryce started.

Gabe chipped in, "That most humans are not allowed to see."

"That's right," Cooper continued, "So my big friend here," he nodded to Gabe, "is going to let me leave you here, providing that you do not tell a soul about what you've seen. You think you can keep quiet."

Percy didn't answer right away.

I have to be able to tell people were I've been. Plus Digby will never believe that I just stopped by. Somebody needs to be a witness to all of this..., he thought quickly.

After a moment, he asked, "And... I am not saying I will, but what if I happen to mention this to someone?" his voice going up and cracking.

Cooper narrowed his eyes, clasped his hands together and squished, "Brain Melt. We'll have to erase everything. Could be messy," he nodded to Gabe who said nothing. "But if you can't keep quiet, we can't take any chances. Gabe, help me over here," Bryce took a step toward Percy.

Percy put his hands on his head, "Okay, okay. I won't say anything. I don't want a Brain Melt. I will keep quiet!"

41

"Well, see that you do," Cooper said, turning away from Percy. As he did, he winked at Gabe.

Gabe walked over to Percy, "We will leave you at the door and have made arrangements for you to be let in."

"Thank you," Percy said, "Thank you for everything. For getting me out of that place and for reuniting me with Digby. Without your efforts," the pale-skinned, auburn-haired man swallowed hard and pushed his glasses back on his nose, "things would have turned out much different. I am very grateful."

"You are very welcome," Gabe said.

"Ditto," Bryce added.

"Now we must go," Gabe said, as Percy enthusiastically shook their hands.

They turned and as Gabe opened the portal, out of earshot of Percy, he asked Bryce, "Brain Melt?"

Bryce shrugged, "Best I could come up with on short notice."

Gabe shook his head and they stepped into the light.

FIVE

"So I've been meaning to ask you. Is this how you always travel?" Bryce questioned Gabe.

"More or less," his protector affirmed.

"So which is it? More or less?"

"Because of your physical limitations, we must walk Between The Veil. Normally, my brothers and I walk through."

Bryce's eyes twinkled, "Really? Anything else?"

Gabe was quiet for a moment, and then gestured with an open palm to the hospital hallway just outside of the room of the patient they came to visit, "Then there is always the Fallen."

Bryce's eyes narrowed as he looked around suspiciously, "The Fallen? Here?"

"There are things that we have not shown you... things you were not ready for," the gleaming man said, "But since you have seen much, you might as well see what we see – at least for a moment."

"See what you see?"

[12]Cooper remembered the first and only time he'd seen Gabe in his current form. Standing at almost twenty-feet tall, and shining a beaming, brilliant white, he was impressive. His thick, feathery, folded wings gave him additional girth, making the Montanan feel dwarfed as he stood next to him.

I'm sure glad he's on my side, Bryce thought, not for the first time.

Leading him to the hospital hallway, Gabe said, "Do you recall what I told you when we first met?"

Bryce's finger came to his lips as he thought back.

That first meeting was life-changing... how could I forget?

Lake Geneva, Switzerland – Four Years Before

It was in Geneva, Switzerland, the night before the LHC's Baseline shot – before the Reset.

"The Reset" was how Bryce came to think of his second chance. He had been working tirelessly at the LHC and through his experiment and contractual work on HAARP in Gakona, Alaska, he nearly singlehandedly caused Armageddon.

Through some quick thinking, the use of the LHC technology, and a little supernatural intervention, Bryce often thought, he was able to "reset" time to three years prior to the ATLAS 7 experiment. In the years since, he'd deduced that the Reset was an alteration to the normal space-time continuum.

With that Reset came a new lease on life. He'd become a Believer in Yeshua Ha-Mashiach, recommitted himself to his family, and walked away from his dream job in Geneva to live at his boyhood home, the Lazy Hoof Ranch in Missoula, Montana.

He was glad that those terrible future events were wiped away, but the memory of the experience was still so vivid, Cooper found that it was sometimes difficult to keep his personal timeline straight.

Chronologically, he had met Gabe more than four years ago. He had been standing on the shore of Lake Geneva, feeling sorry for himself. In spite of his disposition to push through difficult circumstances without whining, he was overworked, stressed and sleep-deprived.

Back then, he and his wife had owned a house on that same

lake. Although it was way down the shore, being in close proximity to the body of water made him realize just how badly he'd screwed up his life at that point.

Because he was a workaholic, his wife Gabby had said she didn't know him anymore. Through tears, she told him that if he intended on spending more time at work, with his "mistress" (that's what she called his work,) instead of with her, he might as well live on campus. And that was that.

It was brisk out and the shoreline was deserted. His mind had drifted back to his wife's and son's most recent visit with him on the CERN campus... it didn't go well.

He remembered exactly what he'd been thinking about: *LJ (his son) has grown up a lot this year. I don't spend enough time with him. I grew up without a father... Now because of my work, LJ's also fatherless.*

"Enough!" he finally said aloud, trying to stave off a spiral of the depression that he was prone to in those days. "Stop feeling sorry for yourself!"

Suddenly, a voice sounded from behind him and he started. "Are you okay, sir?"

Bryce spun around to find a tall, young man of substantial bulk standing about seven feet from him. Before Gabe ever revealed who he really was, this was the persona that Cooper saw.

"Man!!! You scared the bejebbers out of me!" Cooper said, holding his chest.

"I'm sorry. I was walking by and heard you say something. I just wanted to check if you were okay."

"Yeah, I'm fine. I didn't even hear you walk by. I must've been lost in my own little world."

"Sometimes our worlds are interrupted by larger events outside of ourselves, wouldn't you agree?" the large stranger replied in a melodious tone.

"Huh? Yeah, I guess so." *That's a strange comment,* he

remembered thinking.

Bryce also remembered that there had been something vaguely familiar about the guy; he had felt like an old friend. But he was sure he'd never met him.

"Often times we feel like we are alone in the world, left to deal with life's pressures and pain on our own." The young man's voice warmed Bryce's insides as its soothing tone washed over him, vanquishing the chill of the lake.

"I'm sorry. Do I know you?" Bryce asked.

"No, I don't believe we've met," replied the stranger, "My point is... you are never alone, no matter how you feel."

"Maybe so," Bryce responded as he turned back to stare at the darkness, "but sometimes life just comes up and bites you in the butt. I think you have to shake it off and push on. Don'tcha think?"

He swiveled around to look at the stranger, but to his surprise the stocky young man with the soothing voice was gone!

Hospital, Jerusalem – Present Day

Bryce smiled big recounting what was now a fond memory, "Before you pulled your disappearing act, you told me that I was never alone, no matter how I felt."

The two friends paused just outside the room's threshold and stood in the hallway.

"And neither are we," Gabe said, with a wave of his hand.

The walls and air around Bryce pulsed and collapsed inward toward him, shrinking. Then they pulsed outward, expanding, until the physicist's perspective changed completely.

He knew he was still in the hospital hall. The faint outline of its edges and corners faded to thin, translucent representations of the original space, but gone was any sense of depth perception. Cooper had no idea how tall or wide the "hall" now was as his ability to measure his surroundings fled with the onset of this new reality. The physical laws that bound him to his dimension no longer applied here.

Like a high-end HDTV with the best resolution, Bryce's senses came alive with intense clarity of vision and brightness of colors. A strange combined scent of herbs, flowers and sulfur permeated the air. Groaning filled the space and reverberated down the endless hall, not from a human generated sound, but a natural one emitting from creation itself.

He became aware of dozens of menacing, bright-red, angry eyes staring straight at him. Cooper trembled as he realized that the owners of those eyes were humanoid creatures whose faces were contorted in rage. Some of the angry beasts easily stood 25 feet tall. Their muscled bodies were covered with soot-black skin and on their backs were huge, bat-like wings covered with filthy, matted, dull black feathers.

Dark muscles bulged and rippled as the monsters shuffled and fidgeted manically in place. Sweat beaded on his forehead as he recognized the creatures to be exactly like the one that nearly killed him just before the Reset. Now there were dozens.

"What the..." Bryce said under his breath.

To his surprise there were ugly new additions that Cooper had never seen before. These creatures belied explanation, even in horror movies. He shivered, fighting the urge to turn and run.

His eyes darted down the row of ugly darkness and rested on a brilliant, shining being, just like Gabe, right in the midst of the darkness. Relief flooded through him as he saw numerous, illuminated beings in the hallway standing against evil. He and Gabe were not alone. The evil beings gave the far fewer bright creatures a wide berth by staying at least twenty feet away. Other white creatures, also occupied the space, far different from Gabe and defied description.

Bryce's analytical mind froze and the spit instantly dried up in his mouth as he saw the focus of all of those raging, murderous, red eyes. All of them were intently peering at him.

"Where... where are we?" he croaked out to Gabe, "And... and why are they looking at me like that? Like I'm their next meal!"

Gabe gestured toward the black mass, "The Fallen have always been here and constantly interact with humans. Your physical laws just do not allow you to see them. We stand in the space between dimensions, Between The Veil. It is not bound by your physical laws."

"Space between dimensions? I never knew such a place existed. Why are they all standing around? It looks like they're waiting for something."

"Normally, this place is very active. In fact, further on," Gabe pointed to the distance, "war is raging."

"War? You mean between these good guys and bad guys?"

Gabe's eyes narrowed in amusement, "Yes, a conflict that has been going on for many of your millennia. And because it is the end of the Age, the battle is more intense than ever. But this is neutral ground."

"Neutral ground? Here... Between the Veil?"

"Not Between The Veil. Here at the hospital," Gabe answered.

"The hospital? I don't understand. I thought we were between dimensions?"

"Yes, but hospitals are an entry point of sorts. Here, many humans are leaving their physical realm for good. Others are making decisions to follow our Master's Way. Still others will transition to an eternal existence and reject what they have been shown," Gabe paused with a wave of sadness flashing in his eyes, "and will be judged. This place is where much of that begins. It is like a portal. And as such, both sides have agreed to not fight here. Too much to do for both of us."

"Huh... a portal? That's interesting," Cooper said as he looked back to their hate-filled red eyes staring back at him. He swallowed hard, "But why are they looking at me like that?"

"Because they know you."

Cooper swallowed hard at the revelation, "Kno... know me? How can they know me?"

"They know you were chosen. You are a threat to them. If it were not for the Master's protection, they would not hesitate to destroy you."

Still looking at the burning, red eyes directed toward him, Bryce said, "By protection, you mean you..."

"Yes, of course, myself and my brothers," Gabe pointed to the other brilliant-white beings that were scattered throughout.

Unexpectedly, Bryce's vision pulsed outward and then instantly collapsed inward. The sulfur-spewing monsters vanished and the hall returned to normal.

Bryce was holding his breath. At the new scene, he shuddered and let it out, "Thanks, that was unnearv... Hold on... Are those things still here?!"

"Yes, my friend," Gabe turned and led him back to the hospital bed with its unconscious occupant. "They are always around. We have given you back your original perspective so that you can function. It is very difficult for a man to see into our dimension on a constant basis."

"Still," Bryce said, as he looked over his shoulder toward the room's door and the hall that lay beyond, "Kinda changes your perspective."

"Indeed."

A typical hospital bed stood in front of them in the white-walled ICU room. Normally draped in semi-darkness, the area now glistened with Gabe's brilliant glow. Medical equipment stood at attention around the bedside, offering their repetitive beeps, tones and hums as they monitored and supported the life of the near-to-death patient.

Dr. Alvaro Mora's eyes were closed, his face was pale and his breathing shallow. A light blue, ribbed, ventilator hose was stuffed down his throat. Assorted wires were attached to different points of his body and gathered to a single machine that Bryce guessed was another monitor of sorts. Cooper followed the multiple I.V. lines with his eyes down to the black and blue arms of the Professor and winced.

Professor, you don't deserve this.

Dr. Alvaro Mora, or the Professor as his friends called him, was a world-renowned Helio Astronomer with his specialty being all things to do with the sun. He was a naturalized American citizen originally from Costa Rica. He and his beautiful, longtime wife Zoraida, also from Costa Rica, had five wonderful daughters and two great sons, and nearly too many grandchildren to count including one great-grandchild.

The Professor was in his mid-sixties, stood at 5'5" and had thinning gray hair to compliment his friendly wit and thick Spanish accent. His warm personality endeared him to everyone he knew.

The wounded man was a victim of the same cataclysmic plane crash that had sucked Ivy's husband out of the fuselage during flight. The sabotaged flight had nearly taken Cooper's life as well as the lives of a group of scientists that Bryce had gathered together. The party's goal was an effort to try and make sense of a series of natural disasters, scientific exploits and geopolitical events that was threatening life on Earth. Someone didn't want them to find out the truth.

While most of the plane's other passengers escaped with minor injuries, the Professor was less lucky. Mora was skewered by a long metal piece from the disintegrating plane. The modified spear ripped through his lung, spleen and liver, leaving him struggling for his life and in a coma.

Stephanie Mora, the Professor's daughter, also on the plane, had likewise escaped unharmed. She maintained a tearful vigil at her father's bedside until a series of "code blues" shoved her out of the ICU so the doctors and nurses could use a "crash cart" to revive Alvaro several times after he literally died. However, that attentiveness by the staff was waning. It had to.

War had broken out on Israel's southern and northern flanks and a chemical attack had been launched against Tel Aviv. Casualties were already in the tens of thousands. Many of the injured were being transported to Jerusalem for treatment. The original steady trickle of victims was fast becoming a flood.

Already the dedicated hospital staff were beginning to triage their patients. A man in Mora's condition would certainly be put at the bottom of the list for treatment, simply because his chance of survival was so poor. Now was a time of decision for the famous helio astronomer.

Bryce and Gabe traded a look. The companion-in-white subtly nodded. Bryce's gaze returned to the scientist as he walked to the bedside, leaned over, and slowly pulled out his breathing tube. Alvaro didn't wake up.

"Professor," he whispered.

No response.

Bryce reached out and touched him, "Dr. Mora!" he said more forcefully, but still in a quiet voice.

Slowly, the patient's eyes fluttered and then opened with an unfocused stare toward the foot of the bed. He winced.

"Good to see you awake," Cooper said from his side.

Mora's eyes shifted to the sound of the voice on his left. Even before he saw Bryce, he recognized his voice, "Dr. Coop…" he stopped at the sight of Cooper's companion. "Dios mio!" the Professor said in a quiet, raspy voice at the sight of the brilliant creature standing next to the Montanan.

"Am… am I dead?"

Bryce couldn't help but chuckle, "Seeing him, I could understand why you would say that, but me? Doctor, if you think I'm Saint Peter welcoming you at the pearly gates, you better re-think your theology!"

Mora grunted, then gasped and choked to the piercing screams of the monitors.

Gabe reached out and placed his giant hand on the Professor's chest. Immediately his breathing regulated and the monitors went silent.

The Costa Rican looked to the ceiling, "Gracious Padre," and then to his two visitors, "My chest, it feels warm. The pain is gone… how…" he stopped in mid-sentence as he focused on Bryce's clothes.

"Dr. Cooper, are you from the past? All this time I thought…"

Bryce was still wearing the Garments. "No, my friend, this is just an outfit I'm using at the moment."

"An outfit, but…" Remembering the creature that touched him, Alvaro pointed a feeble finger at Gabe, "Aren't you the EMT tech at the crash site? And I seem to remember you standing over me when I first got here. Who are you?"

Bryce smiled, "This is Gabe. He doesn't talk much. We don't have a lot of time. We need to speak with you. Stephanie is coming back and she can't see us."

"Stephanie! Is she alright?! Is she hurt?!"

"No, no. She's fine. She's been here with you. She's just stepped out. But I need to ask you something."

"Ask me? Ask me what?"

"You've been given a choice," Bryce said.

"A choice?"

"Yes, a choice. God knows your heart and has written your name in His book of life. You can choose to go and be with Him now, or you can remain

51

here."

"Go? You mean die?"

"Yes. Die. To this earthly body. In doing so, you will never feel any pain again, but you must leave everything behind."

After a couple of silent beats, "You mean my family."

"Yes, your family." Bryce knew the decision was a hard one for the astronomer. His family meant everything to him. However, with one touch of Gabe's hand, Dr. Mora now felt what real life without pain could be.

"And if I stay?"

Gabe spoke for the first time, "If you stay, you will see and feel much pain. Time is at an end. There will be much suffering. It has already started."

"And if you stay," Bryce continued, "You will have a job to do. I need your help. God wants your help. But it will be very difficult. Those are your two choices."

No further questions were necessary in Alvaro's mind. The Professor fell into a long, contemplative silence and his visitors let him think.

Finally, he cleared his throat, "If my God wants my help, who am I to not help? I will stay."

Bryce smiled warmly, "I kinda figured you'd say that. But you're no good to us in this condition."

Mora peered at the lines in his arm and the breathing tube that lay next to his head, "I suppose not."

Bryce stretched his hand toward the Professor, and authoritatively said, "In the name of the Most High God and by the Blood of the Lamb, get up and walk!"

The crown of Mora's head felt warm and prickly, like thousands of tiny needles. That tingling traversed down his face, to his chest, arms and legs until finally he felt it on the bottom of his feet. When the sensation ebbed away, all of his aches and pains were gone. He felt stronger than he had since he was a youth. As a test, he took a deep breath, filling his lungs. He let out a rush of wind slowly and found that his airway was now unobstructed and he was pain free.

Bryce lowered the bedrail, "You're going to be fine."

Mora didn't need to be told. He was already pulling out his wires to the screeching protests of the monitors.

Unsteadily, he swung his feet over the edge of the bed.

"We have to go now, but you and I will talk soon," Bryce said in a strained voice as he spoke over the alarms.

Mora got to his feet and embraced Cooper, "Thank you! Thank you so much!"

"Don't thank me. Thank God. He did it. I'm just a man."

The Professor pumped Gabe's large hand, "Thank you anyway!" and hobbling to the end of the bed. Remembering something, he unsteadily turned around.

"Señores, you said that you needed me to do something? What is it?" he nearly shouted.

"We can go into that…"

"No," he insisted, "If Padre needs my help, I want to help! Look at me!" he moved his arms up and down in a flying motion, "How can I not?!"

Bryce shrugged and said to Gabe, "He's going to need to know. Now's as good a time as any."

Gabe nodded.

"Professor, we need you to pay someone a visit," Bryce said loudly.

"A visit? You kept me alive for a visit? Who could be so important?"

Bryce cleared his throat, "We need you to talk to," Cooper hesitated, "The Jesuit."

Mora staggered back a couple of steps like he'd been slapped. "The Jesuit?! My God, I haven't seen him in years… and I swore I would not go back again after…."

"We understand, but only you can do this for us. He knows you," Gabe prompted.

Biting his lip, Alvaro thought for a moment, "Of course, of course I will do this…"

Breaking the moment, Stephanie's voice could be heard as she bounded around the corner and shouted, "Dad…." but she stopped in her tracks.

"Wha…" she stammered, "You're… you're awake… You… you can't be out of bed!"

53

"Miha!" Alvaro said as he opened his arms big and smiled, "It's okay! It's gone! The wound is gone! I'm healed!"

Big tears rolled down Stephanie's cheeks as she rushed over to her father, "What do you mean 'it's gone'?!"

Alvaro peeled back the bandages over his chest and side to reveal a tiny scab.

"I… I don't understand…" Stephanie looked at her dad in wonder. He'd been hovering near death, but now he was full of life. His color was back and he was bouncing around with excitement. "How could that be?!" she asked with confusion.

The Professor exaggeratedly pointed behind him, "It was th…"

Bryce and Gabe were gone.

SIX

He found himself on a high peak, overlooking the scene below him. The spring morning air was cool and it bit at his bare skin. He didn't know where he was, but directly in front of him was a man, hands on hips, surveying the valley below.

Short-cropped, white hair rimmed the otherwise hairless head of the man who stood a lean 5'9". He looked to be in his sixties with a few days white stubble on his chin. The back of the man's neck had a deep suntan, like he was accustomed to hard work in the sun.

Bryce looked around for Gabe. The gentle giant was no where to be found.

"Ah ummm," Bryce cleared his throat.

The surveying man's head turned toward Cooper in surprise.

"Where is this place?" Bryce asked.

The man gave his visitor a quick once-over with his eyes, "Oklahoma Mountain Gateway," he answered suspiciously.

"Oklahoma?"

"Yeah, that's right." The man paused and as his eyes swept over Cooper's outfit, asked, "And you are?"

"Bryce Cooper"

The man scratched the stubble on his chin, "Are you real? Or is this... a vision?"

What kind of question is that? Is it every day that someone wearing an ancient dress shows up on his doorstep?

"I'm about as real as you can get," Cooper walked up and offered the man his hand.

The older man shook it, "Larry Taylor. I was told to expect someone," he said in a certain Oklahoma drawl, "I just didn't expect the likes of you."

"Yeah, I get that a lot," Bryce quipped, "You were told that I was coming?"

"Yeah. At least that's the impression I had. Are you from the past?" Taylor asked.

Bryce looked down at his clothes and then back to Larry, "No, this is just my traveling outfit."

"Traveling outfit?"

"Long story," Cooper said with a wave-off. "Why am I here?"

Taylor looked forward again and pointed off in the distance, "Because of that, I suppose."

Bryce focused his eyes off to the distance.

Far below them was a valley surrounded by thickets of lush green pines mixed in with a few deciduous trees. Sparse patches of clearings were covered with white, yellow, red and blue wildflowers. Yet, the beauty of the area was not what caught Cooper's immediate attention.

A short distance from the edge of the trees lay an area that strobed with unnatural blue, green and yellow lights.

"What in the world?" Bryce exclaimed.

Taylor handed him a pair of field glasses.

Cooper was concentrating on the flashing lights when something flew into his field of view at 400 mph. He heard their non-afterburner, turbo-fan engines before he saw them.

Circling just above the tree tops and around the area with the flashing lights were U.S. Air Force A-10 Warthogs, tank killers.

That's strange, Cooper thought, A-10s are flying Gatling Guns.

That's the airplane that flies over a battle and pummels the enemy. Why would they be flying over those lights?

Cooper started to ask, "How long have those been..." He didn't finish the sentence.

An F-22 Raptor popped up from the backside of the mountain and crested the top no more than ten feet above their heads, piercing the air with a roar.

Bryce ducked instinctively, and yelled, "Holy moley! What the..."

The jet dropped down and leveled off just inches above the trees. It banked hard with an impossible-looking fishtail maneuver that spat up a cloud of mist as the plane circled the area of the flashing lights.

Cooper straightened and saw that Larry Taylor didn't even flinch.

"That's the Air Force's newest bird. Pretty impressive huh?" Taylor asked.

"What's going on?" Bryce yelled, trying to be heard over the dying jet noise.

"Military," Taylor said, "Been doin' that all day. Thought they were gonna break my windows," he pointed back to his cabin, "when they first flew over this morning. They must've been doing mach somethin'," he said with irritation.

Just then, Cooper saw another fast-mover hugging the valley floor. It too banked hard around the flashing light area.

"But why? Why here?" Bryce asked.

"They've been at it for a couple of days now. That portal lit up like a Christmas tree..." Larry started to say.

"Did you say portal?" Cooper asked.

With knitted eyebrows, Larry gave him a questioning look, "I was told to show it to you. You didn't know about the portal?"

"I'm beginning to sense a recurring theme here," Bryce

mumbled.

Bryce thought back to his previous life, before his Reset, when he was the ATLAS 7 Team Leader at the LHC, his very own super portal.

"I know about portals, but I didn't know about this one, or that you would show it to me," added Cooper.

"Huh... anyway, this one and the one over yonder" Taylor directed Bryce's eyes to an even brighter spot in the distance, "came on yesterday sometime. I've never seen them so active and I've never seen such interest in them by the Air Force," he pointed to the sky where Cooper saw a huge X written high up.

Bryce looked back down to the planes circling, "When did they do that?"

"They didn't. That X was done by some high-flying big planes. My guess is that they're chemtrails and not contrails, or sky writing."

"Why do you say that?"

Larry's eyes drifted from the sky to take in the face of his visitor, "Cause they aren't going away. They hang there for hours. Contrails and sky writing don't do that. They dissipate. If you know about [13]Chemtrails, you know they stick around for a long time." He turned forward again and spoke to the sky, "Not that it'd matter. Even when they go away, those big planes come back and redraw 'em. The military's never done that before."

"You mean... you've seen this kind of activity before?"

"Oh yeah, from time to time. Same procedures. But never seen them stay so long and never seen the amount of stuff flying out of those portals like the last couple of days."

"What kind of stuff?" Bryce asked.

Larry reached in his back pocket, pulled out some photos and handed them to Cooper, "Like those."

The photos looked like they were taken at night. Some

were from far-away angles and only showing dots against a black, starred background. Others were blown up pictures of strange, snake-like shapes. Still others looked like something from a Star Wars movie.

"These came out of there?"

"Yeah, they did. Used to be that I would only catch one or two, but I couldn't see them. I'd have to snap a picture and get it developed to know what I was looking at. But now..." he stopped in mid-sentence and shook his head somberly.

"Now what?"

Taylor's eyes came up and he looked hard at Bryce. Cooper saw sadness, even pain on his face, "Now the end begins. Darkness has fallen," Larry said.

"Huh," Bryce said, "Don't I know it."

For the first time, Cooper took in his surroundings. Larry Taylor's place sat on the highest peak of the Oklahoma Mountain Gateway. His modest log cabin had a full panoramic view of the surrounding hills and valleys below. Currently they were standing in what looked like Larry's fenceless backyard, on the edge of a steep drop-off. Bryce couldn't see another house for miles.

"You live here all alone?" Cooper asked.

"My wife and I."

Bryce considered this for a moment, "You're sure out in the middle of nowhere."

"Tell me about it! There are times when the phones and electricity goes out and won't come back on for days. Other times they go out for short patches. I think it has something to do with electromagnetic waves coming from the center of this mountain. Sometimes it feels like I live in a third-world country," Taylor agreed. "Wouldn't be here if I had a choice."

"If you had a choice? You mean somebody makes you stay here? Like a prisoner or something?"

Taylor chuckled, "Not like that. I serve Someone who is bigger than myself and I promised I would do whatever He wanted me to do. Whatever someone else wouldn't do. So that's how I ended up here. I guess you could call me a Portal Keeper of sorts."

"Portal Keeper?"

"That's right. I don't know what else to call it. I was placed here to watch over those," he pointed in the direction of the portals, "and I've been here ever since. It's my job to fight in the supernatural realm and boy, let me tell you! These last few days, the battle is raging."

"What has…"

Cooper didn't finish his question.

The F-22 was back, only fifty feet off the deck and in full afterburner. Bryce didn't duck this time, but instead looked up as the jet slashed overhead. It was so close, he thought he could read the tiny lettering stenciled on the plane's skin. Air molecules around them vibrated wildly as the noise shook their chests on the inside like the thumping bass of a rock concert.

After it cleared their peak, it dipped down to just above the tree line and headed straight for the portal below. Instead of banking hard like the first plane Cooper had seen, this one made a beeline for the center of the flashing lights. When it got there, the pilot pulled back hard on the stick and went vertical, in full afterburner.

Bryce tracked it with his eyes and the jet's fire appeared to grow even longer and brighter, as if the pilot gave the plane more gas for the straight-up ascent. It reminded Cooper of a rocket that was launching itself into outer space.

When the plane was at five-hundred feet, Cooper's mouth dropped open.

Another craft, not man-made and definitely not a plane, materialized right next to the F-22 and began to race it skyward.

"What is…" was all Bryce could get out.

Like two funny cars in a dead heat, the two aircraft rose evenly to a height of at least five thousand feet where the other craft paused briefly in midair and then shot off in the blink of an eye.

With its engines still echoing in the distance, the fighter plane cut back its thrust and did a lazy, inverted loop before leveling off and resuming its patrol.

Larry was the first to break the shocked silence, "Huh… never seen them do that before."

"Never seen them do what?" a dazed Bryce said, "You never saw something come out of that portal invisible and then materialize? Or you never saw a human fighter plane race a craft to the sky?"

"I've never seen either. Is it just me, or did it look like to you that those two… aircraft were playing with each other?"

Bryce was slow to answer and said, "Yeah, I think you're right. That wasn't normal behavior."

"Looks like both sides are getting bolder, like… like they're getting used to one another."

"Or…" Bryce surmised, "that they already knew each other. Like they weren't shocked to see one another. I think that's the Air Force's newest, most technological fighter, and that… that UFO looked like it was playing with it."

Taylor faced his visitor head-on, "Bryce, you look like a smart guy. So let me just cut to the chase. Because of that," he pointed with his thumb, "I think all hell's about to break loose."

Bryce narrowed his eyes, "The Veil is thinning He said…"

"Excuse me?"

"Ah, nothing, just something that someone told me. Anyway, don't you watch TV?"

Larry looked confused, "Sometimes, but my electricity and

Internet goes out. Been that way now for over a week. Phone's down too. Happens sometimes and I haven't been ta town lately. I'm kinda isolated up here. Why?"

It was Bryce's turn to have a pained look on his face, "Because my friend, all Hell has already broken loose,,,"

SEVEN

Abdullah Abbas Tabak, also known as The Assyrian, arrived in Tehran for the first time in his official capacity as [14]Caliph of the Islamic States for a New World, or ISNW.

Tabak stroked his salt-and-pepper goatee as he sat thinking. The facial hair was a perfect match for his mustache and bushy eyebrows. Considered an attractive and available bachelor by the veiled women of the Arab world, he always kept his thick, graying hair dyed to a dark brown. Adding to this personage, he worked out his 5'10" frame regularly so as to keep his fit 185 pound weight.

The secret meeting was a high-level gathering of the Islamic leadership, both Sunni and Shia, under the auspices of discussing the current, joint, military exercise throughout the Middle Eastern theater.

The afternoon was filled with plotting whispers against the Zionists in Israel and the Great Satan of America, whose strength and influence in the world had already begun to weaken. However, The Assyrian considered containment of both of these foes, enough for now. As a skilled politician, he elected to bide his time and then strike after his power was consolidated.

Nonetheless, should some kind of provocation occur, the countries of the ISNW and their allies would instantly rally behind him. If that were the case, he would kill both proverbial birds with one stone: the annihilation of Israel and his personal rise to power.

The first, official state dinner was scheduled for that evening. The Assyrian donned military dress with emblems of both the new Assyria and the ISNW. He was the keynote speaker for the event that hosted dignitaries from every Arab country throughout the Middle East and Northern Africa. Even the President of Russia was in attendance, as were representatives from Nicaragua, Cuba, El Salvador, Argentina, China and other ISNW-friendly countries.

A knock on Tabak's door drew a curious look from Farouk, his personal assistant. The beady-eyed man pushed his round, wire-rimmed glasses up on his nose and walked over and opened the door. Shock immediately registered on Farouk's face, but he said nothing.

From behind him, Tabak said, "Please come in."

"Your Excellency, thank you for seeing me on such short notice."

"Of course. You are a welcomed friend," The Assyrian said.

"As I mentioned on the phone, I wanted to give you this present before you took to the podium tonight and addressed the gathering in your new capacity."

"That is very generous of you, but why could it not wait until later?" Tabak asked with a hint of irritation. The Assyrian knew full well that he had little choice in the matter. The Banker was one of the most powerful men in the world, if not the most powerful. If he wanted an audience, he got an audience.

The Banker smiled warmly, unfazed, and continued, "Your Excellency, there could be no better time to bestow such a gift on you than just before you take the reins of what will be the greatest power in the world."

Now The Assyrian was curious. He looked hard at the round, metal case in The Banker's hand.

"Indeed, your assessment is right about the ISNW. Now you have my interest piqued. Your friendship and assistance has been instrumental in the union's development. What better gift can there be than that?"

"May I?" The Banker asked, slightly raising the case and pointing with his chin to a round, waist-high, mahogany table in the middle of the room.

"Please." The Assyrian said.

The Banker walked across the marbled floor, his heels making a sharp, clicking noise with each step. "As a Shia," he asked, "what is the one thing that you wish was different in the world of Islam?"

Tabak thought for a moment, and in a faraway voice said, "That is easy. I would wish that Mecca was not in Saudi Arabia, but in Assyria."

A thin slit of a smile came to the face of The Banker. "I knew you would say that. But it is not Mecca that you seek, is it?"

Again a thoughtful look, "No, you are correct. Pilgrims go to Mecca to kneel and kiss the [15]Black Stone in the Kaaba."

"Ahhhh, and if you had," The Banker asked with anticipation, "your own Black Stone, could you not set it up in Assyria and change the pilgrimage to your homeland?"

As the Emperor, Tabak knew that in time he could do anything he wanted. But first he must have such a stone. And moving the Black Stone from Mecca would be very untidy. "Of course."

Click... Click

The Banker undid the clasps on the round piece of luggage, "My gift to you, my old friend," The Banker suppressed his enthusiasm and lifted the lid of the case, "is a Black Stone of your own!"

Both Tabak and Farouk, who had been observing quietly from a distance, gave an audible gasp.

"This stone," The Banker explained, "is an exact duplicate of the Black Stone in the Kaaba, only smaller. And on this most important day, I place it in your hands," The Banker said as he removed it from the case.

Tabak's jaw was slack and open as his wide eyes sparkled in

awe. The stone was round and bigger than a basketball, black as night and perfectly smooth. The Assyrian noted that despite its glassy surface, it gave off no reflection and judged that by the way The Banker was holding it, it was heavy.

He reached out for the stone hesitantly, slightly pulling his hands back.

"Go on, my friend. It is yours. It belongs with you."

As Tabak stretched his hands to take the Black Stone, a surge of white electricity crashed through the ceiling of the room and struck the Black Stone while it was in The Assyrian's hands.

Tabak's body seized, twisted and shook as he bellowed a guttural howl while holding onto the stone and then he settled and fell silent.

"Your Excellency!" Farouk shouted, "Are you alright?"

Tabak didn't hear him. His face was blank and he stood motionless.

From the high ceiling, a dark, ubiquitous cloud descended upon The Assyrian, enveloping him like a thick, black blanket that melded into his being.

He screamed, "Nooooooo! Nooooooo! I don't want.... Help me!" and started smashing his fist into his own face, while holding the stone with the other. He tore at his skin, gouged at his eyes and ripped at his clothes, trying to get whatever was in him to come out. "Helllppppp meeeee!"

Farouk lunged for his master just as the strong arm of The Banker slammed into his chest, "It's alright. He'll be fine. Just part of the process..."

"The process! Are you mad?!" Farouk spat, "Can't you see..."

Tabak's face shifted, contorting wildly, pulling back and forth like it was made of rubber. It formed into a thousand-different faces, all of them terrifying.

Farouk was frozen as he watched in morbid fascination, until Tabak's eyes burned fiery red.

The aide screamed and bolted for the door. He pulled it open part way and it slammed shut, as if some unseen hand held it closed.

Tabak's convulsions ended with him staggering on his feet. Straightening, he stood there, head down, unmoving and silent.

The Banker was the first to speak, "My Master," and he fell to his knees.

Farouk took a step toward The Assyrian, "Excellency?"

Tabak raised his head and leveled his gaze at his aide.

Farouk's breath caught in his throat.

What's wrong with his face...? It's... it's not human. What happened to his eyes...?

"Allah have mercy..." Farouk prayed.

Tabak's eyes glowed red and locked on his trembling assistant. He thundered in a low, guttural voice, "You should ask me for mercy!" and he reached for Farouk.

Unseen arms lifted Farouk off of his feet, flung him through the air and into The Assyrian's grasp.

Farouk's feet dangled as Tabak squeezed the life out of him, his face contorted with rage and evil. Sensing death close, the aide urinated down his own leg and onto the floor.

"Mas... Master... please..." Farouk choked.

A look of recognition crossed The Assyrian's face.

He dropped Farouk to the ground with a thud.

Farouk choked and sobbed uncontrollably as he spread out prostrate on the floor next to the Banker.

Tabak's laughter roared through the building, shaking the walls and windows.

The Banker exalted The Assyrian in worship as Farouk continued to sob, slimy-snot dripping from his nose, as he lay prone in his own waste.

The odd duo became the first to worship... The Beast.

THE NEW ASSYRIA, HOME OF THE ISNW – PRESENT DAY

A few wispy, cumulous clouds high in the atmosphere lazily trudged along in a crisp blue sky. It was a beautiful day.

A broad field, as far as the eye could see, of vertical steel, glass and cement in the form of skyscrapers reached to the heavens in an effort to mar its beauty.

After all, this was New York which he had visited many times before for both personal and professional reasons. He was always amazed at the harsh contrast between nature and that which was manmade. Despite all of his previous trips, he had never been to the United Nations at its headquarters in Manhattan.

He felt uneasy, dizzy even, like he wasn't quite himself. His gaze shifted from the UN Headquarters to the ground under his feet. He stomped hard on the pavement, making sure that he was really standing.

How did I get here?

He turned at the sound of lapping water behind him, catching the sight of the street sign.

"FDR Drive?"

He stared at a broad waterway of brown and green soot, lined with litter. His nose wrinkled at the smell.

"The Hudson River?" he asked himself, "Smells like dirty socks…"

I'm in New York?

He was on the pedestrian walk along the Hudson, in the back of the United Nations building. He felt a presence before he saw it. Tilting his head to the sky, his jaw went slack and he brought his hand to his mouth, as his breath caught in his throat.

There before him, a white [16]cigar-shaped craft hovered in the sky, slightly higher than the 544 ft. UN building.

"What in the world?!"

It's not that he didn't believe in UFOs. The possibility of their existence had never crossed his mind. He was a man of facts, of order. He dealt with tangibles and planned accordingly.

He was a man of action, not philosophy.

The white craft shown as brightly as the sun. While he gawked, its brilliance diminished; it smoothly and silently drifted lower until he could see that the cigar-shaped craft was at least six city buses long.

He snapped out of his shock and years of honed training kicked in.

"Assess the situation!" he commanded himself.

His jaw muscles clenched and his sharpened eyes narrowed, darting back and forth, gathering data.

I didn't hear anything when it flew up on me. No sound at all. So that means it must run silently, probably with some sort of propulsion other than petroleum. It looks to be about twenty feet wide and a hundred-feet long. No seams or rivets, just a smooth, unbroken skin. No decals or markings. That one window on the front, near the top is the only one I see. It might have another on the other side but I can't tell from this perspective. I wonder if this is the front of the thing. Must be, but I would guess it flies lengthwise. Nobody in the window. Nobody home? No... there has to be someone flying the thing. Probably watching me now... No sudden moves. But why's it just sitting there? And why here?

He asked in a whisper, "What are you waiting for?"

From dark holes high in the sky, tiny specks of light appeared and suddenly bounced toward him, filling his view, before springing back slightly.

He stumbled, tripped over his own feet and fell on his butt.

"Whhhaattt!!!! No!" he cried.

His breath was coming in short, shallow gasps. His hands shook as he sat on the hard pavement. The sky was filled with [17]UFOs.

"Come on!" he chastised himself, "Calm down!"

He forced himself to take in several deep, calming breaths and stood.

Hands on his head, he couldn't believe what he was seeing.

Dozens of ships littered the New York skyline. There were plain orbs, some just made up of lights, metallic-otherworldly vessels, round flying saucers and still others that looked like they were flying [18]snakes and dragons that appeared to be living craft.

How could that...

The tubular-craft shot up, jumping over the UN tower and slowly lowered itself to street level in front of the headquarters.

With the repositioning of the ship, his perspective changed. He now stood at the corner of the main building, looking toward the intersection of 1st Avenue and United Nations Plaza.

The white, cigar-shaped ship sat at an angle across the intersection as the other ships encircled the UN building. Too numerous in the sky to count the UFOs filtered out the sun, giving the midday light the appearance of dusk.

New Yorkers, gawkers and passersby, poured out onto the streets as all eyes shifted to the sky with an uneasy quiet.

Movement at the front door caught his eye. Nervous UN staff filtered out of the main entrance.

Maybe they think it's their job to welcome them....

A puff of air sounded as a seam appeared in the shape of a doorway on the ship's side.

The door's skin dissolved making an opening as a long, metallic ramp smoothly slid out from under the new doorway until it touched the ground.

A tall, white regal figure emerged from the door and slowly walked down the ramp.

EIGHT

The humanoid figure appeared to be male with skin so [19]white it was almost translucent and he had wooly, white hair. His orange-red, lizard-eyes scanned his surroundings.

His clothes were constructed from an unearthly material in a frosted color. As he reached the bottom of the ramp, he peered at the expectant crowd and then shifted his gaze to the UN dignitaries and opened his mouth to speak.

His words were in English, but they reverberated like an echo from a cave.

"I am Dormin," he said, "and we are here to help."

Dormin? the man at the corner thought. *Something is not right. I don't know what it is, but this whole thing feels...*

Black, eerie, shifting, shadows flooded from the same holes that the ships came through and caused the already dim light to grow darker.

What's happening?!

Unfazed, Dormin continued to speak:

"and because of your cooperation, we will usher in a new era for your planet where..."

"What?"

Holes in the ground opened and the same kind of black shadows spewed forth, adding to the numbers from the sky.

As they focused on Dormin, the New Yorkers' expressions changed. Many of them became jittery, twitching and swaying maniacally. Other's developed drenching sweat on their brows and faces. Still others clenched their teeth and shook their fists with their nostrils flaring as they cracked their knuckles.

What in the world? What's wrong with these people?

Dormin droned on, seemingly oblivious to the crowd's change in mood, "We have brought you medicine to help you live longer…"

The shadows grew agitated, darting back and forth. With erratic movements, they swirled around the people, until the humans were overwhelmed and absorbed the black entities.

"…new energy source which will be free to all…"

A tall businessman in an expensive suit turned to the Goth girl next to him and smashed her in the face with his briefcase. Before she hit the ground, he turned to the delivery boy on the other side and ground a raging fist into his head. Like the floodgate to a river of violence was opened, murderous anarchy enveloped the crowd.

Twisted, angry faces found makeshift weapons of sidewalk café chairs, trashcan lids and street signs as they stomped, beat and stabbed each other. A policeman pulled his gun and shot the man standing next to him in the head and continued to fire on innocent people. When he was out of bullets, he held the gun by its barrel and pistol whipped them.

"NO, NO, STOP IT!" the observing man cried.

He watched in horror as a mother with a baby in a stroller, dumped the baby on the street, picked up the stroller and used it as a weapon on those standing around her.

"The baby!" he shouted, "watch out for the baby!"

No one listened to him, nor was he bothered by the black shadows. He was an observer, watching the scene play out like in a movie, unable to make it stop.

Blood was splattered everywhere; on the walls of buildings and cars and in pools on the street. Bodies littered the sidewalks as bloodcurdling screams filled the air.

Still, Dormin spoke unaware:

"So, we have come back to the place where we have planted a seed..."

The observing man felt a strong hand grab his shoulder and turned.

"No! No! The shadows! Help!!!"

Then he woke up.

With unfocused eyes, he saw a familiar face in an oxygen mask.

"Sir!" the face said in Hebrew, "Wake up! You were dreaming! We are almost at the jump point," he held up his hand, "five minutes!"

Burning pain caused him to jerk back his wounded arm from his friend Moshi's grasp, "I'm awake!" he groused.

Zechariah had only allowed himself three naps of a few minutes each in the last seventy-two hours. He was tired and his body was aching. Each time he slept the fluid dream of the UN building, the UFOs, the dark malicious shadows and the good people of New York killing each other - all came back to him.

Sleep deprivation. I'd better be careful. That's how mistakes are made.

He straightened and stretched.

I'm getting too old for this.

With short, dark hair graying at the temples, dark brown eyes and a tanned, deeply etched face, he was in his mid-fifties, far older than anyone else on the plane. He was Mossad, a trained killer who until three days ago led a relatively simple life, embedded undercover as a finance minister in the government.

Today he was paired with the [20]Sayeret Matkal, the elite counter-terrorism and reconnaissance unit of the IDF. Everyone knew that he was Mossad. He had worked with, and fought, with a few of these men before. He had also taken on

Moshi as his protégé, mentoring him in the nuances of covert activities.

He was not military, but this was his operation and he was far more experienced than even the most senior of the team. He pushed his O2 mask up high on his forehead so as to be heard, "Listen up!" he shouted. "You all know our assignment. We are to parachute in and reconnoiter. We will not engage the enemy unless we have to. And we must find our Target. The very life of Israel is at stake. Is that understood?!"

He received affirmative answers from each of the six-person fire-squad.

Tonight, they were doing what was known as a "HALO" jump – High Altitude, Low Opening. They had flown into Assyria in a specially modified, stealth, cargo plane and were at thirty-thousand feet. From here, they would jump into the lightless void of the night and free-fall for twenty-nine thousand feet, finally opening their chutes at one-thousand feet.

Intel placed their Target back in Assyria. Knowing they were probably expected by the enemy, the Israeli assault team chose the extremely dangerous HALO jump as their best means of ingress.

Undeniable proof pointed to the Target as the responsible party for the chemical weapons attack on Tel Aviv and Haifa and there were suspicions that he was also responsible for the small nuclear bomb that destroyed the Islamic holy site of Mecca. He was a madman, bent on murder and he had to be stopped.

What sick person would destroy their own holy site?

The ISNW blamed Israel for Mecca's destruction and declared war on the Jewish State.

Like they ever needed a reason before?

Zechariah's job was to find proof connecting his Target to the WMD, Weapons of Mass Destruction, attacks and bring him back to Israel to stand trial, or as a last resort, take him out.

The latter certainly sounds more favorable than the former. But they warned me... only as a last resort.

Zac would follow orders in spite of his own desires.

In retaliation for the unprovoked attack on Tel Aviv, Israel had detonated a small, tactical nuclear device in Damascus, leveling the city. Between the destruction of Mecca, Tel Aviv and Damascus, all warring factions in the Middle East had taken a step back, worried that they would light the region on fire.

Zac knew that this was not the case with the war raging in America. The U.S. had been hit with several nuclear blasts designed to take out her largest cities and to sever Command and Control. Last he heard, foreign troops were swarming in through her borders and also via the air.

Israel is on her own.

A loud alarm sounded in the cabin, pulling him out of his thoughts.

The red light at the back of the aircraft turned on.

"Alright! One minute!" he yelled, holding out a finger and putting his mask back on. In a muffled voice with sign language, he said, "Jumping positions!"

The ultra-light, ultra-small, stealth insertion plane was so narrow that the team members could only fit in the plane in single file, first man in, last one out. Zac was at the end of the line.

The seven-man team stood and quickly checked each other's gear, front and back to make sure it was on properly with no visible problems.

The red light turned to bright yellow and the ramp at the back of the plane quickly lowered. Air in the cabin went instantly cold and the howling wind buffeted the men in their oxygen masks and jumpsuits.

The men shuffled forward, scooting their lifelines along the safety cable on the aircraft's wall.

The group moved as one to the edge of the ramp.

"Uncable!" Zac commanded.

In unison, the six men released the hook from their belts and hung onto the cable with their free hand.

A piercing buzzer sounded and the light turned green.

"Drop! Drop! Drop!" Zac shouted.

In response, each of the six other men stepped forward and disappeared.

As the last man to jump, Zechariah looked behind him to check the now-empty cabin.

Only then did the Mossad agent step off of the platform into the emptiness of the dark sky.

The hunt for The Beast was on.

NINE

Ash fell like snow against a dark sky laced with billowing smoke. In the distance, lightning leaped from the mountain to the top of the smoke pillars and back again. The air was so thick with pumice that Cooper found it difficult to breathe.

Coughing from the smoke, he said, "I guess this means I'm physically here. I can't breathe worth a snot!"

As he struggled up to the peak, his eyes and face stung with the wind-whipped ash and mountain Cottonwood flowers.

Strange thunderclaps filled the air. The sound could not be attributed to the atmosphere, but something on the ground. Bryce knew the sound's source loomed large over this next peak.

High in the atmosphere, the mushroom plume of gray and black smoke was clearly visible.

Cooper topped the hillside and saw a man standing watch over the scene. He looked tired. From this perch of 9,500 feet above sea level, just northwest of Mexico City, the solemn-looking man wore a bandana around his mouth.

He couldn't hear Bryce's approach with all of the noise.

"That is some sight!" Cooper shouted.

Surprised, the man whipped his head around.

Bryce saw tear lines in the ash on his face, "I'm sorry," Cooper said, "I didn't mean to scare you."

"Aking dios" the man said in his native Tagalog. He pulled the bandana down, "I... I didn't hear you come up."

Cooper walked up even with him and for the first time the physicist saw what the man was looking at.

In the sprawling valley far below, what was once the world's twentieth largest city was smoldering with some parts still burning. Whatever wasn't smoking or on fire was covered in a thick, gray ash.

God... it looks like a bomb went off!

"How long have you been up here?" he asked quietly.

The man's chin dropped to his chest as he fought his emotions. He sniffled, "Since it started. I haven't slept. Over twenty-four hours," the Filipino said in a thick accent.

Cooper's shoulders suddenly felt very heavy at the sight of the devastation.

"You cannot stop what is coming..." he told me.

Even from their location sixty-five miles away, the spewing mouth of the Popocatépetl volcano was an awesome sight as she continued to spit fire and smoke from the caldron in her belly. Her 18,000 ft. peak was gone, blown away by volcanic force equivalent to forty-million tons of TNT.

The man pointed, "The pyroclastic flow did most of that. But the lava flow hasn't abated."

Thick gray and orange rivers of fire were streaming into the vast metropolis that was once Mexico City.

He continued, "I was driving back from a geological conference in Monterrey. I live... lived here. I was almost home when I heard about what happened on the west coast of America. I knew that the devastation would not stop there. But I had no idea that the San Andreas would start a chain reaction all the way down here."

Cooper sighed, "Because of the war, reports on the west coast are spotty, but it's bad all along the Pacific Plate."

"War!" the man spit, "People are dying and countries are

fighting over land?!" Tears welled up in the man's eyes, but embarrassed, he wiped them away quickly.

"Your family?" Bryce asked softly.

"They weren't there.'"

The man's intelligent, brown eyes were red and swollen. Bryce saw a different pain there, perhaps a more personal one.

"My wife and my son Nyhay were killed last year in a car crash. Since then," he made a wide, sweeping motion toward the volcano, "all I've had is my work." He shook his head sadly, "But all of my friends, my neighbors and all of my colleagues were down there!" he shouted, sounding angry for the first time.

"You worked here?"

The man studied the puffy, gray ash under his feet and slowly looked up at Bryce. Ignoring the question, he said, "They didn't have any warning… Popocatépetl just exploded. No one expected it to erupt like that… there was very little seismic activity. We didn't see any real magma movement that indicated it was migrating to the surface and there wasn't any real deformation of the chamber! No temperature increase! No sulfur release," he shook his fist at the volcano, "HOW WAS I SUPPOSED TO KNOW!

"I can't explain it. It was like those earthquakes up north along the Pacific Plate pushed the lava in a southerly direction at super-fast speeds under the earth's crust. It started a chain reaction. First the Aleutian Islands, then the Cascadia Subduction Zone and all the associated faults, then the San Andreas and all the faults attached to that and then down here. It's crazy, it's like the earth is having a temper tantrum. Things aren't supposed to work like this!

"There were almost nine-million people down there," now he was sobbing. "Very few got out! It was my job. To warn them! I'm the volcanologist! This was my area! I was supposed to warn them! They are all dead because of me!" Now he cried openly, tears carving new lines through the ash on his face.

"You cannot stop what is coming..."

Bryce put his arm awkwardly around the stranger, "It's not your fault," he said, "You didn't do this. You couldn't have warned them. Something else is going on. You're not responsible."

Through sobs and anger, the man asked, "Some... something else? What do you mean something else is going on? Are you from the U.S.G.S.?"

A soft smile crossed Bryce's face, "No, I'm not. But what you're seeing here is happening all over the world. And it's happening for a reason. There's no way you could have predicted this."

"I'm," Cooper offered his hand, "Bryce Cooper. It's good to meet you, ah..."

"Romeo..." the man wiped his hand on his dirty trousers, "Romeo Juni. Everyone just calls me Juni," he said, shaking the physicist's hand.

Bryce saw friendly, warm eyes in spite of the gray ash on the volcanologist's face. He was a heavy-set 5'7", but not out of shape - just stocky. Cooper guessed that the thinning, white hair was probably thinning, black hair under the dust and that he was no more than forty. Although his face was covered with ash, his distinct Filipino features displayed the genetic mix of Spanish and Asian influence. The corners of his lips creased up in what looked like a small perpetual smile and to the Montanan, in spite of the circumstances, the man was warm and personable. Cooper liked him.

"Cooper? Are you Dr. Bryce Cooper?" Juni asked in surprise.

"Guilty," Bryce said, "Do I know you?"

"No," Juni said, as he blew his nose in a handkerchief.

"But, of course, I know you," he stuffed dusty cloth back in his pocket, "What scientist on the planet doesn't know who you are?" He blinked rapidly and looked around in confusion, "But what are you doing here? How did you get here?" His eyes ran down Cooper's outfit, "And why are you dressed like that?"

Bryce waved off the questions with his hand, "All good questions, but it would take too much time to explain. I knew I would find you here, Dr. Juni. I came to talk to you about that," Cooper pointed to the belching mountain in the distance.

Juni flinched slightly, "You knew I'd be here? How?"

Cooper's tone was serious, "As I said, things are happening all around the world and they are happening for a reason. But if you thought this was bad, I'm here to tell ya, it's going to get a lot crazier. But I can't really go into all that right now. I came here because I need you to tell me about Popa..." he struggled with pronouncing the long, foreign-sounding name.

"Popocatépetl?"

"Yes."

"I know a great deal about it. Not only on a professional level, because, of course, it is one of the volcanoes that we were watching, but also because I have lived in its shadow for so long. What do you want to know?"

Bryce crossed his arms, "Is it true what I heard?"

"What did you hear?"

"That a government monitoring camera has caught UFO's going in and out of that," Cooper jabbed his finger in the direction of the Popocatépetl, "volcano!"

Juni's lip curled in and he bit on it nervously. After a long pause, he asked, "I don't understand. I thought you were going to ask me some scientific questions... so maybe... maybe we can warn other people around the world if their volcanoes will erupt like this. But you're asking me... about

UFOs?"

Cooper looked hard at him, speaking in a low, steady tone, "Juni, this is really important. As bad as this tragedy is, if what I think is about to happen, happens, then a lot more people than those in Mexico City will die. I need to know. Have-UFO's-really-flown-in-and-out-of-that-volcano?"

Juni shuffled his feet a couple of times, clearly uncomfortable with the subject. "Yes... it was my organization's camera that took that video. And it has happened many more times than you've probably heard. We... we just didn't talk about it because we didn't want people to stop taking our organization seriously. But why is that important to you when we are looking at," he spread out his arms to the valley below, "all of this?"

Cooper sighed heavily, "Juni... believe me when I tell you that something much worse is coming to the planet. Please, what can you tell me?"

Juni's shoulders slouched and he waved his hand in the direction of the volcano, "It is just as you've probably heard... [21]A long, cylinder-type ship was captured on film, diving into the mouth of the volcano in October of 2012 and then another one, a smaller round one, was seen, I believe, in [22]May of 2013 doing the same thing and there were other times... many. We were told not to say anything, but..."

"But what?"

Juni's jaw set and he gestured to the valley below, "but there is no more organization. No one is paying attention now."

Bryce sighed, "That's where you are wrong. my friend. Someones or somethings are paying attention. Just not anybody that you know."

Juni turned his head to the physicist, "What do you mean? Who is left to care?"

"Let me just say that things are about to get a lot worse."

Near The Lazy Hoof Ranch, Missoula, Montana – Present Day

"Who are they?"

"Don't know, but they sure don't look like from around here."

"Regular, Army then? Or maybe Reserves?"

"No… neither. When I say they aren't from around here, I mean they aren't American."

"Not American!" he said a little too loudly.

The two men were lying on their bellies. Danny Mendez was the shorter and he bent his leg at the knee and dropped the toe of his boot down hard on David "Goose" Duckett's calf.

"Hey!" Goose yipped quietly.

Mendez put his finger to his lips, "Shhhhh," he pointed to the armored troop carriers with soldiers disembarking, "You want to get us killed?! Keep your voice down!" he snarled through gritted teeth.

Goose grunted.

The two ranch-hands-turned-scouts were lying in the tall grass near a back road to Missoula. Improvised jungle paint of mud and berries smudged their faces. Not long after they took their positions, they spotted the small convoy. A report on the short-wave radio back at the cave told about strange troop movements with a mass influx of armor and military from the north.

Danny Mendez was a transplant from Los Angeles, California. Cooper had met him on the physicist's first trip up to the HAARP facility in Alaska, before the Reset. The 5'8" Hispanic had straight, short, jet-black hair that he meticulously maintained, which explained why he rarely wore a hat and always carried a comb.

An RF Transmission Systems Specialist by training in the Air Force, Danny had earned his degree in Animal Husbandry, with a minor in Equine Science: Horse Breeding. He also loved the outdoors, so when Dr. Bryce Cooper offered him a job at the famous Lazy Hoof Ranch, he had jumped at the chance.

Far from his childhood in the L.A. barrio, he applied himself to hard work and was quickly promoted to Ranch Foreman. As soon as he thought he had enough pull, he invited his friend, Dave "Goose" Duckett to come up and talk to the Boss about a job.

The two were an odd pair. Goose was a white guy and at six foot, he was built like a Mac truck. He had powerful arms and shoulders, wavy, brown hair and sported a trimmed beard.

Cooper had learned that the men had a "run-in" together when Danny was a kid back in LA. Bryce never got the full story, but apparently through the awkward episode, the two boys cultivated a lasting friendship.

Danny and Goose had, like everyone else in Montana, been dealing with an electrical outage due to an EMP weapon and associated nuclear blasts. Tactical nuclear weapons were targeted at the missile Launch Control Facilities, LCFs, which were spread out all over the state.

Buried deep in the ground in flat, unpopulated, farmland areas, LCF "capsules" had the responsibility to release their designated missiles when a launch order came. Malmstrom A.F.B., home to the 341st Missile Wing Headquarters, was located on the edge of Great Falls, Montana and was responsible for the LCFs and their missiles.

The base was blown into oblivion with a 1 megaton nuclear bomb.

This was the first time since the bombs fell that Danny and Goose ventured out to recon. Prevailing winds blew any fallout in the other direction.

With the effects of the EMP fresh in their minds, they were surprised to see a fully operational military column moving down the road.

They were even more surprised to see who the soldiers were.

TEN

Danny and Goose watched in confusion from the fortified fence around the Lazy Hoof Ranch. Even from this distance, they heard the jets moan in protest as their pilots jerked, twisted and banked them under extreme g-forces in a dogfight to the death.

Two federal U.S. Navy F-18s were chasing two clearly marked Montana State Air National Guard F-15s. The battle ensued after the F-18s strafed with bullets and rained bombs down on the town of Missoula, some twenty-five miles away from The Lazy Hoof. The National Guard sent out its planes in defense of their city.

The U.S. Federal government declared that the city of Missoula was harboring "homegrown terrorists" and dissidents and issued an order for their elimination. Similar totalitarian actions were promulgated against other normal people, all across the U.S.

The dogfight that Danny and Goose were witnessing was the first salvo against Montana in America's new [23]civil war.

The older Air National Guard (ANG) F-15s were not as nimble as the F-18s. After the bomb run, the ANG planes swooped in, warning off the F-18s, but hesitant to fire on other American planes.

The F-18s were not nearly so weary and immediately missile locked on one of the ANG planes, and the fight was on.

Not more than three-hundred feet off the ground, the four planes danced in a ballet of death as fire spit off the wing of one of the trailing F-18s, a missile launch. The two ANG planes split from each other, banking hard in opposite directions. The fighter that had been "painted" by the chasing F-18 blew out chaff that looked like sparklers in a 4th of July celebration. The sidewinder missile took the bait and exploded harmlessly in midair.

"Did you see that?!" Goose said to an open mouthed Danny.

This is for real, Danny thought!

The other ANG plane would not be so lucky.

The more maneuverable F-18 jumped the ANG plane's bank and spit fire from M61A1 20mm automatic gun. At 6000 rounds per minute, the high-velocity bullets ripped the ANG F15c to shreds and the jet exploded in a brilliant ball of fire.

By the time the sound reached Danny and Goose, the pilot was already dead.

"That, that plane just blew up one of his own!" one of the sentries said.

"Not one of his own," Danny corrected, "that exploding plane had the markings of the Air National Guard, one of Montana's."

"Looks like a civil…" Danny never finished the statement.

High up in the ionosphere a giant ball of what looked like lightning erupted. Its tentacles stretched out for miles. As quickly as it came, it faded away.

"What was that?" Goose asked. "There's not a cloud…"

As he was still speaking, the three planes that remained in the dogfight banked hard, two in the rear, chasing the remaining National Guard plane. On cue from the bright flash, all three planes appeared to lose all power and control. None of them recovered from their bank and all three dropped to Earth. Balls of fire erupted on the ground where the planes crashed. Searching the sky, Danny could see only one parachute.

Goose and Danny looked dumbfounded at the other and the other sentries.

"Wha, what's going on Mendez?" one of them asked.

"I don't know, but it looks like a good time to take shelter!" Danny replied.

He reached for the radio at his side. Unclipping it, he brought it to his mouth and pushed the button, "Mrs. C, this is Danny at the front gate… come back?"

No response.

"Mrs. C… you there?"

Still no response.

Danny keyed the radio a few times, but it didn't make a sound. No click, no static, no nothing.

He looked to Goose, "It's dead… try yours."

Goose's radio wouldn't click either. He made sure it was on, but there was no juice. He shook his head, "It's dead too."

"I don't like this," Danny said. Then he looked at his watch. It had stopped.

"Goose, your watch working?"

Goose looked at his watch and thumped it hard a couple of times. "Nope... it's stopped."

Danny's face blanched and he stiffened. With wild eyes, he looked at Goose and leaped off the fence. In a dead run, he headed for the nearest ranch truck by the gate.

"What's wrong?" Goose yelled.

Danny ignored him as he jumped behind the wheel, pumped the gas and turned the key... nothing. Not even a "click". He tried again, still nothing, and again, and again, with the same results.

He staggered out of the truck, slammed the door, and started walking in circles, mumbling to himself.

Goose hustled over to his friend, "Danny! Talk to me, dog-gone-it!"

Danny stopped pacing. He was pale and looked like he was going to throw-up. Locking eyes on Duckett, he swore and spat out the letters, "EMP! I, I never thought they'd use one."

"What?!! What in the sam-hill are you talking about?!" Goose looked back to the ranch hands on the wall who were watching him and his friend.

Danny croaked out in a dry voice, "That's what took down those planes... broke our radios... stopped our watches. That truck won't even click... it's fried." He started moving again toward the men and was about to say something, when Goose grabbed his arm and spun him around.

"Will you talk to me?! What are you talking about? EMP?"

As Goose held his arm, Danny took a couple of deep breathes, calming himself. His eyes focused and he yanked his arm away.

These people need you, Mendez. Now get it together! You're the one with military training. Be a leader! Suck it up!

He spoke in a steady, calculating tone, "[24]EMP stands for Electro Magnetic Pulse. It's a weapon that we have long suspected our enemies had and would use if given the chance.

"Its sole purpose is to fry every electrical circuit in an area. Because we are so dependent on technology, our military leaders warned that it could render our forces deaf and blind.

"It would also make it impossible for us to repel an advancing force or retaliate for a nuclear strike."

He looked at Goose and then to the men standing on the fence, "This isn't some accident, guys. This is all-out war. We've got ta get ta shelter NOW!"

NEAR THE LAZY HOOF RANCH, MISSOULA, MONTANA – PRESENT DAY

Four days ago seemed like a lifetime, Danny thought. *So much has happened since then. It's hard to believe that we're even in the same country. It's more like we're behind enemy lines.*

Danny was still lying on his belly next to Goose as they watched the approaching military column. In spite of the potential danger, he couldn't help but think back to everything that had led up to this moment.

Shortly after the EMP went off and the bombs fell, Dr. Cooper's wife, Gabby, his kids, the ranch staff and all the remaining visitors went to ground – literally.

Underneath the main ranch house, Dr. Cooper had the foresight to build a bomb shelter stocked with a plethora of supplies and a short-wave radio. While monitoring transmissions, Mrs. C heard about the strange troop movements of foreign militaries who were plowing their way south, killing any American they found.

She told Danny that those sweeping troops would eventually find the "abandoned" ranch house and investigate. Such an investigation would most likely do two things:

> 1) Given the ranch's strategic location and ample supplies, those forces would use the Lazy Hoof as part of their logistic, re-supply route from the north. To do that, they'd have to leave some troops there to set up shop, trapping the hiding survivors underneath in the bomb shelter.
>
> 2) Given enough time, they would find the hidden trap door in the basement that led to the shelter. If that happened, there was no question that they would kill every last one of them.

Danny remembered the pained look in Mrs. Cooper's eyes when she told him, "It's time to abandon ship. We need to implement the bug-out plan."

The bug-out plan was possible because of Dr. Cooper's genius foresight. Amazingly, his boss had predicted their current reality.

Their ranch sat within a vast valley and in the shadow of the Bitterroot Mountains. Since Bryce had grown up with those mountains, he had thoroughly explored them as a child. So it was no surprise to Danny that shortly after he was hired, Dr. Cooper took him to a crook in the mountain's side where they shimmed through. What the California transplant saw in the beam of their flashlights was very surprising.

Hidden in the great mountain was an immense cave, or series of caves that appeared to be untouched. Then Dr. Cooper told Danny of his plans.

"And I need you to help me," Cooper told Mendez. "I don't need your help in here," he waved his arm at the expansive space, "I need your help there," Bryce pointed in the direction of the ranch, "to make sure things are running right. You've seen my plans for the place. I need to accomplish what I've laid out. But this," he pointed his chin to the inside of the cave, "this is our bug-out plan… just in case."

Then Dr. Cooper swore him to secrecy.

True to those plans, Cooper surreptitiously tunneled from the bomb shelter under the ranch, all the way to a subterranean entrance of those caves, but he didn't stop there.

A natural underground river ran below those mountains and the master-inventor Dr. Cooper developed a water-turned turbine to provide the cave with off-the-grid electrical power. The Boss literally carved out a place of safety within the mountain's belly. The granite formation of the mountain made it tough going and the costs were enormous.

Danny had suspected that Dr. Cooper was a millionaire. The physicist sent a private jet for Mendez when he was still in Alaska. The Angelino still remembered what Dr. Cooper told him;

> *"Well, Danny Boy, I'm gonna see to it that you're treated like a VIP*
> *your first time out. After that, you gotta earn your keep. Sound fair?"*

Dr. Cooper may not have been trying to impress him, but Mendez was thoroughly impressed. From that first phone call, Danny was treated very well and Dr. Cooper made him feel like an old friend.

The Boss might have been down-to-earth, but Mendez had heard scuttlebutt indicating that his employer was really a very wealthy man. The story said that as a teenager, the physicist invested well with some big Wall Street firm. A few years before the recent collapse of the U.S. economy, it was rumored that Dr. Cooper converted all of his stocks and bonds into gold and silver. The move made him even richer, people said, and it put him and the Lazy Hoof in the perfect position to ride out any storm.

When Danny first heard the plans for the cave, truth be told, the former Air Force Staff Sergeant thought they bordered on paranoia. Not that he'd ever say anything. He was just a hired gun to do a job.

However, Danny reminded himself during the build-out that Dr. Bryce Cooper was a certified genius and wasn't given to delusions. If he was concerned enough to go through the trouble of making a bomb shelter, an escape tunnel and then honing out living space for a hundred people in a cave, that was good enough for Mendez.

And then, of course, he listened to his boss. Cooper had shared with him many of his concerns about the future: the economy, how the government had begun to spy on its own people, a weakened military that just invited an attack on the homeland, the irresponsible opening of America's borders, genetic manipulation, Fukushima, growing seismic and volcanic activity, the potential of extreme solar flares and, most curious to Danny, was Cooper's concern about CERN.

Dr. Cooper came from the science community. Certainly he would know if there was a looming threat from CERN. After all, he used to work there!

The build-out of the cave had only been finished months earlier and although the accommodations were basic, there was enough bed space and supplies to sustain them for years.

Danny and Goose had been tasked with filling the shelter and escape tunnel with supplies because Dr. Cooper trusted them to keep quiet. As far as Danny could tell, no one else had a clue about the shelter, tunnel or cave.

During the bug-out, everyone helped cart supplies through the substantial tunnel to the cave.

Squeaking brakes of a foreign military truck pulled Mendez from his thoughts. Danger was close now.

The troop carrier had stopped on the side of the two-lane road and Danny considered their hiding spot. Did they need to bolt, or were they far enough away. After some thought, he was confident that they were okay for now and he went back to his previous musings.

After all the supplies had been transferred to the cave, he remembered setting explosives at key support structures of the tunnel. When he and Goose were a safe distance away, he hit the detonation switch. The length of the cave-in meant that there was no going back. On the bright side, if someone found the bunker, they couldn't dig through all of the rubble. The cave was safe for now.

While Dr. Cooper had built faraday cages to protect the most crucial electronics from a possible EMP, perhaps the best result of their bedrock cave dwelling, was that it was impervious to EMPs.

They had electricity, they had food, they had water, they had medicine, they had weapons, and other important supplies and they even had a short-wave radio. It could be worse.

Noisy troops piling out of the back end of their truck ripped Danny from his memories for good.

It appeared to Mendez that the men were very confident about their control of the area because they were anything but quiet. As they jumped down and milled around, they were all talking and joking loudly in a foreign language.

"Is that [25]Russian?" Goose whispered.

"Russian isn't one of my strong suits, but I'd say so," Danny agreed.

"I thought all you Army guys wore some sort of identification like patches and stripes? Those guys don't have any."

Danny, "You hillbilly, I was Air Force," he sniped, "but yeah, you're supposed to wear identification. Fact, I think it's in the Geneva Convention or something."

"The what?"

Mendez shook his head, "Never mind."

A tall, burly soldier walked to the back of the truck where the small group of troops were standing, "English, I told you! From now we speak English in case the locals hear us! You understand?!"

A chorus of, "Yes, Major!" ran through the group.

"Good! You have five minutes before we move!" With that, he headed back to the front of the truck.

A skinny recruit glanced at their retreating leader, and said in a combined Russian and Southern accent, "I am sure glad we stopped. I have to piss like Russian race horse!"

A chorus of laughter ripped through the group.

As he walked on unsteady legs, another loud soldier said, "I am glad we stopped too. My butt fell asleep!"

More laughs.

Just then, out of their field of view, Danny and Goose heard an American accent. "I am so glad to see you fellows!"

An elderly rancher walked up on the group holding a shotgun with the muzzle pointed at the ground. The Russians exchanged uncertain glances with one another.

Danny whispered urgently to Goose, "That's Old Man Wilson! We have to warn him!" and started to move.

Goose put his strong hand on his arm and held him down, "Not a good idea, buddy. Look."

The Major walked from the front of the truck.

"We haven't seen another living soul for days!" the kind-looking, white-haired, gentleman said, "And I heard there's chaos down in the city!" he pointed south. "Where you boys from?"

"Hello friend," the Major said in perfect, unaccented English. "Are you by yourself?" he asked, ignoring Wilson's question.

"Me? Naw. My ranch is down over that way. Family's in the house. A few of the ranch hands too. But when all the ruckus started, most of 'em took off, saying they had to find their own families. Power's been out for a while. Got a couple hundred head of cattle. Don't know how I'll manage without enough help."

"Couple hundred huh?" the Major asked impressed. "Where did you say your place was again?"

The rancher turned and pointed behind him, "'Bout a mile up the way, then left on the gravel road. Can't miss it."

Before Wilson's head could come back around, the Major snatched his sidearm out of its holster, leveled it at the rancher's head and pulled the trigger. He was dead before he hit the ground.

Danny and Goose flinched in their hide.

"You four," the Major said, "take the other vehicle and secure the ranch. Remember, English... act like you are there to help. No one left alive, understood? And then I want you to catch up to us. We're moving out!"

"Yes, Major," the four said as they trotted off toward the front of the column.

"You two!" the Major growled, "Get the body off the road!"

"Yes, Major!"

"Lieutenant!" the Major called.

"Yes, Comrade Major?" a younger officer said.

"Make sure you mark the location of the ranch on the map and note the livestock. You will need to add to the report anything else the scout party finds."

"Very good, Major," the Lieutenant replied.

"All of this will be ours," the Major said with a slit of a smile, "I'm sure there are many more ranches with cattle and horses that are just begging to be claimed."

As the small convoy rode off in a cloud of dust, Danny and Goose cautiously got to their feet.

"Many more ranches like The Lazy Hoof," Danny said bitterly.

"They're definitely not friendlies," Goose said.

"And they aren't taking any prisoners," Danny agreed.

"What was that about the cattle?"

"That's what an invading army does," Mendez said, heading back to the cave.

Goose who was still looking in the direction of the departed Russians, asked, "An invading army?" he turned around and quick-stepped to fall in line with his friend.

"Yup," Danny said as he trudged forward through the tall grass, "You send in a recon team. Evaluate targets and assets. Then you make a detailed list of both. Only then do you send in the big guns to take the land."

"Take the land? Like.." Goose paused for a moment, "like in a war."

Danny stopped to face his friend. "Like in a war. But it's not just that. My guess is that it was them that launched those nukes and the EMP bomb. From what we heard on the radio, other strategic sites were hit with nuclear ordinance and the EMPs were set off all over the country. After they think we're softened up, they'll send in heavy forces to clean up," he started walking again.

"But what about those planes we saw shooting at each other?" Dave asked, pointing in the direction of Missoula with his thumb. "Those looked like Americans shooting at Americans. That's a civil war! How are we supposed to stop the Russians from invading, when we're fighting each other?!"

"Exactly!"

"Exactly?" the brown-bearded man asked, frustrated, "What does that mean?!" He grabbed his friend's arm and spun him around forcefully.

"It means," Danny shrugged off his friend's hand and got in Dave's face, "that

93

we are the only thing that stands between them and our land! Get used to it and suck it up!" He backed up, "Cuz I don't know about you, but I'm not going down without a fight."

"Danny, you know me. I'm always up for a good fight. But this… how are we supposed to fight an army?"

"There's that," Mendez replied, "So we gotta get some help. And we gotta get organized before it's too late. I hear a resistance is already forming. Time to report what we've seen and blast it over the short-wave. After that, maybe we can do a little recon of our own."

"I hope it's not already too late," Goose said with disgust as he started trudging ahead of his friend. Dave's shoulders drooped and he looked sullen.

Danny backhanded him in the arm, "Hey, it ain't over. Now come on, we got a war to fight!"

- Part Two -

Unrestrained

ELEVEN

THE BASE OF MT. GRAHAM, TUCSON, ARIZONA – PRESENT DAY

The sharp blue hue of the cloudless sky stretched for as far as the eye could see and the air was as still as a mountain lion waiting to pounce. Reddish sand and dust lay on the narrow road's blacktop, undisturbed. Waves of heat wafted off the long stretch of highway that led back to town, as the temperature spiked to over 110° in the shade.

Breaking the silence, a low rumbling groan quickly grew in pitch until it became a quiet scream. A couple of feet above the deserted road, a thin, vertical line of blinding white light burst through into the empty air, slicing the stillness. The light stretched into a jagged [26]crack in time as it grew in height and width until it stabilized.

Out of the crack, a hand emerged, then a foot, a leg, and then the rest of Dr. Bryce Cooper's body followed as he stepped out of the dimensional slice and onto the road. Behind him Juni stumbled out and Gabe, in his glorified fullness, crossed onto the pavement.

"Wha... What is this place?" Juni asked. "Another dimension?"

Bryce chuckled, "No, just Arizona."

"Arizona? The desert? You brought me to the desert? Why?"

"Because" Gabe answered, "there is someone you must meet here before he goes up the mountain."

Juni looked up the hill and followed the long, windy road

up with his eyes. It was much too tall to see the top, "What's up there?"

"Your date with destiny," Bryce quipped.

"Destiny?" Juni furrowed his brow, "My destiny?"

"No," Gabe offered, "not your destiny. The destiny of the one you are waiting for. He will need... moral support and some of your unique insight about volcanos."

"How am..." Juni started to say when the same moan was heard and the portal opened again. Gabe walked back through without another word.

"What is he talking about, Dr. Bryce? Who am I waiting for?"

"Oh, you'll know him when you see him. He'll be the only one to come down this road and he'll look lost. He'll be here in a jiffy," Bryce stepped back through the opening and disappeared as, with a brief sucking sound, the doorway collapsed in on itself.

Juni blinked and looked around. The desert was still once again.

Regaining his composure, he said, "Ang malaking lang! I cross time and space with two crazies and they leave me in the desert to bake!" He wiped his sweaty brow with his forearm.

He spied a sliver of shade next to a Saguaro cactus and wandered off the road. He plopped down on a large rock under the cactus, and said aloud "With those wormhole things they could take me anywhere. A beach with the cool breeze and a cold drink... the mountains with its pine-scented air... or even..."

He suddenly remembered that there was a war going on and he again searched his surroundings for any signs of life - nothing. "What could be so important that they drop me here to wait? They wouldn't put me in danger."

Little did he know that the world was about to become extremely dangerous for all of mankind.

Outskirts of Tel Aviv, Israel – Present Day

His arms had angry and weeping blood-blisters oozing fluid, and they still felt like they were on fire even two days after the attack. Moans, groans and even screams, resonated throughout the shelter.

He was grateful. For some reason, they'd stuck him in a cubicle with a lone cot. While he could still hear the injured and dying, he didn't have to look at them.

There's so many wounded, he thought, *there just aren't enough doctors and medicine to go around.*

Joe lay on his bed, eyes toward the ceiling and said a silent prayer, one of many this day.

This makeshift shelter and hospital was in a fallback position on the outskirts of Tel Aviv, Israel.

The casualties were a result of a sneak, chemical weapons attack on the city by the new terror organization, ISNW. In their official statement, the so-called Caliphate, or State, said that the attack was in retaliation for the destruction of Mecca by one of Israel's atomic bombs.

That's ridiculous, Joe thought. *Why would Israel blow up the holiest city of their enemy? That's just askin' for trouble! Israel's way too smart for that!*

Although there was no official confirmation as yet, rumors were now circulating that out of the four-hundred-thousand plus of the city's population, two-thirds of them had been killed and many of the survivors were badly wounded.

I was one of the lucky ones… luckier than Eleazar. I'm sorry, old friend. I'm going to miss you.

Josiah and Ruby Wells were Bryce Cooper's uncle and aunt. Ruby was Bryce's mother's older sister. Joe had been Jeremiah Cooper's best friend. Jerry inherited a large, fledgling cattle ranch in Missoula, Montana known as the Lazy Hoof. After he and Bryce's mother were married, the two newlyweds decided to turn the ranch into a Quarter Horse breeding facility and asked Joe and Ruby to help.

It was a labor of love. The two couples worked hard to turn the homestead around. As a consequence, Bryce saw his Uncle Joe and his Aunt Ruby every day. Ruby had become a second mother to him and Joe was a tough second father.

Joe was a second-degree black belt in Aikido and trained Bryce in the art form when Cooper was a small child in their makeshift dojo in the ranch's barn. Josiah Wells was also a numbers-cruncher and often helped Bryce with his homework. Joe smiled, remembering the time at age seven when Bryce brought home a book on Linear Algebra.

Linear Algebra? I didn't even know there was such a thing.

Bryce's dad died when Bryce was eight and the loss crushed the boy. Joe stepped in as a full-time, father figure, while still building the ranch. Bryce had become so close to his Uncle that he'd even started calling him "Pop."

When Bryce's mother contracted inoperable cancer, Joe and Ruby stood helplessly by and watched the boy deal with the long goodbye. Angry, bitter and determined to make it in the world without depending on anyone, a heartbroken Cooper went off to California to attend the University of Stanford at the age of thirteen.

After that, the ranch's success grew exponentially. Joe faithfully saved the substantial profits for the ranch's sole owner, Bryce. Joe invested the funds with a successful money manager on Wall Street and before Bryce finished his Ph.D. at MIT, he was a multimillionaire.

Eventually Dr. Bryce Cooper would see many things that helped bring clarity to his loss and the painful years of his youth. When that happened, he came home.

With Bryce home and Joe and Ruby getting older, their role at the ranch no longer felt necessary because Bryce threw himself into the running of the ranch.

"That's my boy," Joe whispered to the ceiling from his bunk.

Joe and Ruby wanted to go to Israel. Cooper insisted on paying for everything. So fulfilling their lifelong dream, Bryce bought them a beautiful home in an upscale neighborhood in Tel Aviv along with all the furnishings.

That was three years ago.

They could have never imagined that their dream would turn into their current nightmare.

Tel Aviv, Israel – Three Days Ago

Ruby opened the front door and stuck her head out, "Would you two like…"

The shrill of air raid sirens pierced the quiet afternoon.

"What's going on?!" she asked Joe in a panic.

He jumped to his feet, "I don't know!"

He looked at his neighbor and friend, Eleazar who was still sitting in his chair on the porch. The old man shook his head and shrugged.

Joe pulled his eyes from his friend to a swelling commotion in the street - people running. All were moving in the same direction, away from… something. Many had automatic rifles and most carried gas masks in hand, trying to put them on.

Joe raced across his lawn to the street and yelled, "What's going on?"

No one paid any attention.

He tried a different tactic.

A young girl, no more than sixteen, raced by with a rifle slung over her shoulder. As she desperately tried pulling on her gas mask, Joe clamped down on her arm.

"What's going on?" Joe shouted over the sirens.

The girl's deep brown eyes were filled with fear, as she pointed in the distance, "The ISNW! They're coming!"

Joe felt like someone just kicked him in the gut, "What?" He let the girl go.

I knew this day could come… just not so soon.

The girl backpedaled, pointing, "Get to your shelter NOW!" and then she rejoined the running mob.

Joe regained his composure, turning to tell his wife to get their gas masks, but a high-pitched noise stopped him cold.

He had been a Marine in Vietnam… and some things you just didn't forget.

The subsonic whistle of an inbound missile split through

101

the urgent whine of the sirens.

That's close... we've got to get to shel...

BOOM!

The air above him exploded in a blinding flash of light.

The concussive force from the airburst hammered Joe to the ground, knocking the wind out of him.

Gasping for breath, he rolled and forced himself to all fours. Blue Tel Aviv sky had turned to putrid, yellowish-green and a fog descended on the city.

"Joooeeeee! Joe! Look at me! Joe!"

A concussed daze made the voice sound tinny and far away. He craned his head toward its source on his front porch.

He saw Eleazar's odd angled legs and slid his eyes to Ruby with her gasmask on and shouting from the steps.

"Here!" she yelled, "Put this on!" as she tossed his gasmask in a high arcing throw.

The motion snapped him out of his daze. He caught the mask like a catcher digging out a fastball from the dirt.

In one fluid motion, he put the mask on and cleared the filters with a quick powerful breath – just before the deadly chemicals started to rain down on him.

OUTSKIRTS OF TEL AVIV, ISRAEL – PRESENT DAY

There must have been phosphorus mixed in with those chemicals, Joe thought, not for the first time.

It had been a beautiful day on the Mediterranean in Tel Aviv. Like most people, Joe was wearing a short-sleeve, thin shirt during the attack. He had suffered the consequences.

Thankfully his gas mask had a hood attached to it that pulled down over his head and his pants were thick enough to protect him from most of the caustic weapon. The mustard-gas-like substance could account for some of his blisters and later nausea and vomiting, but that didn't explain the burns to

his back and arms. There had to be something more mixed in
with it.

Had to be phosphorus...

He was miserable, but others were far worse off.
Gruesome scenes of oozing green and pink holes burnt right
through people were common in the shelter. Bodies were
scattered everywhere on the streets. ISNW meant to not only
kill, but also to maim as many Israelis as possible.

Those sorry sons... he bit off the thought, *I'm sorry, Lord, and
I know that's not how I should react. I still have it better than
Eleazar... or do I?*

When he had reached the porch, he saw Eleazar's eyes
open, unseeing in death. The force of the explosion had
knocked the old man's chair back. His neck had hit the porch
railing and snapped. He died instantly.

"Are you feeling any better?" Ruby asked as she walked
into the cubicle.

He sniffed and sat up on the edge of the cot, "I'm fine."

She squatted down on her haunches and patted his leg.
"I'm sorry, Joe. I wish I could do something," she said with
narrowed eyes and her brow turned down in concern. She
didn't dare try to hug him, although that's all she wanted to
do. "Has the burning gone away some, at least?" She gently
blew on one of the weeping sores on his arm.

"I'm fine!" Joe said, a little more forcefully than he meant.

Ruby knew her husband well enough to know that he
would not let himself be perceived as weak or hurting,
something about the old Marine in him. She changed the
subject.

"I finally heard from Jerusalem."

Joe leaned forward on his cot, "And?"

Since the attacks on Tel Aviv and Haifa, communication
had ground to a halt. "Any word from Bryce?" he asked
quickly.

Ruby pursed her lips and scratched her head as if trying to decide how to tell Joe, "Well... no. He's disappeared."

Joe dropped his chin into his chest, "Huh... who could blame him? Probably gone to ground some..."

"No, Josiah, I mean he disappeared!"

Joe squinted at his wife and cocked his head, "Come again?"

"The priests said that he went into the Holy of Holies, but never came out."

"Whaaaaat?"

"I know, I know. Sounds crazy. But after that, they didn't dare send someone in after him. Because of the attack, they've evacuated most of the people from the Temple and left a skeleton crew for upkeep. When I asked if they were afraid that the attacks would push toward Jerusalem, they said they didn't think so."

"Doesn't sound too crazy. [27]Muslims have been saying for years that they wanted to make Jerusalem their capital. They won't risk ruining it with a WMD attack... What's this about Bryce?"

"That's all I know," Ruby stood and blew out a long breath.

Joe was quiet for a few beats, trying to make sense of the news.

A smile grew on his face and he said, "Well, you know our boy... he's sure to turn up somewhere."

TWELVE

Zac's ears rang, making it impossible to hear. His eyes stung and watered from the biting smoke that hung in the air after the firefight. His protégé, Mosi, was dead and so was the rest of his team.

How could we have parachuted right into the middle of an ambush?

Before their feet even touched the ground, hot green tracers from AK-47s lit up the LZ and shredded many of his team while they were still in the sky.

Those that weren't immediately killed were wounded. How he managed to land and roll to cover, unscathed, was beyond him.

The battle had thus far been one-sided. He had heard the cries of the remaining team members as each of them succumbed to their attackers.

Our attackers? Who, or what are they?

He was a devout student of The Rabbi, but he wasn't a superstitious man. Yet, this small opposing force, made up of no more than ten men, seemed to be guided by an unseen force.

The night was pitch black, but he could hear them easily moving into position without stumbling or bumping into anything. They were trying to flank him. He'd managed to steal a couple of glances at them and saw that they were operating with the most basic of equipment. They had old

AKs and certainly didn't have night-vision goggles.

So how could they see? How did they know where we'd land? A HALO jump was too imprecise for anyone to know with certainty where we'd land. Yet, they were waiting for us? How?

Zac had drawn blood of his own. Before the rest of his team was killed, they and the Mossad agent killed all but two of the attackers.

One against two... and I have night-vision goggles.

A ricocheting bullet yanked him back to the present.

The attackers had a problem. There weren't enough of them to box in the Israeli. Try as they might, they couldn't flank him, which meant that sooner or later, they would try to charge him. When they did, he would be ready.

[28]Those eyes... It doesn't make sense... they looked just like... No, it couldn't be!

He heard movement to his left. They were trying to circle around him again.

"Amateurs!" he whispered, "I have a little surprise for you."

His mind drifted back to the eyes of his attackers. They were inhuman, even otherworldly. They were...

It can't be!

They were the eyes of Dormin in his dream.

Oklahoma Mountain Gateway, Present Day

He wasn't asleep. Larry Taylor had "seen" himself leave his body. One second he was in a heavy-duty conversation with God about Israel and the next, he was here.

Although it wasn't the first time he had a vision, it never became routine.

When the Holy Land had been attacked a few days ago, something inside of him tripped like a circuit breaker on a house. Larry felt the change in the supernatural and he knew that the attack had repercussions in the dimensions outside of the normal human's perspective. Those repercussions would be immediate and severe.

No doubt about it...

On top of being the portal keeper for this part of the country, Taylor had an affinity for Israel and her leaders, even though he wasn't Jewish himself.

Larry wondered why people didn't ask God to show them more things in the supernatural. He supposed it was because it could be kinda scary for most folk. He remembered out of Exodus 20:19 when the Israelites [29]saw the lightning and thunder on the mountain. They were so scared that they told Moses:

> *"Speak thou with us, and we will hear: but let not God speak with us, lest we die!"*

It occurred to Larry that God had always wanted to speak directly with His people. But he supposed that to have that kind of relationship with the Creator took a whole lot more effort than people wanted to dish out.

Me included sometimes. And how the heck do you see thunder anyway?

He wondered if this was the plan of the enemy all along. If the devil could cause a division between God and Man, people would drift away from Him. The Bible was full of Last Days warnings saying that people would become lovers of self instead of lovers of God.

Sure sounds like today's world.

His attention was drawn back to the vision in which he now found himself.

Christians often called this place "the heavenlies," but he'd come to understand it in a little different way. Through his research, the data pointed to this being an extra-dimensional reality that superseded the earth's 3D physical laws. Here, the limits of his fleshly body were lifted and all of his senses became alive, making colors crisper, his vision sharper and the smells fuller.

He'd come to call this "The Other Place" and the experience of being here couldn't be compared to anything in the physical 3D world. When he tried to explain the experience to people, words failed him. There was no sense of time here and no means of measurement. Those were things related to the physical laws of earth.

He'd been walking alone in a passageway without walls, ceilings or floors. The dark gray fog that surrounded him felt like it was alive, pulsating and vibrating in a translucent sort of mushy solidness.

Walking by the leading of the Spirit, he understood that he was headed in the right direction. More importantly, he sensed that he was going to a place that he'd been to before. As he continued walking, he remembered the first time he'd come down this path.

Just like this time, he was walking alone. Then he had sensed another person walking beside him.

When he'd looked to his side, he saw a gleaming white giant who's very personage commanded authority. Since words were not necessary in this realm, he communicated with the illuminated being through thoughts. He knew him to be Michael, one of the heavenly hosts. The archangel had acted as his guide and protector on numerous occasions both in The Other Place and on earth.

As they walked at a fast clip, the smoke began to clear. Michael slid his hand to the pure gold hilt of his sword, ready to deftly draw it from its scabbard in a moment's notice.

The passageway opened up into a huge chamber and Taylor was filled with both a sense of wonder and trepidation.

A large, clear box at least three stories high sat as a prison at the center of the chamber. Within its confines stood a 25 foot creature that radiated a brilliant violet light. Humanoid in shape, its huge shoulders shifted and rippled as it leaned against the side of the box. Larry walked closer.

In his mind, Larry heard, "I know you."

Glancing over to Michael, his protector gave him an affirming nod, "You're okay. But be careful. He's extremely dangerous."

A Voice with the sound of many waters interrupted his thoughts. "Do not be afraid," and He told him the "name" of the violet entity. Yet, as soon as he heard it, he forgot what the Voice called it.

All he knew was that it was a very long, ancient name that was made up of several words. Although he couldn't remember the actual moniker, he did remember its purpose and attributes; and they weren't good. Larry simply called it Ancient Evil.

The creature's power was immense and incomprehensible to the average man. The being could "erase" anything that stood in its way like a living, black hole. He shivered at the thought.

There was only one thing standing between him and the awesome creature in the box: the Voice of many waters. If it were not for Him, Taylor too would be erased.

"You are the keeper of the mountain," the creature said, "the one that prays for Israel. I too serve the Voice of many waters."

What? How could this creature serve The Creator?

Taylor's focus came back to the present and he found himself walking down the same passageway.

Like before, he had started the journey on his own, but as he looked over, Michael was by his side.

But this time, as they entered the chamber with the three-story-high clear box, Michael didn't prepare to draw his sword. Soon, Larry understood why and he trembled.

The clear box was empty.

Taylor considered the turn of events.

The creature couldn't escape on its own. It had to have been set free.

Set free?!

There could only be one reason why the being was let out of its prison. The last great battle for mankind must be close, because...

Ancient Evil was loose.

THIRTEEN

The men were breathing hard and dripping with sweat. As it turned out, Russian troops had surrounded Missoula. Danny and Goose sprinted, dropped, crab-walked, waited and prayed the whole way. They were dog-tired and still had miles to go.

The men rested against a boulder, in the shade of a Black Cottonwood Tree speaking in low tones. The hundred-and-twenty-foot tree had long ago shed its cotton-like, leaf buds from which the tree got its name.

Danny's eyes were closed and he appeared to be asleep. Goose ran his hand against the stout tree's bark and talked with nervous energy.

"You know," he said quietly, "I bet this tree is at least three-hundred years old. I read somewhere that they can live that long, ya know."

"You don't say," Danny responded, with eyes shut, "Didn't know that."

"Ha, something I know that you don't? Well, did you know that the tree…"

"No, I didn't mean I didn't know about the tree. They're all over the place. I know plenty about 'em," Mendez said, without opening his eyes, "What I meant is that I didn't know the other thing."

"Other thing?" Goose asked, "What other thing?"

Danny opened one squinted eye to look at him, "That you could read..."

"That I could read?!"

Dave elbowed him in the arm.

Silence fell between the two men as they sat alone with their thoughts.

Goose was the first to speak, "Whad-a-ya think is gonna happen? I mean, what're we gonna do? Held up in a cave, no power for the outside world, foreign troops all over..." his voice trailed off.

"Don't know," Danny said honestly, "But one thing's for sure... life will never be the same."

"You got that right," Goose agreed sullenly, "Not only have we got Russians scurrying around like army ants, but Missoula's probably blown to all h... And that's the other thing. How in the world is there suppose-tah be civilization when they dropped that, that EMP thingy?! You said it would fry the electrical grid and all the transformers and stuff. Heck, even our trucks didn't work. How we suppose-tah get them going again with all these troops..."

Danny sat straight up, "That's right... How are we supposed to get the electricity working, our cars... More importantly, how did THEY get them working?

"I'm not kidding, Danny! This is serious! It's not the time to mess with me!"

"No, bro. I'm not messing with you. You are a genius! You know that? A certified genius!" Danny said in an excited whisper.

Eyes narrowed suspiciously, Goose said, "I don't follow."

"That's it!" Danny continued enthusiastically. "The

Russian's vehicles and their electrical stuff would have been fried with everyone else's!"

"But they didn't... so what does that mean?"

"It means, my ugly, genius friend, that they weren't around here!"

"Huh?"

"It means that the Russians knew when that EMP blast was going to happen, so they stayed out of the affected zone."

"But those troops were on us in no time. It must mean that they started out pretty close, right?"

"You got that right," Danny agreed. "You remember that guy, Steve Quayle, that the Boss had up here a few years ago? It was about the time you got hired."

"Yeah, I think so. I never talked to him, but I remember he and Dr. Cooper spent a lot of time together. Something about prepping the ranch?"

"Not only did they spend a lot of time together, Quayle was instrumental in outfitting The Lazy Hoof for a time just like this! The bomb shelter, the food, fuel and weapon stores... all his idea. Anyway, I remember overhearing him tell the Boss about sightings of Russian troops in Canada and northern Montana."

"Really?"

"Really! And judging by the events of the last few days, my guess is that those Russians were hunkered down not too far up north."

"Just outside of the EMP blast radius" Goose added.

"Yep, they probably have a staging area up there."

Danny fell silent for a moment while the wheels turned and then said, "That's it! That's what we're going to do!"

"What we're going to do?"

"You remember the conversations Gabby had on the short-wave with those other people in hiding?"

"You mean from the Resistance?"

"That's right, the Resistance."

"Yeah"

"So that's what we're going to do."

"Huh?"

"We're gonna resist! We're gonna find out as much information about these Russians as possible and how they came into our country unscathed. Obviously they had a plan."

"Whada- yah talkin about?"

Danny rose to his feet, "Logistics, Goose. Every army needs it."

"Logistics?" Goose asked as he stood.

"Supply lines, my friend. Every army has to be supplied. This creates a long line back to the source. In this case, my guess is that the lines will go to the edge of Canada. Those troops didn't just wander in here. They knew where they were going and when to go. Time for a little recon."

"Recon..." Goose mused, "I'm in. Beats sitting around here waiting to be shot."

"Good, let's get back to the cave and let Mrs. Cooper know what we're planning."

The two men headed off at a slow trot. They hadn't made it more than a few hundred yards when they rounded a boulder and found a young woman in a Russian soldier's uniform, squatting on the other side of the boulder with her pants around her ankles and an AK-47 at her side.

Startled at the sight of each other, the ranch hands and the girl stared for a fraction of a second.

Before the men could react, the woman snatched up her

weapon in one fluid motion without getting out of her squat. She leveled the rifle at Danny and Goose.

Mt. Graham Observatory, Tucson, Arizona – Present Day

Cooper was right; when the man in the beat-up, old Nissan showed up down the hill, he did look lost.

"But why am I here?" Juni asked from the overstuffed chair in the waiting room.

Mora appeared to be uneasy as he sat in his chair. He bounced his heel rapidly.

The Professor pulled his eyes from his survey of the room's surroundings, "No sé. But it must be for a good reason. Dr. Cooper and his friend do not make mistakes." As soon as he made the statement, his foot went back to bouncing.

"His friend? You mean that…"

Alvaro's eyes snapped back on Juni before he could finish his statement, "Shhhh… ¡Cállate! Remember, who sent us must remain a secret," he scolded.

"A secret?" Juni was incredulous.

At that moment, one of the tall, mahogany, double doors opened and a secretary came out, "His Holiness will see you now. Please follow me."

Juni's face betrayed his surprise. Tilting his head to the Professor as the two rose out of their chairs, through the side of his mouth, he asked, "His Holiness? Professor, what have you got me into?"

Mora cracked a smile and placed his hand on the man's shoulder, "Just here to see an old friend, one that I swore I would never talk to again."

BEHIND ENEMY LINES – PRESENT DAY

Zac's chest heaved up and down as he tried to catch his breath.

After he'd dispatched the last two ambushers, he grabbed all the supplies he could carry and set out in a dead run in the direction of his objective. He didn't stop until he was well-clear of the hostile zone.

While he escaped from the firefight unscathed, he still had the arm wound he'd gotten in Egypt a few days ago. With all the exertion and dwindling spike of adrenaline, his appendage felt like it was on fire.

"What are you going to do now, Zechariah?" he asked himself.

Of course there were contingencies for mission problems. However, none of them outlined how to succeed if all of the team members and most of the supplies were lost.

Calming himself as he laid on his back, catching his breath, Zechariah did the only thing he knew how to do at that moment. He prayed.

"Adoni, I ask for your favor. I ask for your mercy. And, I ask for your direction. I do not know what, or who, those attackers were, but they were not human. I am in the middle of something I do not understand and I am alone. Please help me."

After blowing out a long, relaxing breath, he rolled over on his stomach and rose to a crouch. While he didn't have any clear answers, the Mossad agent did feel better. He'd wait for the answer to his prayer, but in the meantime, he'd keep moving.

One man or not, he still had a mission to accomplish.

LARGE HADRON COLLIDER, GENEVA, SWITZERLAND – PRESENT DAY

In the Control Room, the hum of the Collider six-hundred feet below them couldn't be heard, but the signs of the world's largest machine doing its work were evident. The overhead lights were wobbling and there was the ever-present vibration as the machine closed in on its targeted speed.

Already, wave-changes in time-space were beginning to pierce earth's physical laws. Unlike Cooper's unintentional experiment results with the LHC, Abbot was [30]purposely tearing a hole in the fabric of space-time.

He was well on his way to completing this job when he heard a radio squawk in the background and someone speaking.

"Dr. Abbot?" a technician said, "It's Corkscrew."

With his concentration broken, he dropped his head and blew out a long, aggravated breath. Looking to his number two, he said, "Make sure we stay on track! Nothing can stop us now. I have to take this."

"Yes, sir."

He picked up the radio, "This is Control, over."

"Control, this is Corkscrew. What is your status? Over," a disembodied voice asked.

Corkscrew is the only person I would allow to interrupt me during this critical juncture. After all, we are both on the same team... so to speak.

"No worries, Corkscrew. We are on track and will be at 100% power in the time we have discussed. Over."

"Very good. We are also in position and have raised the dish. Just making our final checks now. Over."

"Have you had any unwanted interest in your work by the

locals? Over."

"Not really. We are well away from the city, with only farmhouses around us. Soon it will not matter anyway, will it? Over."

"Ha, you are right about that, mate. Soon, everyone will get an eyeful. I need to get back to the acceleration. We will speak again when we are closer. Over."

"Understood. We'll talk soon. Over and out."

Looking at the technician at the power console, Dr. Ian Abbot shouted, "It's time to begin acceleration!"

FOURTEEN

"**H**old on there, pretty lady," Goose said, hands raised and sliding to his right. He stole an urgent glance at Danny and continued, "We don't want any trouble. We're just passing through."

The young woman looked scared. Danny guessed that she was probably no older than seventeen or eighteen. Her face was smudged with dirt and puffy, like she'd been crying. Her Russian uniform pants were down around her ankles, and not because she was using the bathroom. This was something else. Something ugly.

While keeping her eyes locked on the men, the girl slowly stood as she cinched up her pants with one hand and kept her other finger close to the AK's trigger.

Trying again, Goose said in a steady but friendly tone, "Please, Miss. We just want to get home. We…"

Danny slightly shifted at Duckett's side. The move wasn't lost on the girl. She might be young, but not stupid.

"Nyet!" she said firmly. "Don't try anything foolish, or," her glare turned to ice, "you will not make it home."

The men traded a look and Danny breathed out slowly. *She'd only kill us if she felt threatened. Best to relax.*

They were safe - for now.

The wiry, blond teen scanned the area, looking for her comrades as she kept the gun pointed at the men. After a moment, she asked in perfect English, "You two live around here?"

Goose deferred to Danny, who said, "Not far. Your English is very good."

119

She pursed her lips, "I have been here a long time. A sleeper, as you call it."

"A sleeper? So, this has been planned all along?" Danny ventured.

"Unfortunately," she looked around again, "The powers-that-be are never satisfied with what they have. They always want more. They always want," she paused and swallowed hard, "what someone else has."

Ahhh, thought Danny, *she doesn't want to be here anymore than we do. In fact, she's probably a reluctant soldier at best and a prisoner, somebody's sex slave, at worst. Maybe we can help each other.*

After a long pause, it was Danny's turn to look around. "Won't they be wondering where you are?"

The rifle's barrel came down a smidge and she lowered her chin. Remorse filled her eyes, "Not really. We broke for lunch and it's not my turn to cook. So I won't be missed right away," another pause. She gestured with the barrel of the weapon to the side, "Look, you can go. Just don't tell them I saw you," her eyes were almost pleading, "They could make it very difficult for me and..."

"And what?" Goose asked.

Her chin tightened, "They will kill you without hesitation."

"Why didn't you?" Danny asked.

"Huh," she grunted in disgust and dropped the barrel of the gun, pointing it fully to the ground. "Because I am not a killer. And, I have enough of killing! You should have seen what they did on the way here! They killed anything that moved. Men, women, children, unarmed people just wanting to find out what was going on." Tears welled up in her eyes.

"We've seen some of it," Danny said, as he thought back to old-man Wilson.

"I am just trying to stay alive and not get..." her voice trailed off as a tear rolled down her cheek. She wiped it away with the back of her hand. "These people..." she said with a slightly raised voice, "they have taken everything from me. And," she swallowed hard, "They keep on taking me every time they get a chance," another tear. "I've been in America so long, I've almost forgot what Russia was like. I'm probably more American than Russian. But they want to kill America. They want it all for themselves."

now tears freely flowed down her cheeks, "The Americans I've known… People trusted me. I… I didn't know it was going to be like this!

"They took me away from my parents when I was ten years old! Said I needed to be trained. Raised me in a boarding school. I haven't spoken to my mother and father in person since then. They have threatened me over and over and said that if I did not cooperate, they would kill my family. And even now," she swallowed hard, "they think they can take me any time they want to," she said bitterly. "It would be better if I were never born!"

More silence.

After a couple of beats, Danny ventured, "You could come with us. We'll make sure to leave you some place safe. Somewhere away from here," he added.

"Safe?" she scoffed. "Where do you think is safe? What you are seeing here is happening all over the US. [31]Your country… it's being sliced up and divided."

"Divided?" Goose asked with alarm, "Divided by who?"

She waved him off, "It doesn't matter. Besides, if they found out I left with you they would kill us both… and my parents."

"Well," Goose's husky voice was low, "according to you, they'll kill us anyway. Dead is dead," he shared a look with Danny, "If we have to die, at least we'd be helping someone. How do you know that your parents are still alive? Are they in America?"

"I do not know. I don't think they're in America. We came in through Canada before they separated me from them. I think they are still there. Sometimes the soldiers would give me letters from them."

Danny shared a look with Goose. He wanted to help, but he wasn't sure if he could trust her enough to take her to the Cave.

"Well," Danny slowly reached for the AK-47, "we're headed up north to see what we can see. I'm sure we can find a place along the way to leave you," he looked in the direction of her fellow soldiers, "Any place is better than here, right?"

She also looked in the direction he was looking and swallowed hard. She handed him the rifle, "Yes, you are right, of course. Anyplace is better than here. But if we are going to leave, we must go now. Before they

121

notice that I didn't come back."

Goose was already moving, "You don't have to tell me twice. This way," the big man said as he led them north, away from the soldiers in the distance.

"What's your name?" Danny asked.

The young woman seemed to think about it for a moment, "I've had many names in the past few years, like a chameleon blending into the scenery. Whatever the situation called for, I would adapt in order to succeed at my mission."

Goose asked over his shoulder, still moving forward, "Your mission?"

"Yes. I have never told anyone my real name."

"Really?"

"Really"

"So what is your real name?" Danny prodded.

She stopped and so did they.

"My name is Anya. I am a Russian spy."

"A spy?" they started walking again,

"Yes, not regular army. I was sent here to gather intelligence. Which I have done since I was little. And as a reward, they threw me in with those," she looked over her shoulder in distain, "svoloch'."

The group was quiet for a while.

"Were," Danny searched for the right words, "Were they abusing you?"

Anya's face turned red, but she said, "Every chance they got! They just got done with me when you found me. I stopped fighting them after a while. Too many of them and they are very strong," she sniffed.

Again Goose stopped and looked her in the eye. He looked angry, "We promise, you can run with us until you're safe. Then you can make your own way. We just need to find out where all these supplies are coming from."

"Supplies?" she asked, "You mean as in their supply routes?"

The two Americans traded a cautious look. "Auh, that's right. That's why we're headed up north. I suppose it's safe enough to tell you that since you've run off. A deserter wouldn't very well go back and tell the men that abused her of our plans."

Anya's eyes were focused on the ground, as though she were thinking, "You do not have to worry about me telling. I'm done with them. I've been used for the last time. In fact, perhaps I can help with your search. Maybe we can help each other."

"How's that?" Danny asked.

"When they stuck me with that regular army garbage, they made me their logistics liaison. I know exactly where and how their logistics are routed."

"You're kidding."

"No, I am not. In fact, I can do better than that; I know who is in charge and where they are."

Danny and Goose exchanged a look, "Far from here?" Danny inquired.

"Not too far. Just on the other side of the Canadian border near a town called Cranbrook."

They stopped again.

"Wew, not far huh? That's a good two-hundred-plus miles," Goose said.

"And across rugged Montana terrain," Danny added. "Maybe it wasn't such a good idea after all."

"That is no problem," Anya said, "Up here is a motor-pool. I can get us a truck and," she looked them over, sizing them up, "Some regular army uniforms that should fit. We can drive there unimpeded in a few hours."

"Really?" Danny asked stunned.

"Really. Remember I'm the logistics liaison. I can get whatever I need. Plus, some of those people owe me a favor. If you don't have to talk to anyone on the way, we just might be able to get to the base."

"Base?" Goose asked, swallowing hard.

"Not really a base. Just a makeshift, forward operating point. The town was wiped out when they swooped in," she looked down, ashamed and then regained her composure. "Those animals killed a lot of innocent people. There's no resistance up there now. Security is lax. They think they've caught everyone by surprise."

"Well, they sure caught us by surprise. No way we saw this comin'," Goose said.

"I will help you get all the way to the base on one condition."

"Condition?" Danny asked, "What's that?"

A sly smile formed on the young woman's face, "That when we get there, you help me capture and interrogate someone."

"What?!" Goose asked in surprise. "Look, little lady. We'd like to help, really. But capturing and interrogating people... we're just ranch hands. We don't know nothin about interrogation."

Danny held up a hand to his friend to silence him. "Who is this person that you want to capture and interrogate?"

Anya cleared her throat, "The head of the base is a general. I believe he will know where my parents are and how I can find them. Last I knew, they were in Canada still. Perhaps we can..." she corrected herself, "Perhaps I can go find them after. But at the same time, you will be able to ask the general questions about his plans for your country. You may be able to stop some of the bloodshed, at least."

"Look, he's a general, for cryin' out loud," Goose said, "There's no way we'll even be able to get close to him, much less snatch him. This is a way bad idea."

"Not to worry," she said, "As I said, I am logistics and people owe me favors. Not only can we get close to him, I can probably get alone with him."

Goose raised his eyebrows, "Do I wanna ask how you know that you can get alone with him?"

She blushed, "No, you do not. You'll just have to trust me on this."

Danny thought hard. *At least stopping some of the bloodshed would be better than stopping none of the bloodshed. Maybe we can find out where their next offensive will be. Maybe we could even blow some stuff up while we're there to slow them down. At least we'd be doing something. If she's telling the truth. She could just be talking crazy.*

"Alright, I'll play along for a minute. What makes you think you can get within an inch of this general if he's running that base. Heck, if he's running the base, he's probably running this invasion," Danny said.

"Yes, you are correct. At least, he is in this part of the country. There are other branches of it coming up out of Mexico. They were easy to preposition when America dropped her defense of the southern border."

"That's all well and good, but you didn't answer my question. Why do you think you can get close to the general?"

"I told you. People owe me favors," she said cryptically, "And others will simply want to help me. Besides, I'm logistics and that is a logistical base. I am supposed to be there. We can go up there to look around. If it is too dangerous, of course, we cannot go for the general. At the very least we should try. That way, you will know who it is that is hunting you."

"When you put it like that," Goose said, "I don't like bein' the hunted. I'd much rather be the hunter."

"But if you got ahold of the general, what would you do with him?" Danny asked.

"I am a spy. We have been trained to… shall we say… extract information. I will make him talk."

"No offense, little lady," Goose said, "but you don't seem the type to me to…"

Before he could finish his sentence, Anya closed the distance between them, swept his legs out from under him with a roundhouse kick and then, while he lay on his back, she slid behind him, locked his torso in a vice grip with her legs and wrenched his head between her arms in a choke hold.

Without even breathing hard, she said, "From this position, I can put you to sleep or snap your neck."

Danny held out his hands, "Okay, okay. We believe you."

Anya unclenched her legs and let go of Goose's neck. He jumped up instantly and started dusting himself off.

Goose said with clenched fists, "Look, lady! I otta…"

Danny shoved him, "Stow it. You're three times the size of her. She had you dead-to-rights. She was just making a point," he reached down and helped her to her feet.

"Yes, I was. I am sorry, Goose." She bowed at the waist, "I needed you to take me seriously. Often times I am underestimated. But it is important for you to know that I am telling you the truth."

"Well…" Goose said, still flustered.

Danny smacked him on the arm and motioned him to follow as they walked out of earshot. "Can you excuse us for a minute?" he asked.

She nodded.

When they were far enough away, Danny asked, "What do you think?"

Goose was still red in the face, "I think I otta slap her sil..."

"No, about her proposal. To go up north and find this general."

Goose exhaled heavy, "I don't know, D. We just met her. And she's a Russian. How do you know we can trust her?"

"It's a good question, but I don't think she set the whole rape thing up just because she thought a couple of American cowboys would stumble upon her. And did you see the look in her eyes? She hates them for what they've done to her. I think she wants payback."

"Yeah... but what about headin' up north? Do you really think she can pull it off?"

Danny scratched his head, "She seems to know where their stuff is. She speaks the language. It might be worth a trip."

"I don't know about this kidnapping the general, though. I think she's crazy if she thinks we can snatch him."

"Agreed, but we'll have to play along to see if she's telling the truth. Still, it beats sittin' around here and waiting for them to come for us. And come for us, they will."

"What about the Resistance that Mrs. Cooper was talking about. If we could scope things out, we could always report back to them, right?"

"My thoughts exactly. If for nothing else, we could give them some intel."

"Hum... I guess it's worth a shot. We just have to go slow."

"Right, we'll go slow," Danny said, and slapped his friend on the back while they turned back around to face Anya.

"Okay, you have a deal. We'll go up north with you and we will seeeee if it's possible to snatch this general. We're not into suicide, so if it looks like it can't be done, then we're out. Agreed?"

"That's sounds fair," she said.

"Alright, it's a plan. Let's go find us a truck."

FIFTEEN

"**A**valito! How good it is to see you! But what are you doing here? And on such a day as this? Didn't anyone tell you that there is a war going on?" the Pontiff walked over and gave the Professor a bear hug.

Embarrassed, Mora accepted the gesture, but as they broke, said, "Your... your Holiness... I..."

"Pleassse, my friend. We have known each too long to rest on formalities."

The Pontiff's given name was Emmanuel Jesus Bianachi, the first Pope from Argentina as well as [32]the first Jesuit to hold the office. Now in his seventies, he was a slight man who stood a mere 5'6" and sported a white, friar-tuck hairline.

Although he was born in South America, his father was from Italy. Consequently, he was considered an Italian Pope which endeared him all the more to the Vatican.

While the Pope is regarded to be the current "Peter" by the Catholic faithful, many secretly believed Emmanuel to be the actual reincarnation of the Apostle Peter, if such a thing existed in Church doctrine. As evidence, the people gave him the name Pope Peter II because he was so beloved.

All of us are human and have our faults, my friend. But if they knew what you were really like, I doubt that they would have given you that name, much less this position.

"Of course, of course, I am sorry, Emo. Tradition dies

127

hard."

"That is alright, my old friend. And who do we have here?" the Pope asked, gesturing to Juni.

The Professor made introductions.

"Do you know, Juni, that this man has known me longer than anyone still living?"

"No, your holiness, I didn't."

"In fact, he and I grew up together. Our families were close friends and I would visit him and his cousin..." he looked to Alvaro, "Alfredo?"

The Professor nodded, "Sí."

"That's right, Alfred! In the city of Limon, Costa Rica, on the Caribbean coast! His parents had an old fishing boat and they used to take us Marlin fishing! What a grand time!"

Mora chipped in, "Alfredo loved that boat so much that he eventually bought it from his parents, as well as a couple other boats. He started Blue Marlin Fishing out of Limon, which he still runs today."

"How does he find the time?" Pope Peter asked. "Isn't he a medical doctor as well?"

"Yes, but he doesn't actually practice. When he does, he donates his services to the needy."

"God bless him!" Turning back to Juni, the Pope continued, "And in the spring months, Alvaro would come over to Argentina to visit my family. We would spend days in the Atacama Desert. Alvaro saved my life there once!"

The Professor shuffled his feet and his ears turned red, "It was nothing."

"Nothing? I would have died if you hadn't got me out!"

Mora looked at Juni, "He got lost in a cave. I just helped him find a way out."

"You make it sound so simple," Emo turned to Juni to explain, "There was a rock slide, you see. We were camping in Peru... in the desert of all places! Two days walk to civilization. We were on our own. I would have died in that cave if he had left me, I'm sure of it," he turned to Alvaro again, "I am forever in your debt," he said with a slight bow of his head.

"No era nada," The Professor said, waving off his longtime friend.

"But without my getting stuck in that cave, I would have never... we would have never... found those giant skeletons."

"Ah, yes. The skeletons. The giants. They left quite the impression on you."

"They did, my friend," the Pope agreed, "I've never forgotten. It is the reason why I think this place is so important," he said quietly. And then, as if remembering that there were other people around, he abruptly changed the subject, "By the way, how did you know I would be in town? This visit was unannounced. As I said, it is very dangerous out there right now."

"Let's just say," the Professor said sheepishly, "I heard from a highly placed source that you were here. I had to see you," Alvaro made a show of looking all around. "Speaking of a war outside, things around here appear to be normal, that is, except for your visit. Are they not afraid of an attack?"

"I'm glad you came, war or not. As far as being afraid, well," he pointed to the sky with his index finger, "we have... other protection."

He didn't say Godly protection. While such a statement would not be out of place for a man in his position, there is something else going on here. And I have seen that look in your eyes before, Emo. Could there be more to this... ah... extraterrestrial relationship after all?

"Now please," Peter II said, "Join us for lunch. We can catch up and afterward I will arrange a special tour. How wonderful that you've come today! Today of all days! This is a very important day indeed."

The Professor inquired of God silently: *Today of all days? What is so important today? Does his being here have something to do with why I'm here? We are so different! I've stayed away for a reason! It was one thing to get a Christmas or birthday card, and maybe the occasional phone call. But now, after not seeing him all of these years... Padre why are you making me face the one person that I've purposely avoided?*

The door opened and in walked a priest in his mid-forties.

"Father Federico! Father Federico is the Director of the Vatican Observatory here," the Pontiff winked at Alvaro, "He's also a Jesuit."

"Of course," Alvaro smiled.

"Your Holiness, lunch is served," the priest said.

"Very good. Can you please have two more places set at the table? Our friends will be joining us."

"Already done," Federico said with a forced smile.

Ha, he doesn't' want us here. We're intruding... on the Pope's visit? Or is it something else that we're not supposed to see or hear?

"Excelente!" the Pope quipped, "We have a substantial Jesuit community of scientists here and I'm sure you will enjoy the table conversation." He stole a glance at Federico, "There have been, and will be, several interesting developments. I'm sure as a Helio Astronomer you will find the disclosures fascinating."

This was hardly the Emo the Professor remembered. This man was polished, decisive and charismatic. Yet, it seemed to the Professor that something was bubbling just under the surface - something that started in a young Emo a very long time ago.

COSTA RICAN RAIN FOREST – MANY YEARS AGO

It didn't matter if he was spending time with Emo in Argentina or if the older boy was visiting Alvaro in Costa

Rica. Emmanuel would always disappear for long stretches at a time.

"¿Dónde te desapareciste? (Where do you disappear to?)" Alvaro would ask.

With a dismissing wave, Emo always gave the same answer, "Sometimes I just need to be alone."

Alvaro accepted these lone sojourns as a quirk of his personality and he would give Emo his space. Most of the time. However, one day when the young Argentinian was gone for an exceptionally long time, Alvaro went looking for him.

Those times in the past, when he went searching for his friend, young Mora walked and called for Emo. Inevitably, the boy would pop up in the oddest of places after hearing his name shouted. On this particular afternoon, Alvaro decided to give him a lesson by scaring him, but first he'd have to find him.

The rain forest of Costa Rica offered many places to hide and because he'd been gone so long, Mora had the distinct feeling that his friend was hunkered down someplace.

Perhaps he fell asleep. If so, I will scare him so bad that he dare not disappear again.

Mora had been quietly searching for almost an hour when he came across an outbuilding in the forest, a storage shed for maintenance workers. It was a neglected cinder block structure with an old, rusty government sign that said "keep out".

Alvaro knew Emo's stubborn streak and that such a sign wouldn't deter him from having a nap in there. He quietly checked the knob. It was unlocked.

Putting his ear to the door, he listened and was rewarded with the sound of low moaning.

Emo's in there. Probably dreaming. You're going to get it now!

Alvaro took in big breath, turned the door knob silently

131

and burst through the door, "Argghhhhh!!!!!"

Emo wasn't asleep. He was sitting perfectly still, eyes wide open and staring straight ahead. He was in a trance.

His best friend sat in front of the remains of a rainforest monkey. The poor creature had been killed and skinned.

The carcass was pinned down to the wooden floor by all four extremities and flayed open. A strange symbol was painted around it.

Not just any symbol, Alvaro corrected himself, *a pentagram, surrounded by small, lit candles.*

"Dios mío!"

To this day, Alvaro wondered where the candles came from.

Alvaro shoved his friend on the shoulder, "What are you doing?!"

Life came back to Emo's glassy eyes and he realized Alvaro was looking at the dead monkey.

Emmanuel found his voice, "Alvaro?" he said weakly and then caught himself, and said "Alvaro! Is... isn't this terrible?! Who could have done such a thing?" and like a train picking up speed on a downhill straightaway, the lie flooded out, "I... I was wandering around when I found this old building. I... I opened the door and, my god, I found this poor creature. I, I was just sitting here praying that God would avenge the poor little thing. Whoever did this terrible thing must pay!"

MT. GRAHAM OBSERVATORY, TUCSON, ARIZONA – PRESENT DAY

He knew it was a lie, even if he didn't want to believe that the boy he trusted with his life could be so cruel. However, for the sake of the friendship, he said nothing.

Even if he told someone, who would believe him? *Emo was*

an altar boy for his local diocese. He had very good grades and had never been in trouble. Emmanuel Jesus Bianachi was the model citizen who was even rumored to have been being groomed for the priesthood. He always said he wanted to be part of the Church full time.

Look at you now...

"That sounds interesting," was all the Professor said.

"Wonderful," the Pontiff said as he clapped once, "Let's eat!" he added as he turned and put his arm around Juni, leading him to lunch.

"So Juni, tell me, are you Catholic?"

Juni licked his lips, thrust his hands in his pockets and replied, "Your Holiness, where I'm from, we were all raised Catholic."

"And now?"

"Now? Now, I'm... I'm just trying to sort things out."

"Ah... pity, perhaps we can help. Are you open to bribery with gourmet food? I hear they have an excellent Jesuit chef here!"

Alvaro thought back to [33]Father Malachy, the Irish priest born in 1094. Malachy had a vision which, thus far, had been 100% accurate. He named all of the pontiffs from his time until now. It was the name of last pope on the list bothered The Professor. That pope's tenure would throw the world into a terrible time of distress just before the second coming of Christ. Malachy named the last pope "Peter The Roman".

Emo's father was Italian and immigrated to Argentina. That blood association in biblical times would have made his friend - Roman. When Emmanuel received the name Peter, The Professor's alarm bells went off.

Could he be Peter The Roman and if that were so, what did it mean for the immediate future? Given his old friend's dark proclivities, The Professor had no desire to ever speak with him again.

And that was before Alvaro had heard some other disturbing accusations against his long-time friend. Emmanuel Jesus Bianachi was, in fact, being tried in absentia. The [34]International Tribunal into Crimes of Church and State had witness testimony of sexual abuse and even murder as a result of occultist practices, perpetrated by the Jesuit.

Murder? Nooo...

The Professor's mind went back to the monkey in the rain forest and he involuntarily shivered.

Padre, please give me wisdom!

Sixteen

"**S**ay again, last. Over."

"I said zombies, over."

"Zombies?" Gabby asked stunned, forgetting all radio etiquette.

"That's right, Big Sky, real live zombies, or at least what looks like them. Over."

"Zombies aren't real!"

"[35]Zombies in the movies aren't real, but these things, ah, people, are probably the closest that we're gonna get. When the [36]President dropped protection of the southern border, all kinds of people started filtering up. First, we had the [37]drug cartels who moved into the south U.S. with a vengeance. They took over whole ranches, killed and threatened anyone who would not cooperate. Then, of course, we had the [38]terrorists of the ISNW. With no one to stop them from getting into the country, they simply walked into the States and hunkered down into their preplanned positions until the war kicked off. When they did - well, let's just say it's been brutal. There have been [39]beheadings everywhere, mostly Christians, but even non-religious people too. They're equal-opportunity haters. Like the cartels, they try to obtain obedience by intimidation. And then came the zombies. Over."

Gabrielle's face was tight with worry. If what she was hearing was true, then things were much worse off than she thought.

"That still doesn't explain what you mean by zombies, over."

"These are the people that have been plagued with [40]Ebola, or the hybrid of Ebola. People are saying its airborne. Ebola's never been airborne before, only transferred through fluids. Many of them weren't symptomatic until they crossed into America, but others - well, they had sores on their body and were leaking blood through their eyes, or ears, nose or mouth. I don't know how they kept moving, but they managed to come here, infect people and die. Now we have people sick all over and I'm sure you'll be seeing it up there soon enough. But that's not the worst part, over."

"Worst part? You mean there's more?"

"I'm afraid so. The reason I call them zombies is because these people aren't just sick, they're acting funny."

"Acting funny?"

"Yeah, they're angry and mean, even evil. I don't understand it. It's like they're possessed or something."

Dead air.

"Big Sky, are you there?"

"Yes. Yes, I'm here. It's just a lot to take in, over."

"I hear ya, but down here we don't have the luxury of trying to figure it out. Not only is there a war going on, but we have to deal with all of this. Really makes you wonder where things will end up, over."

"How long do you think we have until we start seeing that kind of thing up here? Over."

"I don't really know. There's still a war going on and both the cartels and the zombies can be held in check by soldiers with guns. My guess is that you're safe for now. Over."

"Alright, as I said earlier, we have men out in the field doing some scouting. If we find anything of significance, I will get back with you. Over."

"Roger that. We're trying to sort things out down here and figure out how many men and how much equipment we have. The military and police forces were the first to be hit. Most of the people that were left in those groups went into hiding. We need to organize. Soon as I have some sense of where we are, I'll figure out a way to get a coded message to you. We can't be talking about specifics on the open air. I'm sure they're listening, over."

"Ah, Roger, understand."

"Okay, I guess that's it for now. Keep your heads down and be safe. We'll talk soon. Southwest Resistance, out."

"Big Sky, out."

Gabby sat back from the short-wave and hugged herself, rubbing her arms like she was cold as she blew out a long breath.

It's hard enough to come to grips with the fact that our country has been attacked, but cartels and zombies too?

She moved her hand to her lukewarm coffee, but she didn't bring it to her lips. Instead, a lone tear rolled down her cheek and then another, and soon she was sobbing.

"God, I can't take this! I'm just a wife! How am I supposed to run a resistance? And what about my family, my friends? Ebola? God! How do we protect ourselves from something we can't see?"

She was shaking now, still sobbing but trying to muffle the sound with her hands over her face.

She thought about LJ, and Sarrah and her newest baby, Aaron Eleazar Cooper, only a few days old. It was all she could do not to imagine them with bleeding sores all over their bodies.

Then she heard her husband's voice in her head, "Now Gabby," he would say soothingly, "you know that Elohim will not give us more than we can bear and that He is able to do exceedingly, abundantly above all we can ask or think," he would normally kiss her forehead at this point in the pep talk, "So buck up, young lady. We have people depending on us."

She stopped crying, blew her nose and wiped her eyes. "There are people depending on us," she said aloud and touched her forehead.

"Where are you, Bryce? Are you even still alive?" She considered the thought. "Don't be ridiculous Gabrielle! Of course he's alive," she chastised herself, "Until then you are in charge, so get it together!"

A curtain closed off the radio room from the other parts of the cave. On the other side of the flimsy divide, she heard someone clear their throat, "Ms, Mrs. C, can I come in?"

Gabby wiped her nose and eyes again quickly with a tissue, "Of course, come in."

One of the ranch hands stuck his hand between the curtains and slid into the room.

Gabby winced, and looked over his shoulder, "Did you hear very much of that?"

"Not really," the young man lied, "And besides, it's okay. You're entitled. You've been pretty strong in front of everybody, but you're only human."

"Thank you," she said, "What did you need?"

"Oh yeah, almost forgot. I came to let you know that Danny and Goose are back and you're not going to believe what they have!"

LARGE HADRON COLLIDER, GENEVA, SWITZERLAND – PRESENT DAY

The process of running up the LHC to its highest speed was easier said than done. Seconds stretched into minutes, minutes into hours, and hours into more than half a day.

Although Dr. Cooper was brilliant by human standards, he could never have made this leap, Abbot thought. This grand experiment required more than human technology. It required, he chuckled to himself, Nephilim technology.

"Nearing 90% power, sir," a voice from behind him said.

Turning to face the small group, Abbot said, "Very good. Remember, at 96%, the Tachyons must be infused, not a moment sooner or a moment later. Understand?"

"Yes, sir."

Tachyons, he mused. Humans didn't understand them. In fact, most physicists discarded them as a myth. They couldn't understand. Tachyons were a gift from the Nephilim and truly out of this world.

[41]A tachyon is a hypothetical particle that always moves faster than light. Most physicists think that faster-than-light particles cannot exist because they are not consistent with the known laws of physics.

Known laws of physics! Their known laws only conformed to this 3D reality. They had no idea about what life was really like on the other side of the Veil.

Because of their limited understanding, these same scientists think that if such particles did exist, they could be used to build a tachyonic antitelephone, which according to special relativity, would lead to violations of causality.

"Causality!" he mumbled. "They just cannot grasp the fact that the universe is bigger than them."

"Excuse me, sir," the tech behind him said, "Did you need something?"

"Ah, no, no, I was just thinking out loud. How is our progress?"

"Approaching Infusion Point shortly. Should I give you a five-count?"

"That would be fine."

Despite theoretical arguments against the existence of faster-than-light particles, more enlightened human scientists have conducted experiments on the search for them. No compelling evidence for their existence has been found. "Ha!"

No compelling evidence indeed! All they'd need to do was look at our earlier work here at the LHC. That slip up in [42]September 2011 from my predecessor was a report that a tau neutrino, a faster-than-light particle, had travelled faster than the speed of light. It was a major release by CERN. That was a mistake. Word should have never gotten out. It took a lot of effort to pull back the information on that test in later updates from CERN. Finally the media did swallow the line about how the [43]OPERA project indicated that the faster-than-light readings happened because of "a faulty element of the experiment's fibre optic timing system." He snorted aloud and raised his eyebrows, *So easily swayed.*

That's why the previous Director had to go. He'd become too emotional and easily excitable, far too human for our purposes so we eliminated him.

"Nearing infusion, sir."

By introducing a stream of Tachyons from the other side of the dimensional Veil (the Tachyon Universe as some physicists had come to call it) into the LHC's beam acceleration, the experiment will take on a definite, non-human attribute. As the beams rotate in opposite directions, infused tachyons will cause the beams to break the speed-of-light threshold and set up the world's largest tachyon field, even before the beams are coalesced. Then with the help of Corkscrew, acting as the master-key, we will be able to unlock the [44]giant portal that the LHC really is. When that happens, all of the other locks, portals, around the world will be opened. And my brothers will finally be free!

"Then we will be set in our rightful place as kings," Abbot brooded.

"Infusion in five... four... three... two... one..."

Seventeen

"Literal? You mean Hell is about to LITERALLY be let loose?" Bryce asked Gabe.

The large, gleaming man nodded, "It is as you say," and added, "We are here. They mustn't see me like this."

With a shimmer and a vibration, Gabe's brilliance dimmed as he shrank down to his human size.

"You know, you outta charge for that. Trust me... people would pay to watch it!" Bryce said with a grin. "So where are we?"

"You will see," Gabe said, as he stretched out his hand and made a ⁴⁵whistling sound. He used his hand to slice the air, making it a vertical crack of light which opened up at his fingertips. Pulling the crack back and forth, like he was kneading dough, he soon made the opening large enough for them to walk through.

The man sat numbly on the edge of his cot, hardly able to comprehend the horror that was being reported on the radio:

> *"If you are hearing this report, you are obviously not in an area affected by the ongoing, nuclear crisis around the world. We, ourselves, are safe for now, away from the effects of radiation and the EMP, that is, Electro Magnetic Pulse, associated with nuclear blasts. We will continue to report as*

long as we are able.

So here is the latest:

What can only be described as the [46]breakdown of civilization is taking place throughout the world. Because of the collapse of the world's economies, rioting and looting are taking place in virtually every country on the planet. Store shelves are bare and the world's citizens are hungry and desperate. Governments around the world that haven't already collapsed are teetering on the edge of anarchy as they contend with social disorder and war.

Reports from America are still sketchy; however, what we can confirm is that there have been several small [47]nuclear detonations in numerous cities all along the West Coast. These explosions appear to have been in the kiloton range, rather than the megaton range, which as far as damage from a nuclear bomb goes, is good news because the majority of the infrastructure has been spared. However, early reports of radiation sickness have indicated that the strikes produced a great deal of radiation and millions of people within the vicinity of the blasts are already sick. Although not a comprehensive list, we can confirm that numerous airbursts occurred in San Diego, Los Angeles, San Francisco, Oakland, and in the area around Silicon Valley. It also appears that Seattle and Portland have been hit.

In addition, there have been key nuclear strikes in many Midwestern states designed to take out the United States' Command and Control and their ability to launch a retaliatory nuclear attack. Some of these strikes were much more significant than those of the west coast. Thus far we can confirm that megaton blasts were targeted at key missile bases like Malmstrom Air Force Base in Montana, Cheyenne Mountain and Warren Air Force Base in Wyoming. Minot Air Force Base in North Dakota was also attacked, but it appears that it was done with the smaller kiloton nuclear weapons.

Although no nation-state has taken credit for the attacks, we have unconfirmed reports of [48]Chinese submarines surfacing off the coast of California. Eyewitnesses have credited those vessels with launching a salvo of ordinances which we can only assume were nuclear in nature, given the destruction we are now seeing.

There are also reports that Russian and Chinese ground troops are easily moving through the country in the west and Midwest with little to no resistance. In addition, there are unconfirmed reports of... What? Unconfirmed reports of Germans fighting alongside the Russians?

Is this right?" he asked someone in the studio.

"Um, by all appearances this is definitely a coordinated invasion. The exact number and names of the invading countries are unknown. Hold on! My god!"

Silence and the sound of weeping.

"We have just gotten word that there have been additional nuclear explosions along the east coast

of America. New York City has been totally destroyed by a very large nuclear explosion. That means that the island of Manhattan, home to Wall Street and the United Nations, god!"

Sniffles

"I apologize, it is too much to bear," he swallows hard, "In the meantime, back in the Middle East, Israel has mobilized its forces in response to the tactical chemical weapons release in Tel Aviv and Haifa. The IDF, Israeli Defense Force, appears to be moving in mass to meet a combined, military advance of Russian and ISNW forces. The face-off appears to be headed for the Jezreel Valley which," he swallows hard and speaks slow, "is also the biblical location of what Christians call Armageddon?" he said, sounding incredulous.

A silent pause is heard while the speaker gathers himself.

"Internationally, America's allies around the world have also been attacked. London, Tokyo, Ottawa, Canada and Canberra, Australia have all received nuclear bombings as well as other major cities whose country's sided with the United States. The degree of damage in those cities varies, depending on the size of the blast. It is noteworthy to mention that, because the radiation from the Fukushima Daiichi nuclear power plant meltdown, most of Japan was slowly contaminated and the vast majority of [49]Tokyo's population had already relocated to the disputed Senkaku Islands. It appears..."

Wiping tears from his already bloodshot eyes, the man

wagged his head in sorrow and turned off the radio.

As he lifted his head to blow his nose, a piercing, bright light cut into the small cubicle where his single cot was set up.

Cooper stepped through, followed by Gabe.

The dumbfounded man opened his mouth to speak, but words would not come.

"Hi, Uncle Joe."

Lazy Hoof Cave, Missoula, Montana – Present Day

"Are you crazy?!" Gabby asked in a hushed angry voice. Her face was bright red and she was visibly shaking.

"You know, Mrs. C," Danny said, as he pushed his hands down in the air to calm her, "that I'm not. Just hear me out."

"Hear you out? Hear you out! You know that you could have just sentenced all of us to death?"

Gabrielle Cooper had met Bryce in Bonn, Germany many years ago when he was in town for a conference. She had long, curly, black hair and deep blue eyes and was slight in stature, standing 5'7". With only the smallest trace of a German accent, from the very beginning, the physicist found the sing-songy rhythm of her voice intoxicating.

Today, however, Gabrielle's voice was anything but sing-songy. She was an angry woman. In the last three days, out of necessity, she'd transformed into an army general for the new Big Sky Resistance. And just like his days in the Air Force, Danny Mendez was now being called on the carpet by his commander.

"You have ten seconds to convince me why we shouldn't shoot her!"

"Shoot her?!" Danny's voice rose an octave in surprise.

"That's right, shoot her," Gabby said. She started counting on her fingers, "One, she is the enemy! Two, her people have slaughtered our friends and neighbors! Three, if she leaves here alive, she can tell them where we are! Do I need to go on?" she spat through gritted teeth.

"Okay, okay. I hear ya. But I think we have a solution to our problem."

"A solution to our problem? What solution is that, Danny? That a whole bunch of evil men with guns have overrun our country?! What were you thinking?!"

Danny's boyish smirk returned and he leaned in confidently to his lady general, "The problem of knowing who is attacking us and how. Mrs. C," he declared, "I think we have found a way forward for the Resistance."

BEHIND ENEMY LINES – PRESENT DAY

Zac didn't know exactly when he stopped. He had walked for as long as he could and collapsed somewhere near his objective, or where he thought his objective would be.

Crawling into a dark shadow under the brush, he finally made himself rest. Before he slept, thoughts of how he was supposed to track the Beast all by himself kept running through his head. Now he was only one man; his team was gone. And although he was supposed to be the hunter, judging from his welcoming party, he distinctly got the feeling that he was the prey.

Events had taken on an eerie, supernatural feeling. Those things may have had human bodies, but their eyes certainly weren't human. Whatever was inside of them wasn't human. But they could be killed, as evidenced by the fact that he was here and they were dead.

"How am I supposed to fight what I don't understand?" he whispered to himself, more as a prayer than a question. Before he drifted off to sleep, he said, "Adoni, help."

Oklahoma Mountain Gateway, Present Day

Larry Taylor stood in his backyard, overlooking the portal. Since the strange interaction between the fighter jets and UFO that morning, it had been quiet. Yet, after his vision of Ancient Evil being loosed, he knew deep down that the quiet was only the calm before the storm.

In concentrated prayer, he asked, "Father, please show me what's really going on."

As if in an answer to that prayer, the ground below his feet rumbled.

Another earthquake!

Oklahoma was not known for earthquakes, but over the course of the last couple of years, they had grown in frequency and intensity. This one was big.

Taylor stood like a sailor on a boat being whipped by waves, shifting his weight back and forth as he tried to maintain his balance. His dogs were howling in the distance. Ten seconds stretched into twenty, then thirty. The shaking intensified.

He heard a thunderous crack from behind him as the main "I" beam of his log home's roof split down the middle, sagging the roof.

A bigger jolt accompanied the shaking and it took him to his knees.

The ground wouldn't stop moving.

Rocks began to split and he heard a scream come from the portal area far below.

Dust and smoke wafted up from the ground as the soil in the portal area began to tear.

The scream didn't stop and Larry had to cover his ears.

After what seemed like an eternity, the shaking subsided along with the scream of the earth.

Larry got to his feet and dusted himself off. An uneasy feeling hung in his gut. After the intense noise there was only a chilling silence.

Turning back to his home, he saw that its roof had collapsed. "Great..."

Roofs could be repaired, but he couldn't say the same about the valley below. Off in the distance, a long, jagged, mile-length, tear in the earth stretched across the portal area.

"Why there?"

His question hung in the air as he headed back toward the house to see what he could salvage. It would be dark soon and he'd have to have some place to sleep. He was glad that his wife was at work in Dallas for the week.

As bad as the shaking was, he had the distinct feeling that what was coming next was going to be worse.

YEMEN COAST, SEA OF ADEN – PRESENT DAY

"Unmi! (Mama!)" the little boy cried out in Arabic, "Unmi!"

Like hundreds of other people washed away by the tsunami which occurred a few minutes before, the boy's whole family disappeared under the sudden, angry torrent of water.

Those waves were preceded by a shallow, mega earthquake that registered 9.3 on the Richter Scale, just off the coast of Yemen, at the portal area which Gabe showed Cooper.

In the place of the super-secret human and extraterrestrial portal structure was a great, pulsating canyon that had been ripped open on the ocean floor.

For the moment, it was still... and it was waiting.

- PART THREE -
CONVERGED
SPECTRUM

EIGHTEEN

LAZY HOOF CAVE, MISSOULA, MONTANA – PRESENT DAY

Gabby's shoulders relaxed, "Danny, your plan has merit, but I'm going to have to limit our exposure to her. We'll feed her," Mrs. Cooper looked over her shoulder and through the large cave at their new Russian visitor, "but she mustn't overhear what we are doing or how we are doing it. Is that understood?"

"Yes, Ma'am." Changing the subject, Danny asked, "Any word from Dr. Cooper?"

Worry lines around Gabby's eyes grew deeper at the question and she bit her lip. "No, nothing."

"Don't worry, Gabby," Danny patted her on the shoulder. "The Boss is one tough dude. I'm sure he's fine. With all the chaos, he probably hasn't been able to get to a radio."

Mrs. Cooper exhaled long, "I know. Still."

"Have we had any contact with the outside world?" Danny asked, pointing to the radio."

"Oh! I meant to tell you. We've had quite a lot of radio traffic which is strange, considering the EMPs."

"How so?"

"Well, most of the chatter is in Russian. I do know a few phrases here and there, but I can't make out the main conversations. They do sound military."

"That makes sense. According to our new, ah, guest, she said the Russians control not only the northern part of the U.S., but they are well in control of southern Canada too."

"There's something else."

"What?"

"Foreign transmissions that I can understand."

"Yeah?"

"German"

"Ahhhh, Anya did say that they were playing a role in this invasion."

"But how can that be? They were supposed to be our allies?"

Danny exhaled loudly and shook his head, "War makes strange bedfellows, I guess."

"I guess so," Gabby agreed, "But I also have better news."

"What's that?"

"I spoke to the Resistance down in the southwest. No one wants to go down without a fight."

"Then why aren't they fighting?" Danny asked, frustrated.

"There have been a lot of casualties. It's only been three days. They need to find out who's left to fight and what they have to fight with, instead of throwing good men at battles they can't win. They're gathering intel and making plans."

"Plans? What kind of plans?"

"Of course, they wouldn't say on an open line, but word is that there is a large concentration just over the border at Medicine Hat. Seems the Canadians and Americans have thrown their forces together. Apparently, there is a big meeting up there in two days."

Danny pinched his forehead as if trying to find a memory, "I think that's pretty close to where we want to go."

"Where you want to go?" Gabby asked, with a confused look on her face.

"That's right, Mrs. C. I think it's time to get into the fight ourselves. And we have an ace in the hole."

Danny detailed for Gabby how they intended to kidnap the head of the Russian base camp.

MT. GRAHAM OBSERVATORY, TUCSON, ARIZONA – PRESENT DAY

After lunch, Pope Peter was whisked away for private conversations with the astronomers of the observatory. However, before he left, the Pontiff sternly told the group that Dr. Mora should be shown everything.

Although the table conversation was light enough, a few hints to potential revelations were dropped. The Professor would have no idea how this day would change his worldview forever.

His guide gave the Professor a clearly uncomfortable look as he glanced at Juni standing by Alvaro's side.

"It's okay. He's with me."

The young Jesuit cleared his throat and said, "And this is our Large Binocular Telescope Near-Infrared Utility with Camera and Integral Field Unit for Extragalactic Research."

"Uhhh humm, you mean the [50]Lucifer Device," Dr. Mora pointed out.

"Lucifer device?!" Juni asked in surprise.

Alvaro locked his eyes on him and put his finger to his lips, while shaking his head. Be quiet!

Juni got the message and fell silent.

The Professor was well aware of the device's history, although this was his first trip to the observatory and he had never laid eyes on it.

Why would they name it after the devil if they didn't want to invoke a little help from the dark side?

The instrument was chilled to -213 Celsius and mounted on the Large Binocular Telescope to allow for near-infrared observations. It also had three interchangeable cameras for imaging and spectroscopy in different resolutions.

Seemingly reading his thoughts, the Jesuit who was called Father Joshua, said, "It was not we who named the device. Rather, it was the scientists from the five German universities who designed the device."

"And yet," Mora said with raised eyebrows and a knowing smile, "you've kept the name."

"Yes, well, it is not our device to rename," the young priest said, befuddled.

The Professor chuckled, "It's quite alright, Father. I'm just having some fun with you," he said, gently patting him on the back. "So how effective is it?"

Letting out a breath, the priest said, "It's very effective." He looked toward the door, "The Holy Father did say to tell you everything. Are you sure you're ready for such disclosures, Doctor?"

What could be so shocking?

A smile creased his lips, "In the words of the younger generation, 'bring it on!'"

"All right, as you wish. As you probably know, the device is designed to help us understand the formation of stars and planets as well as allowing us to see very distant stars and very young galaxies."

"Yes, that's right."

"However, we often make observations that are not released to the general science community, or, the public-at-large."

"Such as?"

Now it was Joshua's turn to smile, "It's better if you see it for yourself."

The Professor stood rigid for a moment, licked his lips and simply said, "Alright."

The priest walked over to a console, punched a few keys that brought up a high-resolution view of what the telescope was pointing at, "Tell me what you see."

Alvaro hesitated for a moment and then hunched over the monitor with his lip stuck out in concentration, "Those stars don't look familiar. So I'm assuming that this is one of those distant galaxies that you were speaking about."

"That's correct. Keep watching..."

After a moment, something like a star shot across the screen, "Whatttt? What was that?"

"Keep watching."

Two more flew through the view spectrum, "Those are shooting stars..." Three more blips crossed the screen slowly this time, "Are those what I think they are? And are they flying in formation?"

"They are exactly what you think they are."

Dr. Mora turned from the screen to face his tour guide. He was pale and his eyes were glassy, "But how? Why are you not surprised?"

Joshua remained silent with an impish smile on his face.

Answering his own question, the Professor said, "Because you see them all the time don't you? This is normal, isn't it?"

"[51]In fact, we see them all too often. They get in the way of our work here."

"Whattt? Why haven't you told someone about this?"

He waved off the suggestion, "We've told too many to count. Do you think we're the only ones that see such activity? I'm sure you've heard of the rumors coming from the [52]ISS (International Space Station)."

"Of course, how can any astronomer not? Most of the time it's just chalked up to astronauts being too long in weightlessness."

"And yet you wonder if it is true?"

"Yes, of course. But any respectable scientist could never voice such thoughts. We would be debased by our peers and the public. The damage to our professional reputations would be irrevocable. You would never be able to publish a paper again, much less find, and hold, a respectable position."

"Indeed, and yet," Joshua pointed to the screen, "there they are."

"Indeed!"

"You ever think about the kind of people that have seen UFOs? Reputable people, like scientists, astronauts, politicians and world leaders. Nonetheless, we play this game – like they don't exist. Why?"

"I suppose it's because if such a thing got out…"

Of course I believe in UFOs. But that belief is tempered by a [53]*biblical view. I've had glimpses, but those experiences are seasoned with the knowledge that they are not what they appear to be.*

"They would change the world forever," the Professor finished his sentence. "That includes the political and religious structures of the world. Those in charge probably fear such a change. It would not only mean that they would lose their power, but that there might be turmoil throughout the earth."

"That's exactly right. Now you can understand why we sit on one of the best kept secrets of mankind. But that won't go on for much longer."

"Humm, what do you mean. What are you saying?"

"Ahhh, for that," he reached down to the keyboard and made a few mouse clicks, "we don't need the Lucifer Device. In fact, we don't need very much magnification at all."

The screen changed from a field view of distant stars, to several ships flying in a close-knit formation.

"Dios Mío!"

"That's right! They are here."

JERUSALEM, MOSSAD SAFE HOUSE – PRESENT DAY

"Are you saying," Percy asked, "that everything which occurred the last few days was planned?"

"Not necessarily planned," Diggs said in measured words, "just foreseen. The Bible is full of what are called prophecies that spoke of a time like this."

Percy's appearance at the door of the safe house stunned both Diggs and Mac. In an exercise of caution, the men questioned the geneticist at length. Although Percival was short on details, he did know that Bryce had been wearing the Garments. That was good enough for the physicists.

The Professor's daughter, Stephanie, had also made it back to the safe house. All flights in and out of the country were frozen and no one was going anywhere.

London was decimated by a two-megaton nuclear missile. Fallout throughout the other parts of England would make it uninhabitable for hundreds of years. Diggs and Percy were never going back.

Hindering the American's travel plans was the fact that foreign troops had invaded the U.S. Even if she could go back, Los Angeles was destroyed and with it, the Mora homestead. For him, Mac's last posting was in Geneva, at the LHC, and he didn't have any family to return to.

The future was equally uncertain for all of them.

As efficient as they always were, Mossad "cleaners" disposed of the bodies left by the gruesome event which had taken the lives of Ivy and the two guards. The organization was concerned that the safe house was compromised, but a war outside made it impossible to change locations. They had plenty of food and water and were told to stay put.

The guard was doubled, but no one expected the extra security to last very long. Israel was fighting for her life and every able-bodied person that could carry a weapon was needed. They knew that, soon, they would be on their own. When that happened, they just hoped they'd have weapons.

Voicing a question that no one else would, Percy asked, "So, where does that leave us?"

Diggs started to answer but Stephanie, who was sitting next to him on the couch, put her hand on his arm and answered instead, "It leaves us in the middle of [54]the land that God calls His own, with [55]His people. While it is true that many people here do not serve Him, His covenant is clear. None of us knows what the next few days or even hours hold. But we do know this: God is bigger than this war and He is more than able to protect us."

Percy didn't understand.

We're in a bloody war here and these three are acting like they're on holiday. Has the whole world gone daft and I'm stuck in the middle of the daft? Yet, I did see Dr. Cooper's luminous friend. I walked in... what did he call it? "Between the Veil." Maybe I'm just as crazy, but I still don't understand how these people can be so calm!

Stephanie continued, "Ask yourselves why all these things are happening."

"And," Diggs interjected, "we've been working on that very answer. "Have you ever heard of The [56]Group?"

Nineteen

The main support beam of the cabin's roof had a gaping split running horizontally through its center. It needed to be repaired, but that would require time and energy. At the moment, Larry was running low on both. Instead, he placed a blue tarp over the hole as a temporary fix.

Standing on the roof, he scanned the sky for anomalies. There were no UFOs in sight, but the azure of the heavens had been replaced with angry, twisting [57]Undulatus Asperatus clouds that hung thick over both the portal and his home. With their yellowish hue, they made the earth look like something from a distant planet.

"Clouds didn't used ta look like that..." Larry scratched his head.

The air was sticky, but it didn't smell like rain. The clouds blotted out the sun, adding to the ominous feeling in the pit of Taylor's stomach.

Larry had seen this type of cloud formation before but only after a thunderstorm and never on the heels of a significant earthquake. He had the distinct feeling that the Veil between dimensions was seriously thinning.

He needed to check his property for damage and decided to walk the perimeter. It would be dark soon, so as he always did this late in the day, Taylor armed himself with a flashlight

159

and his .45 sidearm.

Living in the wild called for caution. He may not have to worry about people this far from town, but an enormous black bear shared the former policeman's mountain top. Taylor thought the bear was a novelty and named him Putin after the Russian President.

As he tramped through the brush, he noted that the atmosphere felt charged with static electricity. [58]Electromagnetism was nothing new to this mountain. Batteries would drain unexpectedly, TV satellite dishes would fry, rocks would split and electronics were known to fail. Taylor didn't know if it was a direct result of the portal below, or if it was something that was buried deep within the mountain itself.

Just in case, tonight he added an electro-magnetic meter to his inspection arsenal as he walked in a circular, clockwise, downhill route. The path led him to his dog pens, a short distance from the main house.

The animals were still jittery after the earthquake. He fed and watered them and thought back to the baying he'd heard during the quake.

Poor guys, you must've been scared to death.

He was turning to go when something on the ground, toward the back of the large pen caught his eye. The ground had opened up a crevasse big enough to swallow a man.

No wonder why the dogs were going nuts.

As he moved in for a closer look, the hair on his arms stood on end.

That's strange.

Stopping in mid-stride, he pulled out his meter. The needle was bouncing between halfway and three-quarters.

He took a couple steps.

The needle leaped to the top half of the gage.

Walking to the edge of the crack, he saw that the meter pegged out at the highest reading.

"Something's down there."

Looking around at the fading light, he shrugged and took a step into the abyss.

OUTSKIRTS OF TEL AVIV, ISRAEL – PRESENT DAY

"Bryce?" a stunned Uncle Joe asked, "Is that really you?"

"It sure is," Cooper said as he reached over the bed to hug his surrogate father.

"Awwwww...." Joe nearly screamed, "I can't, son. I'm sorry. I'm nearly skinned."

"What happened?"

"Chemical attack. We were in the middle of it."

"My God! Is Aunt Rub..."

"She's fine, but that's better than ol' Eleazar fared."

"Don't tell me!"

"'fraid so"

Bryce swallowed hard as sobs stuck in his throat and tears pooled in his eyes. The old Jeweler meant a lot to Cooper. Although most of his experience with the gentle man occurred before his Reset, he had learned much from the holocaust survivor. Bryce glanced at Gabe who simply nodded in affirmation.

"I'm sorry to hear that, Pop. I know you and he were good friends."

Josiah hadn't allowed himself to think about the loss of Eleazar. When Joe spoke again, his voice was monotone and he slumped on the edge of his cot, "It's tough, but I will see him again." He stared at his empty hands, trying to compose himself.

He cleared his throat and croaked, "Never mind that! What in the world was that Houdini trick just now?! And how did ya get here? I thought you were stuck in the Temple. They said you never came out. And who is this?" Joe pointed to Gabe. "I must be losing my doggone mind! You can't be here."

Cooper took his uncle's hand, "You're not hallucinating. I really am here and this is my friend, Gabe."

Joe nodded at the burly, blonde man in recognition.

"And as to how we got here... well, that's a little more complicated. But I can tell you that we just came through a [59]wormhole."

"A wormhole?" Joe said in an astonished voice, "You physicists, I swear!"

"Uncle Joe, look. A friend of yours needs your help."

"My help? Son, I hate ta tell ya," he held up his blistered arms, "I'm in no shape to help anybody. Besides, anyone tell you there's a war going on? I think we're stuck here for a while."

Bryce grinned, "We're not stuck. And as far as your condition, well..." Bryce placed his hands gently on his uncle's head, "Father, Joe is your child. By Your Hand, the universe was created and is held together. You've made our bodies and You breathed life into them. So, God, we ask that You touch Joe's body and heal him in order that he may complete the task that You've given him. In the mighty name of Yeshua HaMashiach."

Joe opened his eyes and realized that the intense burning and pain he felt on his open wounds was gone. He flexed his arms, "Hey, they don't hurt anymore!"

Bryce asked, "Are you ready?"

"Ready? You mean now?"

"Yes, Joe. Now."

"Sure, I'm ready enough. But you know I have to say goodbye to your aunt. She'd be worried sick if I just disappeared."

"Right. Okay, go let her know, but try to leave out the wormhole stuff."

"Okay, I'll be back." Joe took off in search of Ruby.

"He will be returning with your aunt. You had better get changed," Gabe said, "There will be no need to travel with the Garments after that."

"How am I supposed to get changed? I don't have any clothes."

"We are at a shelter. There are clothes here that will fit. One moment," Gabe disappeared around the corner for a couple of minutes and returned with clothes that were Bryce's exact size.

While Bryce was pulling on a boot, Gabe said, "It would be better if we said as little as possible to your aunt."

Bryce grinned at this friend, "You got that right. She wouldn't understand anyway. Hey, I was thinking."

"Yes?"

"Is it because I'm with you, that I don't need the Garments?"

"You are partially correct. You needed the Garments to find the space between dimensions on your own. While I have been with you, you have not needed them. However, I will be leaving you for a while after our next stop."

Bryce tilted his head and narrowed his eyes, "Then I don't

understand. How are we supposed to get around?"

A cross between sadness and expectation filled Gabe's face, "Things are about to change forever. The end is very near now."

"Humm... I was afraid you were going to say that."

Just then, Aunt Ruby rushed around the corner, "Bryce! You're alive!"

JERUSALEM, MOSSAD SAFE HOUSE – PRESENT DAY

"Hold on," Percy knitted his eyebrows, "Digby, you don't really believe all of that [60]Georgia Guidestones lunacy, do you?"

Diggs and Mac had just spent the better part of the hour taking Percy through the conspiracy theory of The Group and particularly, the site known as The American Stonehenge.

Percy continued, "You're telling me that all of this has been done to reduce the population to five-hundred-million? And what about the natural disasters? I suppose The Group can wave a magic wand and cause earthquakes and volcanoes to erupt!"

"It's not just the reduction of population, but we'll get back to that," Diggs said, "The Group is trying to solidify their power base.."

"Digby, I've known you for a long time and I never thought you were a conspiracy nut."

Mac added, "A theory is only a theory until it's a fact. I used to think the same way you do," he held his palms up at his sides, "but..." he let his point dangle.

"So you're saying that everything: the work I was involved in, those Gray creatures on the tables, this war, the martial law, etc. etc. is all because some megalomaniacs are trying to consolidate power?"

"There is something else," Stephanie said, glancing at Mac.

"Something else besides murdering almost the whole population?"

"Yes..." she hesitated, "The woman that was killed here?"

"I'm sorry about that. It must have been horrible," Percy empathized.

Mac was looking down at the carpet. In a hollow tone, he said, "Her name was Ivy. She was my ex-wife's sister."

Percy didn't know what to say, "Again, I'm sorry."

"The thing is," Diggs added quickly, "did you know she was a geneticist?"

"A geneticist?" Percy asked in surprise. "No, no, I didn't."

"She had a Ph.D. in Medicinal and Pharmaceutical Chemistry from USC," Mac added.

"I see."

"She talked about things she saw. Disturbing things," Diggs said, "That's what got her killed."

"Is that so?"

"Yes," Mac injected, "Particularly disturbing were her revelations about," he made quote marks with his fingers, "The Plan."

"Hold on," Percy said, scooting to the edge of his seat, "Did you say the Plan?"

"Yes," Diggs added, "Have you heard about it."

Percy blanched, "It is something my supervisors would refer to often."

"It can't be the same plan, can it?" Stephanie asked.

"It is a very curious moniker," Diggs responded.

Mac continued, "She used to work at a well-known pharmaceutical company in Pasadena, California, where she

165

had come in contact with…"

"Chimeras," Percy finished for him.

Mac didn't hide his surprise, "How do you know that?"

"Because, I know this company well. We worked closely with them on parts of this so-called Plan. All of us did."

Mac, Diggs and Stephanie all shared a look of astonishment.

"All of us?" Diggs asked.

"That's right," Percy answered, "As I said, we were working on [61]transhumanism to make the human race better." He held his face in his hands, "These experiments are being done all over the world."

TWENTY

"How is this possible?" Danny asked their escort as he fiddled with the collar of the Russian uniform he was wearing.

"It's not hard to understand," replied Anya, "We control the air, the roads and most of the back country. This is a Russian truck and we are simply Russian soldiers headed back to our supply point. So long as you two do not have to talk, we will be fine."

"Da," Goose said, exercising one of the few Russian phrases she had taught them,

"Ty pakhnesh', kak vam nuzhno prinyat' dush! (You smell like you need a shower!)" Danny replied with a grin.

Goose held his arms up and made a show of sniffing both of his armpits, "Da!!!" to which the three burst out laughing.

After the laughter died down, Anya reminded the men, "Seriously, if you use that line at a checkpoint, the guards will certainly relate to you," She told Mendez, "You need to work a little more on the accent, though. And try not to laugh. Be serious."

"Okay. It's not as easy as it sounds, "Ty pak... Ty... Ty pak"

"So where do you think we'll have the biggest problem on

this road trip? The border?" Goose asked.

"No, not the border. Remember, when America, ah, fell," her cheeks turned red, "so too did Canada. There's no border anymore. Highway 93 continues up through Canada and runs into 95. We go left and the base is just outside Cranbrook," she looked over at the fuel gage, "But we need fuel, or we'll never get there."

"You're telling me!" Goose agreed.

They were passing through the small town of Whitefish, Montana. "There!" she pointed, "Pull into that Zip Trip on the right. They should have diesel and because it's small, only one or two guards at most will be posted."

Danny and Goose exchanged a nervous look. It was their first real chance to get caught. If they did, they'd be dead.

"Are you sure?" Goose asked. "Shouldn't we go to a bigger place like a truck stop? There were a couple of huge ones down the road. We could blend in."

"That's the problem," she said patiently. "There will be many more soldiers there and you may have to talk to them. Because this gas station is out of the way and small, we have a much better chance of success. Trust me."

"Famous last words," Goose muttered.

The awkward deuce-and-a-half pulled up next to a diesel pump under the high awning. The lot was void of cars. The men could see through the store window. A scared local man sat behind the counter. A single guard leaned lazily against the wall, his AK-47 slung over his shoulder.

"That child-soldier's probably no older than eighteen," Danny observed.

"Nope," Goose agreed, "And it looks like he's the only

guard."

"See!" Anya said, playfully socking the big driver in the arm.

"Yeah, yeah! I know! Trust you!" Goose said with a half-smile.

"Ah, huh. Now let me out."

Danny opened the passenger door and slid out. Anya exited and as the door closed behind her, turned back to the Americans, unbuttoned the top button of her shirt, and said, "Watch how it's done."

Rounding the front of the truck with her best model walk, she sauntered toward the guard. He met her halfway between the truck and the entrance to the store. They were within earshot of the nervous Duckett and Mendez.

Although the Americans couldn't understand the words, the body language was unmistakable.

Through gritted teeth and in a low voice, Danny said, "I bet that kid has never talked to a girl that pretty before."

"That's not nice. What about his mother?"

"Look at him. I doubt his mother was that pretty."

"You got a point."

"What's your business?" the soldier asked in Russian. His eyes swept her body from head to toe, but paused where her button was undone.

She leaned forward slightly while she fished out a string that held her logistical I.D. badge. The soldier's eyes grew large and he brought his hand to his mouth.

"She eviscerated him!" Danny said, under his breath.

"Yeah, it ain't fair, is it?" Goose replied.

"Nope."

They took a step toward the truck.

"We're on," Danny said in a whisper and in a loud booming voice, he added, "Ty pakhnesh', kak vam nuzhno prinyat' dush!" and socked Goose hard in the arm.

Again, Goose sniffed at his armpits, "Da! I vodka (And a vodka!).

Anya reached out and gently touched the guard's arm. In her best helpless woman's voice, she asked, "The shelves inside are empty? Is there any water left?" She put her hand to her throat and slowly licked her lips, "I am soooo thirsty."

The kid froze and any interest in an inspection of the truck evaporated.

He wiped perspiration from his forehead with his sleeve and said, "I believe that the clerk has hidden some in the backroom for, um, special visitors. I will order him to bring some out for you. Also, there are American snacks that I think you will love."

She looped her arm in his and led him to the store's glass doors, "I love American snacks. Do they have any of those crunchy Cheetos? Oh, I almost forgot, can they pump the fuel?"

The guard carelessly looked over his shoulder, "Yes, yes, of course."

"Boys," she shouted in Russian, "Go ahead and fill it up!"

Anya and the guard walked into the store.

The Americans looked on from the cab.

"Eviscerated..."

"It just ain't fair."

JERUSALEM, ISRAEL, THE THIRD JEWISH TEMPLE – THREE DAYS AGO

The ground shook with swarming mini-earthquakes and the charged, ionized air smelled fresh and crisp, as it did after a thunderstorm.

His body twitched and tingled as static electricity throbbed up out of the ground, through his bare feet to the crown of his head. Goose bumps ran down his back and arms and the hair on them stood on end.

His mind was fuzzy and his eyes blurry. He worried that he might pass out as the low drone of pure, electrical power vibrated through his ribcage.

As he progressed to the curtain, he saw clear waves breaking up through the ground, bending and distorting the light as they rolled and crashed. He paused briefly, looking over his shoulder for the source of the sound that was building to a piercing roar and realized that it was coming from in front of him.

He willed his feet to move forward, each step heavier than the last. The pressure in the room felt like a pile of stones heaped on his shoulders, threatening to collapse him.

Reaching the thick Veil, [62]the barrier between worlds, he heard a sound like rushing waters from the other side. His senses were overwhelmed and he licked his lips, before beginning his petition.

He reached to part the thick curtain, whose fabric was densely laced with pure gold. As his hand drew close, static electricity jumped off of the curtains and bit into his fingers with a snap.

He yelped and recoiled in pain, rubbing his stinging hand.

Gritting his teeth and closing his eyes, he lunged for the fabric and hung on in spite of the pain. Power surged off of the curtain and into the flesh. He shook as small shock waves coursed through him.

Slowly, he parted the heavy curtain and walked Between The Veil.

Blinding light slapped him in the face as he broke through to the other side. He raised his hand quickly, shielding his eyes from the light's assault.

Squinting, he viewed his surroundings as best he could.

No wonder I can't see.

A pillar of brilliant, pure, white light ran through the room's ceiling. Its illumination wrapped itself around every angle and pervaded the space, eliminating all shadows. It was permeating even him, washing over and through his body.

The sound that he'd heard on the other side of the curtain was coming from the pillar of light.

How can light make sound?

The pillar wasn't fire and it wasn't electricity, yet he felt its heat that did not burn. He sensed that the white light was alive as its thunder filled the small room. He was frozen, transfixed at the sight with his hand still in front of his face.

The perfectly cubed space was free of any furnishings except for the one piece at the back of the room where the [63]Ark of the Covenant sat. The pillar of light was beaming into the Ark itself and had materialized just before he entered the Temple.

He heard another sound, distinctive from the rest, like someone's rhythmic breathing. With his hand still shielding his eyes, he saw the Ark's gold-clad, wooden sides moving in and out in concert with the breathing sound. His knees nearly buckled as he realized what it was.

He forced himself to take a few paces forward, but the heaviness of El Elyon's presence was overwhelming. Unable to stand any longer, he dropped to his knees and then to his face.

Realizing that he couldn't complete his task if he were lying flat, he struggled to push himself up to a vertical kneeling position. God's people, and the World, were depending on him.

During the cleansing ceremonies, he'd heard whispers about the attack on Tel Aviv and America. If the World ever needed a Reset, it was now.

Slowly he reached into both breast pockets and carefully removed the two crystal cylinders, the [64]Urimm and Thummim, from the Garments' breast pockets.

The Archangel Gabriel had visited the rabbis and priests of the [65]Third Jewish Temple and convinced them that he should enter into the Holy of Holies. This was a marked deviation from the Law which said that only the High Priest was supposed to go before the Ark.

His hands were now occupied and he was defenseless against the bright light. His eyes were clamped tight, in reverent whispers, he made the people's petition, repeating it again and again. Finally, after a moment, with shaky hands, he brought the crystals chest high.

He opened his eyes one last time and uttered his own personal petition, "Adoni, please give me wisdom, courage and strength to do Your will as the darkness falls."

Holding his breath and grimacing, he touched the ends of

the Urimm and Thummim together.

A loud crack erupted out of the pillar and a brilliant ark of light in the shape of a man's hand reached out and snatched him up.

Dr. Bryce Obadiah Cooper was gone.

Twenty-One

<u>Between The Veil, Present Day</u>

"Very soon, everything will change," Gabe said.

"And not for the better, I take it?" Bryce quipped from the illuminated being's side.

"You've been doing this for a while."

"Seems like forever."

"Indeed, but soon, it will be only a memory in eternity."

"And they will beat their swords into plow shears…"

Gabe smiled at Bryce.

I didn't think he could smile.

"All of the heavenly hosts have waited for that day since the beginning of time. No more war, no more tears with Him who sits on the throne in His proper place. What a glorious day it will be."

"Yes, it will. And very soon now, I take it?"

"In the twinkling of an eye, really, on your side of the Veil. But the earth and its inhabitants must endure much pain and hardship before that day."

"Long days ahead, huh?"

"Unfortunately."

Uncle Joe followed behind, in a daze and muttering to himself. He kept looking around and when they stopped, he nearly bumped into them.

"Do you remember the tone I gave you that opens the portal?"

"Yeah, it's really that simple?"

"It will be after the portals are open."

"But... if they are open to anything..."

"Do not worry, the Others cannot come this way."

"That's a relief."

Joe spoke up, "Am... am I dreaming? Or is this a hallucination?"

Bryce put a reassuring hand on his shoulder, "It is as real as you and I, Pop. You're not crazy."

"That's funny; that's what a hallucination would say."

Bryce chuckled.

"We are here," Gabe announced. "Remember, you must get out of the portal, with as little light, and as quickly as possible. Keep your head down. Find your contact and get him where he needs to go. Remember what you were told? You will be used to bring about the fulfilment of what the prophets warned."

"I understand," Cooper said.

"Ready?"

"Let's do it."

Gabe raised his hand, whistled a tone and cut open a crack of light with his hand, large enough for both of them, "I will see you soon."

Cooper and Uncle Joe stepped out of the portal and into hostile territory.

STONEHENGE, ENGLAND – FIVE DAYS AGO

"It is good to see you, Professor. But what happened? You look as though you were run over by an articulated lorry (semi-truck)?" the redheaded Diggs said, his eyebrows pulled up.

"Huh, funny you should say that. It's good to see you too. Thank you for coming on such short notice."

"Of course, of course. Whatever I can do," the now-Ph.D. Williamson said as his sharp blue eyes shifted over to Stephanie Mora standing off to the side. Her ears turned red and she looked down to her feet.

"Oh, I'm sorry," the Professor said coyly after seeing the look, "This is my daughter, Stephanie. Mija, this is my prize student Dr. Williamson. The one I was telling you about?"

"It is a pleasure to meet you," Diggs said as he gently shook Stephanie's hand, holding her gaze a little longer than normal.

"Thank you. You too," she said.

The Professor cleared his throat.

They let go.

"Well," Diggs said, red-faced, "Professor, what have you got yourself into? Meeting here," he gestured with wide arms, "in the middle of all of this craziness."

Sun-worshipers, new agers, druids and witches gathered at England's Stonehenge for the [66]Spring Equinox. Dr. Mora chose to meet in the middle of this mayhem in order to thwart the efforts of those who were trying to kill him.

Digby had been one of the Professor's brightest students when Alvaro taught at the University of Cambridge some years ago.

"Of course. I can see how it looks," the Professor said, "but it was one of the easiest places to blend in and..." he bit off the last part of the sentence.

"And?" Diggs prompted.

Dr. Mora shrugged with embarrassment, "And, you can see people approaching from a long way off."

"People approaching? Oh my! Are people looking for you?"

The Professor swallowed hard, "I'm afraid so."

"Perhaps you'd better tell me what is going on."

"Yes, of course, but first, did you bring the data I asked for?"

"Yes, just as you asked," Diggs said, patting the backpack over his shoulder, "But I've had no time to review it."

Dr. Mora exhaled. "Finally, some good news. Come, let me tell you a story that you won't believe."

The Professor related the attempt on his life and what he found out about the potential [67]destruction of Planet Earth.

MT. GRAHAM OBSERVATORY, TUCSON, ARIZONA – PRESENT DAY

The question is: are these two things related? I have to find out.

"Hold on," Mora said to the priest, "of course I've always thought that such a being could exist. It's hard for any intellectually honest astronomer to not believe in the potential for extraterrestrial life. But, are you telling me that it is replete?"

"Not only is it replete," Joshua said, "It is," he gestured toward the screen, "here now. Soon, the whole world will know what you know."

Mora held his chin in deep concentration as he tried to absorb what the Jesuit was saying. An important memory niggled at the recesses of his mind.

"I need to ask you something before we delve too deep into, ah, [68]Disclosure."

"Yes?"

"Five days ago I was at Stonehenge in England."

"Really? Five days ago would have been the Spring Equinox? That's funny, you don't seem the type," Father Joshua said with a slight grin.

"Huh, I'd agree, but I was meeting someone. Anyway, this year the Spring Equinox was supposed to coincide with a total solar eclipse. Now, I've been a bit distracted, but I don't remember hearing about one."

Father Joshua sighed, "His Holiness did say to tell you everything."

"Yes."

"Well, that solar eclipse WOULD have been visible here."

"That's right. Remember, the sun is my specialty. I should have seen it in England because Europe was supposed to see it as well as the Middle East."

"Correct, but it didn't happen."

"Whatt? What do you mean it didn't happen? How can it not happen?"

178

Joshua bent and hit a few other keys on the keyboard. When he was done, he straightened and asked, "Dr. Mora, in the course of your work, have you noticed any strange anomalies within our solar system?"

Mora's eyes narrowed, I don't like where this is going.

"As a matter of fact, the reason that I was meeting someone at Stonehenge was to discuss some of those very anomalies. However, events of the last few days have caused us to diverge from that undertaking."

"And?"

"And although I wasn't able to discuss them then, my concerns over certain anomalies remain."

"Such as?"

"Such as, [69]gravitational and orbital perturbations throughout the solar system. Rotations of various planets appear to have been altered. In addition, Jupiter's great red spot is shrinking. And even [70]a wobble in our own planet's rotation has been noted.

"As anecdotal evidence of something being askew, all one needs to do is to look at the shortened, almost non-exist, growing season throughout the world these days. Likewise, [71]weather patterns throughout the world for the last few years have been extremely erratic.

"It makes no sense. Or should I say, it makes as much sense as the [72]North Pole wandering into Siberia" and then he added, "which it has.

"So none of this makes any sense unless something else is causing this phenomena," Dr. Mora concluded.

"In answer to your question," Joshua said, "the solar eclipse will take place shortly."

"Take place shortly? When? How? Since when do eclipses happen later?!"

"Exactly. It is another anomaly that is being caused by..." the priest's voice trailed off and he studied the floor.

"By what?"

Joshua let out a sigh and gestured toward the computer screen, "See for yourself."

The Professor studied the monitor and then backed away like he'd just been slapped.

"Speaking of Disclosure," Joshua said, "We hope that they can help with that. If not, then we are all in serious trouble."

The Professor's eyes were glazed over. I was right...

JERUSALEM, MOSSAD SAFE HOUSE – PRESENT DAY

"What?" Percy asked, "I thought you said that according to the Georgia Guidestones, this... this..."

"Group," Stephanie added.

"Right. This Group was trying to kill everybody. Now you're trying to tell me that they are involved with transhumanism too? That makes no sense. Either they are trying to kill off mankind or they are trying to make it better. It can't be both."

Diggs breathed out a heavy sigh, "This is very complicated, but believe me when I tell you it is both and for a very good reason."

Percy sat back and crossed his arms, "I'm waiting."

Diggs asked, "What do you know about the days of Noah?"

His cousin scoffed, "You mean like in the Bible? Noah's Ark and all that?"

"Yes, exactly."

"Look, you went to the same Anglican Churches as I did. They will tell you that all that is allegory, designed to teach a broader lessen."

"Yes, I've heard the lessons. But, I've come to believe that the Bible is literal and when God puts something in there, it's more than a good story."

"So you're saying that [73]the flood was real?" Percy asked, his voice going up an octave.

"That's right; I believe it was real, but the larger question is why? Why did it happen?"

"I'll play along, cousin. Why did it happen? I suppose it was because of sin and all that. People rebelling against God. Evil in the world, etcetera, etcetera."

"Okay, you're going to find this hard to follow, but you asked."

"I'm ready."

"Did you know that the reason God chose Noah was for his genetics?"

"Sorry?" slack-jawed Percy asked.

"DNA, my dear Percy. His genes! While the vast majority of people who are familiar with the story of Noah's Ark will say that God destroyed the earth because of sin, or evil or blatant disobedience, it had much more to do with genetics."

"What on earth are you talking about?"

"Genesis 6:4 talks about how fallen angels, or The Fallen, mated with women in Noah's days. These women..."

"Hold on. Back it up! You're trying to tell me that angels and women had sex?! Are you daft?!"

"Look," Diggs spoke slowly, "I don't expect you to believe everything I'm telling you. In fact, many supposed Christian scholars don't believe what I'm telling you. However, if you are to understand why we," he looked at Mac and Stephanie who both nodded, "believe that there is a direct connection between transhumanism and the murdering of the masses, I have to briefly take you through this."

Percy let out a long breath, "You know, Digby, if it was anyone else but you telling me this story, I wouldn't pay any attention. However, because it is you, I will indulge you. For the moment."

"Fine," Diggs continued, "The offspring of this mating were called the [74]Nephilim in verse 4.

"As a geneticist, you should find this next bit interesting. In the original Hebrew language in verse 9, it says that God favored

181

Noah because, wait for it. His gene pool was pure and uncorrupted."

Percy squeezed the bridge of his nose, "Digby, I cannot possibly guess why this is important."

"Because, in verse 11, when it says that the earth was corrupt…"

"Let me guess," Percy ventured, "In the original language it means that human beings were genetically impure."

"That's right."

"So?"

"So, this may not mean much to you, but it meant a great deal to God. You see, when the [75]Messiah came to earth, according to Genesis 3:15, He would be a descendant of Adam, and the seed of the Woman."

"Wait," Percy said, as his forehead wrinkled and he looked off to a blank wall. "And since the Nephilim had corrupted the gene pool, then the Messiah's genes would be corrupted?"

"Yes," Diggs said slowly.

"And," Percy continued, "since Noah's genes were pure, the Messiah could come through his genome uncorrupted."

"That's right."

Diggs let Percy think. After a moment, his cousin said, "You know, this makes no sense unless you're a geneticist."

Mac piped in, "Tell me about it!"

"So here is the connection," Diggs continued, "Ultimately, The Group is controlled by the Fallen, who have instituted The Plan to either kill off the vast majority of mankind, or change the remaining population's genome with transhumanism.

"From the very beginning, the devil, who is the chief fallen angel, has been trying to corrupt mankind, not only with sin, but physically in man's DNA. Ergo, if he cannot kill every last creation of God, he will corrupt them until they no longer look like God's creation, [76]but a creation of his own making."

Percy swallowed hard, "Like in [77]homosapien 2.0."

"I'm afraid so."

"My God! That's what transhumanism is all about!"

The Americanized Diggs said, "BINGO!"

IN THE SKY – PRESENT DAY

A light rap at the door brought him out of his reverie. The Man With The Book had long given up trying to pull any more information from its pages. He was lost in thought.

"Enter!"

His aide slipped into the room and said, "The pilots just told me that we will soon start our final approach. We should be on the ground shortly."

"Hummm," was all he said. After a few beats, The Man With The Book asked, "Any problems with radiation up here?"

The aide considered the question for a moment, "No, sir. As specified, the aircraft is heavily shielded. Our onboard instruments aren't showing anything dangerous. I'm sure after the fallout circumvents the world a few times, it'll be another story. However, as you know, most of those bombs were [78]Neutron Bombs. They are smaller, no more than a few kilotons each, so as to keep the physical damage at a minimum. They are designed for a greater release of radiation than the standard fission bombs. Since they use [79]tritium, the half-life is only twelve point three years. That means that the land can be re-inhabited within a few decades rather than the millenniums with standard nuclear weapons."

"And re-inhabited with a lot less people."

"Yes, sir. That was the Plan."

"And has the media picked up on the fact that they've used Neutron Bombs rather than the other fission type?"

"No, not really. Those news outlets that are still up and running are reporting the smaller blasts as good things."

"They have no idea how efficient the [80]culling process will be with the greater release of radiation, then?"

"Not a clue. In fact, there are not a lot of news sources left. The ones remaining are hiding like everyone else."

"If they started talking again, a couple of those guys could really throw a wrench in the works. What about [81]Alex Jones?"

"Phewww! That guy was taken out a week before the attack. We should'a done it sooner, but the action would have drawn too much suspicion."

"How 'bout that pain, [82]Matt Drudge?"

The aide was less enthusiastic, "I'd like to say that his elimination was successful, but…"

The Man With The Book glared. He didn't like surprises. "But what?"

"Well, apparently he took his own advice."

"What do you mean, his own advice?"

"A couple of years ago he tweeted something that should have tipped us off."

"Which was?"

"He said," the aide made quote marks with his fingers, "[83]Have an exit plan."

The Man With The Book brought his hand to his chin in thought, "Have an exit plan?"

"Yeah, I guess he saw this coming and bugged out before we could tag him."

"You're kidding me?!" The Man said with narrow eyes and a raised voice, "What about [84]PRISIM? Surely you could have tracked him with that, after all the money we dumped into it?"

"No, sir. I don't know how, but he just disappeared."

The Man was quiet for a moment and then conceded, "Doesn't surprise me, I suppose. He had the best sources. We should have eliminated him while we could," he said pointing his finger at the aide.

"Yes sir, except it would have been the same problem we had with Jones. Too soon and people would have asked questions."

The Man waved him off, "Ah, I guess it doesn't matter now. Drudge can dig all he wants. No one will be around to hear him. It's a brave new world."

"Yes, it is, sir."

"What is going on with the [85]weather-modification end?"

"Well, [86]HAARP is still at it and so are our [87]laser-based programs. Currently there is a typhoon that we generated in the South Pacific to keep people's heads down. We haven't got much control over some of those small island countries. As you know, we have significantly shortened the growing season throughout the U.S. and as a consequence, people are already starving."

"So I've heard. [88]Seems that riots have broken out everywhere."

"That's right. Anywhere that there isn't fallout killing them off, they are killing each other."

"Unbelievable," The Man With The Book said as he played with the [89]gold ring on his finger. Like the book, people took issue with his selection of jewelry.

"And," The Man said, "how goes the other assault."

The aide's brow furrowed, "Are you referring to the Ebola?"

"That's right."

"Ah," a smile slit across the black man's face, "that was brilliant, you know. It's now [90]airborne and is spreading exponentially. The [91]Useless Eaters are calling them zombies."

"Zombies," The Man chaffed, "Like in the movies?"

The aide chuckled, "Yep."

"Simpletons!"

After a moment, The Man asked, "And the, ah, festivities?"

"Won't be long now. I put a call into Dr. Abbot. He and Corkscrew are on schedule."

"Good," The Man With The Book said as he gazed unseeing at an empty bulkhead wall.

The aide cleared his throat, "Well, time to buckle in. We'll be on the ground shortly." The aide turned on his heel and exited the cabin.

To the blank wall, in his native Arabic, The Man With The Book said, "And then we will rule."

TWENTY-TWO

BENEATH THE OKLAHOMA MOUNTAIN GATEWAY –
PRESENT DAY

Warm tentacles of darkness wrapped themselves around Larry as he cautiously made his way through the hollow earth.

There was much more to his mountaintop than what people saw. The electromagnetic anomalies pointed to unseen [92]geomagnetic currents. Perhaps those currents acted as the canary in the coal mine foretelling a [93]pole shift that was long overdue.

The conductive forces of that electromagnetism would partially explain why the battery in his phone, his satellite dish, his computer and other [94]electrical components all failed before they were supposed to. He'd even seen [95]ball-lightning in his house and bolts of light going from room to room. Yet, that wasn't the only reason why the former policeman thought something odd lay underneath.

The [96]Heavener Runestone was just a few miles from where he lived. Long believed to be an ancient site, its brief glyphs were so strange that most scholars could not interpret them. Taylor had discovered that the writing was a form of ancient Hebrew, but no Rabbi would reveal the glyphs' meaning.

Only two reasons would prevent these scholars from providing the translation: 1)The writing was a curse that would not be repeated, least the curse fall on the one who translated, or 2) The writing were the very words of God. In this case, translation would be considered irreverent.

What could be so bad that you didn't even want to speak about what's on that rock? Larry thought as he picked his way through the dark tunnel.

The town of Heavener was at one time called "Heaven-er". The dash had long since been dropped and the pronunciation changed. The land had been altered since then. Strange and ominous things now occurred in and around Heavener and the monument. Perhaps it had something to do with the writing.

Larry thought that a portal or stargate was in the area of the Runestone. However, the main tunnel system which lay under the stone had been dynamited long ago, hiding all secrets in the blast.

Could this tunnel be part of the Heavener tunnel system?

Taylor's intent was to follow this tunnel and find out who, or what, had caused things to change.

Recently, Taylor had found someone who was willing to translate the writing. What was revealed was that the land and its purpose no longer resembled the statement made by the Runestone glyphs, which said:

"Yahwah's Territorial Boundary Marker"

This land was originally marked as belonging to the Creator. Now, it was not. Why??

BEHIND ENEMY LINES – PRESENT DAY

His breaths were coming in short gasps as he held his own hand over his mouth to keep from screaming. In all of his time in the IDF and then the Mossad, he had never witnessed such inhumanity.

Hunkered down under dense cover, all Zac could do was watch in horror. He was but a single man, behind enemy lines, in search of The Assyrian. The politicians said that the only way for the attack on Israel to be stopped was to capture the man responsible for the attack. The problem was that The

Assyrian was not just an Arab thug. Abdullah Abbas Tabak was the Caliph of the ISNW.

Now, with all of his team dead, the odds of Zac's success had dropped close to zero.

Tabak had ordered The Assyrians to slaughter their own people. [97]Christians were being beheaded, and even crucified. Any [98]Muslim who did not swear allegiance to the new Caliph was also mercilessly killed.

At the moment he was frozen by the sight unfolding before him. Zac saw firsthand streets that ran red with blood.

Through his field glasses, he watched as a [99]toddler, no more than four or five, was chained to a fence. The bound child was forced to watch as her parents were brutally tortured and then dismembered while they were still alive.

The Mossad agent was too far to hear the conversation, but the child's screams were carried to him on the wind. He assumed by the rebels gestures that the family were Christians.

Zechariah wanted to scream. He wanted to take out his weapon and kill every last Jihadist. He wanted to run over to the little girl, unchain her and cradle her in his arms.

Yet, none of that would happen. He couldn't risk the mission. A silent tear rolled down his cheek.

"Mamzers!" he spat, "Tisaref B' Azazel!!!" he swore under his breath in a rage.

Tabak's position lay on the other side of all of these murderers. He couldn't go around and he certainly couldn't fight his way through. He had to wait them out. So he sat in frustration, watching.

The snapping of a branch less than twenty feet from where he was hiding caught his attention.

Slowly he turned his head to the right. A patrol had flanked him as they haphazardly performed guard duty. His eyes settled on the nearest member, a bearish man with a pock-marked face and the same lizard-like eyes as the group that attacked his team.

To his rear, he heard warning sounds. They were almost on him. If they didn't alter their path, they would stumble over him.

Looking back to the murderous group torturing innocents in the distance, he saw that they were too preoccupied and too far away to notice what was about to transpire.

With at least three rebels around him, Zechariah prepared himself to take at least two of them out, but he knew that doing so would reveal his position.

He wasn't going to go down without a fight.

Knowing that death was near, he began to pray, "Adon olöm Asher mö-lach..."

Canadian Border, Hwy 93 – Present Day

If someone were to have told me a week ago, Danny thought, *that I'd be dressed in a Russian uniform, traveling in a Russian truck, accompanied by a beautiful Russian spy, in an America that had been invaded and on my way to kidnap a highly-placed Russian officer, I'd have never believed it.*

And yet, here I am!

As they traveled the road, they saw bombed-out buildings and cars. Some dead bodies littered the pavement, but it was apparent that the Russians hid the dead.

Going through one town, the three travelers saw that it was completely flattened.

"Must have been resistance," Goose observed, as he carefully navigated the bomb-pocked road that had, no-doubt, been damaged in an overwhelming shelling.

On the other side of the decimated town, Danny said, "I just don't get it."

"Get it?" Anya asked, from her position seated between the

driver, Goose, and Mendez.

"Why attack us? America's huge. As big as the Russian army is, it's not that big. They'd need a much bigger force."

"Remember, I told you that the Germans were fighting alongside?"

"And what's with that?" Goose threw in his two cents. "Weren't they supposed to be our allies or something?"

"Yeah, in NATO," Danny added.

"You have to understand," Anya explained in a serious tone, "America's demise has been planned for a long time.

"My, ah, general used the term The Group. I have heard that the Iranians, the ISNW, the North Koreans and especially the Chinese are all involved. The Group is using this coalition of countries to do their bidding.

"In return, those countries will receive the spoil of America's natural resources, food and land. More importantly, this Group will have the U.S. out of the way so their Plan can move forward. This conspiracy isn't just about America. These people want to rule the world and they are ready to launch The Plan's final phase.

"The Chinese," Goose thought aloud, "now that makes sense. They have the numbers."

"You said that they're ready to move on to the last phase? So am I to assume," Danny asked, "that the attack on the U.S. was only one part of The Plan?"

"You assume correctly."

"So what is the final phase?" Goose asked.

"I do not know," Anya said. "You must understand. I wasn't privy to these conversations. I happened only to be in the area where they were taking place in unguarded moments. From what I can understand, the final phase is a highly kept secret, even from the leaders of the coalition."

They were quiet for a few moments when Danny said to the windshield, "I've heard that they are starving over there."

"Where?" Goose asked.

"Both in China and North Korea. There's even been some reports of cannibalism in the rural areas.

"The Chinese government began to lose control over the masses," Anya added, "And in some cities, pollution is so bad that they are becoming uninhabitable."

"Not to mention," Danny continued, "that they've [100]consumed almost all of their natural resources. Their economy was once the envy of the world because of how robust it was. Now, it's 101ground to a halt."

"Yeah," Goose added, "but wasn't their government 102buying up a bunch of gold? They had to know this was coming."

Danny said, "In light of what's happened, it sure looks like that. Most people thought they were positioning themselves for their currency to take the place of the Dollar. I guess there was a lot more to it than everybody thought."

"You think it's the same story for North Korea, too?" Goose asked.

"The same, but different. Their people have been suffering for a long time. Starvation is a powerful motivator. In fact, when people go hungry and economies fail, governments start wars. Wars build up the economy and people will focus on the enemy rather than their incompetent leaders." Danny said.

"Each coalition country has their own reasons why they want to destroy America," Anya added. "The North Koreans are China's long-time allies. They will always do what China wants. But make no mistake, their people are starving and they need food. As far as the Chinese's motivations; well, the Dragon believes they are destined to be the next superpower. They can hardly do that with America in the way.

"But the Iranians want to usher in the 103Mahdi. Because they are more closely related to the Arabs, they are aligned with the ISNW. The ISNW are just plain blood-thirsty and want to bring in an apocalypse which they believe will usher in the Mahdi."

"Strange bedfellows," Danny mused.

Anya turned to look at him, "Greed does that."

"Indeed!" Danny nodded.

"The Mahdi?" Goose inquired, "What's the Mahdi?"

"104The Mahdi, or Twelfth Imam, is the Islamic Messiah," Danny said. "A [105]Caliphate is an Islamic nation or State. The person that runs this so-called country is the Caliph."

"Wait... like that guy Tabak for the I-S whatever?"

"Exactly. And in addition, the last Caliph is supposed to come into the world just before their Mahdi."

"Why haven't I heard of this before?" the big man asked from behind the wheel.

"Because there hasn't been a Caliph for decades," Anya added.

"Decades?"

"No," Danny resumed, "the position of Caliph was abolished in Turkey in, ah, 1924, I believe. I guess that the Turks thought it old-fashioned."

With eyebrows raised, Anya said, "Not a simple ranch hand after all?"

Goose chuckled, "Nope, ol' Danny Boy here is edge-a-ma-cated."

Mendez' ears turned red, "I read a lot."

"Ah huh," Anya nodded in approval.

"Look!" Goose said. The group had been so involved in their conversation that they didn't realize how close their objective was. Duckett was pointing to a sign that said, "Welcome to Canada. Please be prepared to stop."

Rounding a bend down the road, they took in the sight of what was left of Canada's border checkpoint booths. Several of the booths had been completely flattened and in their place, Russian tanks sat end-to-end, with their turrets pointed toward the U.S. in a haunting greeting.

Although the civilian population was mostly exterminated, security was still tight in southern Canada. The two remaining booths were used to control the flow of traffic in the area. As such, Russian vehicles lined up, making their way to the forward operating base.

On the other side of the checkpoint was a neat line of at least thirty Russian tanks. There were also troop carriers and other armored vehicles nearby.

A sheen of sweat developed on Goose's forehead, "Looks like an invasion force!"

Danny did a quick count. "Those tanks are battalion strength," Danny said, as he looked at Anya. "I thought you said there were no borders now. What's all this?"

"I had no idea this was here. It appears to be a staging area."

"I thought you said the staging area was the base we're headed to," Goose asked with narrowed eyes."

"It is. They must have parked these here after I went down," she said, watching as Danny laid his rifle in his lap and flipped off the safety.

"Everybody just be cool," he said, "Remember, we're just some soldiers headed back to base."

The muscles in Goose's jaw flexed as he down-shifted.

TWENTY-THREE

LARGE HADRON COLLIDER, GENEVA, SWITZERLAND – PRESENT DAY

"**T**achyons infused!" the tech announced from his console.

"Speed?" Abbot asked a different station.

"Slightly below the speed of light. With the next few rotations, we should break the barrier."

"How long?"

"Fifteen minutes at the most."

"Keep me updated!" Abbot demanded, "I have to coordinate with Corkscrew when we bring the beams into alignment for the collision."

"Yes, sir!"

Abbot picked up the radio handset and squawked, "Corkscrew, this is Control."

"Corkscrew, here," a focused voice on the other end said.

"Fifteen minutes. Be ready."

"Roger, we are standing by. Out," the line crackled and went dead.

What was about to take place was inconceivable to Man.

Humans throughout history have tried to harness nature's power. Mankind has successfully produced electrical power from rushing water with hydro-electric dams and solar technologies. However, never before had Man ripped energy from the very atmosphere that encompassed the planet... until now.

Dr. Valery Roux Durand was the head of the MAAPELS project, currently located less than fifteen miles from the outer ring of the LHC. Durand's name loosely translated meant "a foreign power with [106]red hair that was strong and lasting."

At 6'9" and 225 lbs., he was intimidating to the average 5'9" Frenchman. He looked middle-aged with stylish, shoulder-length, gray hair which had long-since faded from its youthful, bright-red color.

His renowned temper was every bit as caustic as the LHC's Scotsman, albeit with renowned French finesse. Durand had the sharpest of tongues and was able to dress down a colleague in a voice just above a whisper.

Genetically, Durand and Abbot were closer than the European was to any of his countrymen. The fact that the Scot and the Frenchman shared the same ancient bloodline was unknown to anyone. They were cousins and citizens of another civilization that predated the modern world. Moreover, they both walked amongst a clueless mankind... waiting.

LHC, UNDERGROUND – THREE AND A HALF YEARS AGO (BEFORE THE RESET)

Two minutes, fifteen seconds...

"So... Abbot, I... ah..." Bryce looked at the LHC Collision Chamber. *I have to get closer,* "So you are a... a Nephilim?"

"That's right, human. I am a Nephilim," he said proudly. "My ancestors, my cousins, were the fallen angels who took human women and had their way with them. I come from a [107]generation of Nephilim, now genetically manipulated to fit into your primitive society without notice," the creature said.

He chuckled, "Some of us come down in space ships as [108]UFOs. You humans are so gullible. One day you'll welcome us as the solution to all of your earthly problems. You are nearly ripe for the Great Deception."

Keep him talking, Cooper.

"I don't get it. Why all the..." Bryce was side-stepping toward the Chamber while he spoke, "Why get me the HAARP job if you were just going to kill me before I was successful?"

The creature was so caught up in the moment that he didn't notice Bryce inching closer to the Chamber. "You mean to tell me that the great Dr. Cooper still hasn't figured it out?" the creature cackled and howled.

"This was never about your experiment at the LHC! This was all about your work at [109]HAARP!"

Cooper stopped in his maneuvering.

One minute, twenty seconds... It's time for answers. If I'm going to die, I want to die knowing!

"What are you talking about? What about HAARP?"

"You fool!!! You think you're so smart! We needed your knowledge to open the Abyss! It is in the eighth spatial dimension, as you call it!

"My ah... cousins and I, can only move freely in the first two spatial dimensions beyond your 3D world. But youuuu... you were chooosennn," he said snidely. "You've been put here on earth to bridge the gap between dimensions! You're a Levite, and a descendent of Aaron," he said sarcastically.

"We didn't care about this puny experiment," Abbot said, gesturing wide with his arms. "We needed you to release the prisoners before their time. By doing it this way..."

Bryce was side-stepping again. The creature had exited the cubicle and circled back around him, blocking his escape route. Now Bryce's back was no more than three feet from the Collision Chamber.

I'm not going anywhere! Fifty seconds...

The dimensional warping effects were pummeling Bryce. His head was swimming and he could barely focus. His knees were weak and he felt like he was going to puke.

Just a little longer...

The creature was saying, "... by doing it this way, you have given us the ability to unlock the Abyss for the Generals and their legions sooner than anticipated.

"It's quite brilliant, you know. It means that we will be able to launch a surprise attack and kill a third of you humans in the process! You have been very helpful, Dr. Cooper. We couldn't have done it without you."

Forty seconds...

Just then, Bryce saw the bomb leads that went to the black box on the floor. He followed them up to the C-4 with his eyes. A look of horror registered on his face.

"Ah, the brilliant Dr. Cooper is finally beginning to understand," Abbot shouted condescendingly. "Those explosives will go off at the same time as the particle collision.

"With my little present there, and your acceleration of the beams beyond the Speed of Light, we should be able to incinerate most of Europe, perhaps the earth! And all of this, even before we set the Generals free!" he howled and laughed maniacally.

Twenty seconds...

Bryce pulled out the Urimm and Thummim from the Garments' breast pockets.

Catching his breath, the creature saw the crystals in Bryce's hand. For the first time he noticed what Bryce was wearing. "What is that you have on there? And what is in your hand? Do you honestly think you can outsmart me? It's too late!"

Ten... Nine...

"You know," Bryce said, "They say that 'close' is only good in horse shoes, hand grenades and thermonuclear war. I think this is close enough! This is for Mac, you arrogant..."

Three... Two... One...

Bryce brought the crystals together.

The creature roared and lunged at him - but it was too late.

The crystals connected at the same time the collision occurred and... just a millisecond before the bomb detonated.

With a blinding arc of hot light... Dr. Bryce Obadiah Cooper was gone.

MAAPELS, GENEVA, SWITZERLAND – PRESENT DAY

"Corkscrew" was Durand's call sign for his position in charge of MAAPELS, the Mobile Atmospheric Arresting Plasma Energy Laser System. The program was an upgrade to the aged HAARP technology in Alaska.

It was a combination of the newest laser experiments on the planet - technology from [110]the Pentagon-sponsored, super laser research program and the [111]High-Repetition-Rate Advanced Petawatt Laser System. The latter system was referred to in pop-culture as "The Death Star".

Officially, it was an atmospheric experiment in which the system was placed on a mobile structure and moved from location to location. The criteria for its placement depended on weather conditions which were suitable for the experiment to drain energy from the sky. Unofficially, all of the money and effort spent in the system's design was done so for this very day. And it had nothing to do with an atmospheric experiment.

The gargantuan, starfish-like, dark-gray dish rested on four oversized, semi-truck, flatbed trailers. Its distinctly otherworldly appearance was augmented by several other space-age vehicles. When assembled, MAAPELS was seven-stories high and the width of a football field. It fired a one-quadrillion-watts, oscillating plasma beam into the atmosphere.

The [112]machine harvested excited particles right from the air and drew them back down to the support equipment. Those particles were converted to energy and fed back into the laser, thereby increasing its power. The laser's burst would further excite particles, generating electrical charges in the form of lightning. This cycle continued as converted energy increased the power, speed and width of the beam until it was either shut off or melted down.

If left unchecked the beam could rip a hole in the sky, or spin a hurricane greater than the world had ever seen.

Like the LHC, preparation for the experiment took weeks. When setup and safety checks were complete, the army of technicians would withdraw to at least fifteen miles.

A MAAPELS experiment had never been scheduled to run this long, with so much power and in conjunction with a particle collision at the LHC.

The combined experiment would only happen once because it would literally slice a hole in the sky.

Durand looked at the large dish in the distance through his field glasses and spoke softly, "Et puis nous allons gouverner (And then we will rule)."

JERUSALEM, MOSSAD SAFE HOUSE – PRESENT DAY

"So what you are saying," Percy asked, "is that unknowingly I've been involved in a plan…"

"Not a plan," Stephanie interrupted, "[113]The Plan."

"Alright, The Plan, to kill off or enslave all of mankind."

"I'm afraid so," Diggs admitted.

Percy was quiet for a moment, trying to fit all the pieces together. "So, what is the purpose of those… those Grays that I told you I saw?"

"The Plan has multiple facets," Diggs said, "Those Grays are supposed to make people think that aliens left the seed of Man on this planet thousands of years ago."

"It's called [114]Panspermia Theory," Mac, the astrophysicist, said, "And it's easy to see how the multitudes could fall for it. After all, people's belief in God has waned considerably over the last few years. Both Catholics and Protestants alike will believe when the Pope and mega-church preachers start telling their flocks that ETs were used to [115]plant the seed of Man on earth. Then, when Aliens bring medical cures, free energy and peace planet-wide, people will see the true Gospel as irrelevant. That's how you get The Great Deception."

"But wait a moment," Percy said, "All of that sounds pretty good to me. What's to say that the gospel isn't irrelevant when they come?"

"That's a fair question, except for one thing," Diggs said.

"What is that, pray tell?"

"It's a lie! You need to remember who these things really are. Their goal is not to bring a better world; it's a ruse to take down humanity. While we may have free energy, and what not, for a while, the cost will be higher than you'll want to pay. Besides, after three-and-a-half years, it won't matter."

"Three and a half years? What's that got to do with aliens?"

"Look," Stephanie said, "It's not like we don't know what's going to happen. The Bible talks about a covenant being made for seven years. In the middle of that, they go back on the deal and it gets very ugly. That's what Digby is talking about."

"What does all of this matter anyway," Percy said smugly, "If you lot are correct, you'll be gone, right? Oh wait, I thought you were already supposed to be gone? Which is it?"

"What on earth are you talking about?" Diggs asked.

"With all that's happened the last few days and this Great Deception about to take place, aren't you people supposed to fly away or something?"

"You mean the [116]Rapture," Stephanie said.

"Yes, that's it! The Rappppturrrrre."

Mac, Diggs and Stephanie traded a look and Diggs nodded to Stephanie.

Stephanie started slow, "You're only partly right."

"Partly right? You're either here or you're not."

"That's what I mean by partly. I don't like the term Rapture and I'll tell you why in a moment. But specifically what you are referring to is the," she made quote marks with her fingers, "pre-tribulation Rapture."

"Come on, I don't want to get into all this religious mumbo..."

Stephanie held out her hand, "Hold on, you brought it up. And considering what's going on, you need to hear this."

Percy was quiet for a moment, "Alright, I'll concede the point for a moment. But I'm telling you right now, I don't want to be proselytized."

"Fair enough," Diggs said.

Stephanie continued, "The Tribulation is a terrible time for humanity and it is foretold about in the Bible. Unfortunately, it looks a lot like what we are seeing now. And more to the point, it's only going to get worse."

"So?"

"So, this doctrine of a pre-tribulation Rapture, or catching away, is one that most Christians believed because it was convenient."

"Convenient?"

"It's loosely based on 1 Thessalonians 4:17 which says that we will be caught up with the Lord in the air when He comes back."

"That is what I'm saying! You think you're not supposed to be here for all this mess! So if you're wrong about that, what else are you wrong about?!"

"That's the same thing that many Christians are asking themselves right now. They're disillusioned because they expected to escape all of this craziness. So much so, that they doubt God's very existence."

"And," Mac added, "making them ripe for the Great Deception."

"I'll say," Percy exclaimed, "If they are disillusioned now, can you imagine what will happen when these little Grays start showing up?"

"Now you understand," Diggs said, "That's why we call it 'The Great Deception'."

"So you agree this whole God thing is wrong."

"No," Stephanie said, "The verse in Thessalonians is right, but the idea that we are snatched away before all the bad stuff happens is wrong."

"You mean that Christians were lied to?"

"No, I'm not saying that," Stephanie leaned forward in her chair, "That verse out of Thessalonians uses the word "harpazo". It means to be snatched away. But nowhere in the verse or in the sections before or after does it say that this catching away will happen before the bad stuff starts happening."

"It doesn't?"

"No! That's the problem with that pre-tribulation doctrine. In fact, when you compare it to the totality of scripture, the opposite is true. For instance, in Mark 13:24 Jesus said He wasn't coming until AFTER the tribulation and Matthew 24:29 says the same thing, AFTER the tribulation they will see Him."

"Look, I told you that I'm not religious, but if most Christians believe in this Rapture, then why do you think you're smarter than they are?"

Stephanie was quiet for a moment, "Not smarter, just unwilling to believe something because it's convenient. And this is why I have a problem with the word [117]Rapture. The doctrine was popularized with books from famous so-called experts and Christian pop-culture movies.

"The [118]origin of the word rapture comes from Latin. And it gives the connotation of being dragged away to be raped.

"So, not only do I think it's a bad idea to translate from a translation, in this case the Latin Vulgate, but it seems to me that the doctrine is a reflection of what is really going on today with the Church."

"What do you mean?"

"This pre-trib doctrine has been used by the enemy to drag Christ's Bride away and... well, you know.

"We have a whole generation of Christians who are facing perilous times for which they are unprepared, because they thought they would escape!

"I'm no smarter than those people who believe in a pre-tribulation Rapture, but I'm willing to look at the truth, even if it's uncomfortable."

"Well, that's harsh."

Stephanie's voice sounded sad, "Not harsh! Real! Based upon the totality of scripture. Christians have work to do during this time and in the future. We are called to be salt and light to a dying world. That's not convenience; that's doing what we were born to do. We will meet Jesus in the air, but at a time of His choosing, not ours."

Percy waved off her comment, "I didn't want to talk about religion."

Diggs said, "Cousin, you can't separate what is going in the world now and what the Bible talks about. We are living in those times of the end. We are seeing these things come alive before our eyes. We," Diggs looked at Stephanie and Mac, "aren't trying to convert you. You wanted the truth. In fact, you were right in the middle of this deception in your lab. The point is that - this is not about religion, it's about truth."

Percy cleared his throat, "Well, you may be righter than you know."

"How's that?" Mac asked.

"Those little Gray creatures?"

"Yeah."

"The last I saw them... they were waking up."

TWENTY-FOUR

L arry Taylor had been walking for a long time and now had a sheen of sweat on his forehead.

Why is it so warm down here?

As soon as he thought it, the darkness began to ebb.

Is that light?

Rounding a bend, the glow turned bright and Larry's pulse quickened.

Another bend in the tunnel snaked the opposite way. As he rounded it, Taylor found himself at the mouth of a mammoth cavern.

"What?!"

Warm light beamed from all directions and was amplified by [119]giant, white crystals, both glowing and bending the light.

Larry took off his baseball cap and ran his hand over his slick head and scratched his jaw.

After a moment, he walked up to the nearest crystal. It was more than forty-feet long and ten-feet thick and the glassy surface felt warm as he ran his hand over it.

As he touched the glass, his head started to swim, his ears rang and it felt like he was being pulled out of his body, up, up and... He jerked his hand back.

"My God... What is this place?"

Modern electronics use silicone and crystals. This mountain must act as some kind of circuit. I knew it! That explains the electromagnetic fluctuations!

He explored the crystal cavern, being careful to not touch the luminous glass for very long periods of time. Sensing there was more to discover in his mountain, he hesitantly moved on.

Finding an identical tunnel on the other side of the cavern, he pressed on and noted that the ground no longer sloped downward.

He ran his hand over the tunnel walls.

Only a little dusty and smooth... Not blasted, more like they were... machined. What could dig through solid rock like this and leave the walls without gouges or scars?

Larry thought back to the world's biggest tunnel-boring machine, [120]Big Bertha, digging under Seattle. It was Man's best tool to cut through rock, but it couldn't touch the precision carving of this cave.

Somebody... or something, made this place and they're a lot smarter than us.

Behind him the glow from the crystal cavern receded. He turned on his flashlight and looked at his watch. It wasn't working. "Huh?" He stopped and thumped it with his finger. Nothing.

"Electromagnetics..." he said and started walking again.

Another glow appeared down the tunnel. It wasn't the warm, incandescent light that he'd seen heading into the cavern. This illumination was sharper, and didn't look natural.

Rounding another bend, Larry stopped cold.

As the tunnel opened up into a cavern bigger than the last, a giant, domed building stood in front of Taylor, hewn right into the rock.

Dozens of sconces with the same glow as the huge crystals were attached to the walls of the building and cavern.

Not only could they cut through that rock of the cave, it looks like they cut through those solid crystals for those lights. And that stuff's a lot harder than rock.

There were seven, sweeping, rounded steps that led up to what he guessed was the front door. He walked over to them and stepped up.

Taylor knew that the standard step had about a 7 ¾ inch rise and was approximately 11 ½ inches deep. But these steps had a rise of at least two feet and were four feet deep.

These are some big steps... for big people!

He climbed all seven and found himself on an ornate landing that had strange carvings in the stone. He didn't know if it was writing or just decoration, but it was nothing like he'd ever seen.

Next, he ran his hand over the outside of the building. Like the tunnel, it too was smooth and felt machined. When he brought his hand away from the stone, to his surprise, there was no dust on it.

No dust on the walls?

He knelt down and ran his hand on the ground and then looked at it.

No dust on the ground?

He stepped back, taking in the full height of the cocoa-colored building. Crossing his arms and cupping his chin, he stood thinking for a moment.

"This thing must be thousands of years old... how can there be no dust?"

He took a step toward the door. Its shape was long and horizontal, wider than it was tall. It looked like it was made out of bronze, but Larry couldn't see any patina and it didn't look old. In fact, the whole building looked like it was just built yesterday: no dust, no scratches, no wear.

Taylor studied the door. It didn't have a handle or knob. He scratched the stubble on his chin.

He started to run his hand over the metal and... it silently slid open.

MT. GRAHAM OBSERVATORY, TUCSON, ARIZONA – PRESENT DAY

"Is that what I think it is?" The Professor asked the priest.

Joshua replied, "The question is: what do you think it is?"

Juni couldn't help himself. Seeing the concern etched on the Professor's face, he asked, "What's wrong? Why do you look like that?"

Joshua and Alvaro traded a look and the Jesuit nodded.

"[121]Hercolubus…" Dr. Mora said.

Juni's brow furrowed and he shook his head, "I'm sorry, Professor. I don't speak Spanish."

Alvaro was lost in thought, staring at the ground. He pulled his head up. His eyes were glassy and jaw tight, "Hercolubus is a name."

"A name? A name of what?"

"It goes by many names: [122]Planet X, [123]Nibiru, the [124]Blue Star Kachina, [125]The Destroyer, [126]Wormwood, [127]Nemesis… Hercolubus," Dr. Mora was back to staring at the ground.

Juni walked up even with him and placed a hand on his shoulder, "Professor, what has got you so upset?"

Alvaro blew out a long breath and turned back to Joshua, "So I suppose you're expecting the [128]Anunnaki? That's why you are preparing for [129]Disclosure?"

The priest stuck out his lip and shrugged, "Yes… but it is time anyway."

"How close will the [130]flyby be?"

"Of course, there is no data from the last time this happened, but we anticipate the closest ever," Joshua said smugly.

Juni raised his voice, "Professor, will you please tell me what you are talking about?"

Mora turned to his new friend, "Juni, have you not heard of Nibiru?"

"Nir… what?"

"Nibiru"

"No."

"There has long been speculation that there was an Interloper in our solar system."

Juni scratched the back of his neck, "Professor, I'm a volcanologist, remember? I have no idea what you're talking about."

"An Interloper is an unseen celestial body, a planet, or star that is in our solar system."

"How can that be? We've named the planets all the way to Pluto. In fact, didn't they say that one is too small to be a planet so they [131]un-planeted it or something? Anyway, if they can see all the way to Pluto, why wouldn't they see this, this interloper?"

The Professor shook his head and sounded like he was lecturing students again, "It's not that easy. You see, many people think this is not a planet at all, but a brown dwarf star with heavy mass and a small constellation around it. Supposedly, it is on an elongated elliptical orbit that takes it to the furthest part of the sun's gravitational influence and requires 3600 years to complete its rotation. "

Juni looked to Joshua and then back to the Professor, "I still don't understand. How could they not see it?"

"Most solar systems," The Professor continued, "are at least binary systems, meaning that they have at least two suns and sometimes more."

"A sun?" Juni asked astonished, "Of course we would see another sun."

"Not," Joshua answered, "if the sun in question is a brown dwarf star."

"Yes," Juni turned back to the Professor, "you mentioned that brown thing."

"Not just a thing, Juni," Dr. Mora said, "A [132]brown dwarf is a star that is too small in mass to sustain a hydrogen fusion reaction but has the mass as a light star."

"If it doesn't sustain a reaction, how can it have light?"

"No, I don't mean light as in shining, I mean light as in not heavy. But understand, it is much heavier than any of the planets of our solar system. Because of that, other celestial bodies orbit around it like our own sun. The Anunnaki supposedly live on one of those planets," the Professor looked Joshua in the eye.

Joshua nodded.

"The what?" Juni asked.

"The Annunaki were introduced by a man, [133]Zecharia Sitchin, who said…"

"Not just him," Joshua corrected, "we have ancient texts that also point to them."

Alvaro paused. Sitchin supposedly translated those ancient texts. Collaborating evidence is an issue, but he decided to ignore the comment and continued, "He said that these Annunaki were extraterrestrials who had made their presence known to the people of earth on previous flybys."

"Aliens?" Juni said, "It's not too hard for me to believe in aliens. I've seen them... or at least their ships with my own eyes. They like to hang around volcanoes. In fact, they like to fly into volcanoes."

"What?" The Professor looked over at the priest who had a confused look on his face and just shrugged. "What do you mean they like to fly into volcanoes?"

"Just what I said," Juni replied, "All kinds of UFOs. Saucer-like, long tubular UFOs. They hang around these volcanoes and then they just dive right down into the cone. Craziest thing you ever saw. Like they had some kind of death-wish or something."

"But..." the Professor started to protest and then bit off his sentence. His hand went to his mouth as he pinched his lower lip in thought. Juni started to say something, but the Professor held up his hand and began to pace.

Juni traded a look with Joshua.

The Professor stopped pacing and asked, "You are certain that these craft have gone into volcanoes?"

Juni's eyes narrowed defensively, "Absolutely. It's also been caught on video on many occasions."

"And you say that this activity has happened at more than one volcano?"

"Yes... and sometimes when they have been erupting. But like I said, I don't know why they would want to kill themselves off like that. It seems to me that they're not too smart."

"I don't think that is the case at all."

"What do you mean?"

"Why didn't I see it before?" the Professor said, lightly punching his fist into his palm.

"Professor, what are you talking about?" Juni asked.

"I believe I know why Dr. Cooper and his friend put us together."

Juni cocked his head, "Why?"

"He put us together to figure out that they," Mora pointed to the computer screen, "are not just coming. They are already here and they are using portals to get back and forth!"

Behind Enemy Lines – Present Day

Zechariah slowly rolled onto his back. His camouflaged paint and netting
had thus far made him invisible to the enemy... but not for long.

Twelve feet.

Zac centered his Uzi on the chest of the jihadist. He figured he could
take out two, maybe three of them before the rest of them rushed him.

Ten feet.

He let out a slow, steadying breath and slid his finger to the trigger.

Six feet.

The fighter dropped his head to see where he was walking. His lizard-
looking eyes went large, as he realized there was a man with a gun pointed at
him.

Zac was about to squeeze his trigger when he heard a crack. A light
sliced through the air just behind the jihadist. The rebel heard it too and
began to turn.

The arms reached through the light for the head of the rebel, pulled his
body back toward the light, but not inside. At the same time, one hand
covered his mouth and twisted the fighter's neck, until it snapped.

The fighter's corpse went limp and the bodiless arms lowered him
slowly and silently to the ground.

Then a man exited the light.

Noise to his right caused Zac's head to swivel in the direction of the
sound.

He turned just in time to see another man in hand-to-hand combat with
another jihadist.

The second man used the jihadist's own movements against the rebel as
the fighter lunged at the man with a knife. The man side-stepped the lunge
with the grace of a dancer and latched on to the rebel's wrist. The man
forced the arm to keep going in a 360 degree motion, until the shoulder
dislocated with a sickening pop. He dropped the knife and howled.

In one fluid motion, the man picked up the knife and sliced through the fighter's neck, severing his voice box and arteries.

A third rebel, not fifteen feet from the fighting men, raised his gun to fire.

Too late! Zac put a clean, silenced headshot through the jihadist's forehead.

The Mossad agent spun around on his stomach and brought his field glasses to his eyes. The larger group of jihadists in the distance had been too caught up in their bloodlust, yelling and shooting their guns in the air. They hadn't noticed the brief noise and scuffle.

On both sides of Zac, his rescuers dropped to the ground.

"Josiah? Dr. Cooper? How did you two get here?!"

TWENTY-FIVE

SOUTHERN CANADA – PRESENT DAY

The checkpoint was little more than a pause for the trio in the Russian truck. When they reached the front of the line, Anya simply held up her logistics I.D. with a sultry smile.

The young guard smiled back, nodded to the driver, Goose, and waved them through the barrier. That was over an hour ago.

"I gotta pee," Anya said.

"I could go too," Danny added.

"Alright, we can pull into a rest area as soon…" Goose started to say.

"No," Anya replied, "No place where we might run into other Russians, remember? You don't want to have to talk to anyone. If you do, we will all die."

"She's right," Danny agreed, "There!" He pointed to a wooded area.

As soon as the truck stopped, Anya pushed on Danny to get him out. When he did, she slid out behind him and hit the ground running.

She skidded to a stop a few yards from the truck and ran back to the cab. Opening the glove box, she pulled out a roll of toilet paper.

With a red face, she looked at the slack-jawed Danny and said, "American toilet paper… got to love it!" and she ran off to the woods.

Goose chuckled and headed in the direction of the tree line. Danny followed him and facing the woods and bushes, the men unzipped to relieve themselves.

"How far are we?" Goose asked.

"If I had to guess, I'd say probably twenty-five miles," Danny replied.

"Ahhhh. Guess it's a good thing we stopped when we did. I bet there's a lot more Russians that way. Hate to run into one and have to explain myself."

At their rear, they heard the squeaky brakes of a heavy truck parking behind them.

"Ah, oh," Goose said.

Through gritted teeth, Danny said, "Just be cool and don't talk!"

They zipped in a hurry and were about to spin to make a break for the truck.

Before they did, two Russian soldiers lined up next to them in their makeshift latrine line.

Danny and Goose nodded and turned to their truck which was parked at least ten yards away.

The men were Russian bears. One was at least 6'6" and the other one was a little shorter, but solid muscle.

"Ahhhh," the shorter man groaned and then looked over his shoulder at the retreating Americans and said something.

They pretended not to hear the Russian and casually kept walking.

The taller man looked over his shoulder with a scowl and yelled something at Goose and Danny. The ranch hands could hear the inflection in his voice. They stopped, traded a knowing look, and turned around.

The Russians finished with nature's call and turned to face them.

The large, angry Bear gestured with his chin to his partner and growled something to the Americans.

Danny and Goose made a show of shrugging their shoulders and turning their mouths down as if to say, "Who knows?"

The tall Russian's face scrunched in confusion.

The shorter Russian pointed to the American and said something, eliciting a belly laugh from the big guy.

Goose and Danny did the only thing they could do, shrug and laugh with them.

The big Bear's joviality evaporated; he pointed his finger at the Americans and then pointed to the symbols on his lapel.

The shorter Bear nudged his friend on the arm and said something else in Russian, to which the men laughed.

Danny and Goose laughed too.

The Bear's jaw tightened and he pointed emphatically to the men, and then to their truck.

Danny and Goose looked over their shoulder at the truck and shrugged.

Big Bear went ballistic, shouting as he held out his hand in demand. Danny assumed he wanted to see their I.D.s. Then the Bear pulled his sidearm.

The shorter Bear also pulled his sidearm.

Big Bear yelled something and held out one finger, as if to say, "I'm going to ask you one last time."

Danny closed his eyes because he knew he was going to die.

In the corner of his eye, Goose saw Anya's head pop up in the cab of the truck; she had a rifle in her hand.

Duckett clamped his big hand on Danny's arm and hit the deck, pulling Danny down with him.

The Bear's eyes followed them going to the ground and never saw the beautiful young woman with the gun.

Anya opened up on the Bears with full automatic.

Danny and Goose held their hands to their heads as if their flesh could protect them from flying lead.

The Bear's heads exploded in a crimson puff of torn flesh, shattered bone and gray matter.

The short burst of fire stopped.

The bodies teetered as if they didn't know they were now

headless and then fell backward to the ground with a thud.

LARGE HADRON COLLIDER, GENEVA, SWITZERLAND – PRESENT DAY

"We've crossed the Speed of Light!" the tech nearly shouted.

Abbot didn't need to be told. He was already feeling, and seeing the effects. The Control Room filled with translucent vapors, spirals and rolling, clear waves that bent the light as the effects of dimensional warping began.

The humans around him couldn't see what was happening.

For Abbot, this was normal. He'd traveled many times beyond the speed-of-light and experienced the warping of time and space in the [134]flying crafts that The Others manufactured.

He picked up the radio handset.

———————————————————————

"Corkscrew, this is Control, over." the radio sounded.

Dr. Durand hit the button and said, "Go ahead, Control, over."

"We have speed of light rotation, over."

Durand didn't need to be told. He too felt the effects of the speed-of-light being broken, even though he was fifteen miles away.

"Roger, we are ready for Starburst, Control."

"Well, laddie, let's get this party started!"

"Roger that!"

Durand asked the technician next to him, "Are we ready for the firing sequence?"

"Yes, sir. We have been harvesting power from the atmosphere for the last half hour. The charging units are almost at capacity and we need to fire soon, or shut down the harvester. Whenever you are ready to go, sir."

Durand slid his hand over to the five-inch, red ignition button that sat under a clear protective cover on a hinge. He flipped the cover open. Looking at the technician, he said with a slit of a smile, "Very soon now, mon ami."

"Corkscrew, are you there?"

"Roger, I am here and we are ready for the firing sequence."

"Roger, I am ready to bring the beams into collision. On my mark, then."

"Roger, on your mark.

"And Corkscrew?"

"Yes, Control?"

"It is a glorious day!"

"Indeed it is, Control. And then we will be kings!"

"And then we will be kings!" Abbot said with glee, "Ready?"

"Ready"

"See you on the other side."

"On the other side."

"Ignition on my mark," Abbot said again.

Durand swallowed hard and placed his hand in the air, six inches from the top of the red button.

The radio squawked, "Five... four... three... two... one... Mark!"

Durand slapped the red button down with his palm.

JERUSALEM, MOSSAD SAFE HOUSE – PRESENT DAY

Percy was up and pacing while he muttered to himself.

"Well," Mac said, "You gotta admit, it's a lot to take in."

"I'll say," Stephanie said.

"But he needed to hear it," Diggs added.

"So this [135]Group," Percy said, as he stopped pacing, "Surely they have to have more to their plan than just killing everyone?"

"Oh yes," Diggs admitted, "They have everything worked out, except..."

"Except what, Digby?"

217

"Except that they think they are..." Diggs looked at Stephanie and Mac, "To use an American saying: they think they are calling the shots."

"What do you mean; they think they are calling the shots? They're not?"

"The Group consists of the wealthiest and most [136]powerful people on the planet. It is built from families that have long [137]royal bloodlines."

Percy's eyebrows raised.

"And yes," Diggs added, "that includes ours." Both Diggs and Percy were distant relatives to the House of Windsor.

"This sense of power and entitlement was bred into their families and encouraged by another group, even more powerful and longstanding than their own."

"More longstanding than the royal families?"

"[138]This group is ancient."

"Ancient?"

"That's right. They are called, The Others."

"I've never heard of them?"

"You have indeed, in this very room."

"No, no, I would remember such a thing," Percy insisted.

"You heard us speak of them by another name."

"Which is?"

"The Nephilim"

"Ohhhh, bloody... not this again!"

"Percy, either you want the truth or you don't. Which is it?"

Percy sighed in frustration, "Alright. But I'm warning you, Digby, I don't want to get into all of that religious thing again."

Diggs held up his hands like he was defending himself, "Like we told you, we're not trying to convert you, but you needed the background to understand what is going on and why."

"Fine"

"Individual families have always been in control around the world in one way or another. Yet, they were always autonomous kingdoms, if you will, and their power was limited.

"Sometime at the beginning of the twentieth-century, The Others, the Nephilim, came to them with a Plan that would unite their efforts and give them total world domination. To accomplish this Plan, They offered these families their [139]Nephilim technology, but said it needed to be introduced into the world slowly, so as to not raise suspicion.

"Thus, they formed these families into The Group and set down the road of making the Plan come to fruition. But something happened a few years ago that The Group didn't anticipate."

"What happened?" Percy asked.

Stephanie stepped in, "The Group had come to think of The Others not so much as partners, but servants. They took for granted that The Others had altruistic motivations for helping them.

"It was true that The Others were not as creative as humans, but their intelligence was far advanced. For some reason, their egos probably, The Group thought their creativity made them superior to their servants, The Others."

"And that was a mistake," Mac said, "The Others had [140]embedded themselves in every part of the world's structures: politics, science, financial, religion, etcetera, etcetera. In doing so, because of The Group's dependence on them, they leveraged that dependence to become the very core of the world's leadership."

"What are you saying?" Percy asked.

"It's hard to know when it happened exactly," Diggs said, "But sometime just a few years ago, The Group who had been on the inside looking out at the rest of the world, implementing their plans for world-domination, found themselves on the outside, looking in... at The Others."

Percy scratched his receding hairline, "I don't understand. I thought The Others' goals were the same as The Group's. What would it matter?"

Mac said, "That's what The Group thought too."

"Wait, so The Others don't want world-domination?"

"They couldn't care less," Mac said with a frown, "They've been around for thousands upon thousands of years. And always manipulating mankind for their own ends."

"So, that begs the question," Percy said, "what do they want?"

Diggs said, "They want what they've always wanted. They want to institute their cousin's plans."

"Their cousin's plans? What cousins?"

"Percy, you said that it didn't make sense that The Group was trying to take over the world at the same time that they were trying to kill it off."

"Yes, and... and I stand by that," Percy said, not sounding nearly as confident as he did when he first made the statement.

"We are going to share something that will help you understand everything that is happening," Diggs said, "It is the glue that holds all of this craziness together..."

"Yes?"

"That glue is the fact that The Others are now doing the bidding of their cousins."

"Yes, you said that."

"What I haven't said is that their cousins are The Fallen... As in [141]fallen angels, demons if you will, and they hate mankind.

"It is they, The Fallen, which are trying to use The Plan to wipe out mankind, God's creation, once and for all."

The already-pale face of Percy lost the rest of its color.

"Crikey..."

TWENTY-SIX

IN THE SKY, ON FINAL APPROACH – PRESENT DAY

There were few times in his life that The Man With The Book felt inadequate. This was one of those times.

Over the years he'd taken hundreds, if not thousands of meetings. He'd learned a long time ago that it was important to give an air of competence and authority, even if he was totally in the dark about the subject matter.

This meeting was the most important of his life and he was in the dark. He'd given up all of his leverage, did everything he was told to do and took the brunt of all the bad press. The question was: would his efforts be rewarded? He was about to find out.

He looked down at the book in his lap again.

This book was prophetic. I doubt its author thought of a literal world without the United States. While I'm sure the people at the meeting will be happy at what's going on in the country, how can they be sure that a world without America will be any better? And more to the point, can I do business with these people? I guess I'm going to find out.

He felt the plane shudder and heard the thump of the landing gear locking in place.

A pale Danny stood on unsteady legs. He'd been bent over throwing up.

Wiping his mouth with his shirt sleeve, he said, "I've never seen anyone killed close up."

Goose patted him lightly on his shoulder, "It's okay, buddy. I don't think I've ever seen anyone throw up that much."

"It was necessary," Anya said curtly, "You see those uniforms?"

"Yeah"

"Spetsnaz"

Danny swallowed hard, "141Russian special forces?"

"That's right. They're all over up here and they were insulted that you didn't answer them. They already think they are better than regular army. Then after insulting your mother, they..."

"My mother?"

Goose piped in, "Must be a universal insult."

"When you still didn't respond," Anya continued, "they said something about sticking your head... well, you get the picture."

"Another universal insult!" Goose said.

"They asked you about the truck and where you were going. The taller one started flashing his rank so you knew he was serious."

"Trust me," Danny said looking down at the dead bodies, "I knew they were serious from the beginning."

"When you still didn't answer, they concluded that you were American spies, and demanded that you show them your I.D. They were about to shoot you - really."

"I know. Thanks," Danny shivered.

"Now we have to hurry," Anya directed, "Someone might have heard the gunshots and may come to investigate."

"Hurry and do what?" Goose asked.

"Take off your clothes."

Goose and Danny traded a look of surprise. "Excuse me?" Duckett said.

"Take off your clothes. We have to move the bodies and you don't want to get blood on your uniforms. That would lead to questions later on."

Just then, the rumble of a plane passing overhead caused them to look to the sky.

"Is that what I think it is?" Danny shouted to be heard.

Three sets of eyes stared at the blue-and-white passenger jet with its landing gear down, headed to the forward operating base.

"There's not an airport around here large enough for a plane that size." Danny said.

Anya pointed in the direction they were headed, and with a raised voice said, "Our military must have finished the temporary landing strip."

"I guess, but... why is that plane landing there?" Danny asked confused, "And how is it flying at all after the EMPs?"

"Maybe an emergency landing?" Goose guessed.

"Regardless, if they are here," Anya quipped, "then they must have known where to go and what they needed to avoid."

"Huh... strange bedfellows?" Danny said wearily to Goose.

"You just never know, Danny boy. You just never know..."

Anaya clapped her hands twice, quickly bringing them back to their situation, "Now come, come, boys. Get undressed!"

Goose looked at Danny with a grin, "Somehow I imagined that invitation would sound different."

Danny slugged him in the arm.

BENEATH THE OKLAHOMA MOUNTAIN GATEWAY – PRESENT DAY

Larry's heart was pounding as he stepped across the threshold of The Chamber.

Like the steps at the front of the building, everything in the place was way larger than for regular humans.

I hope nobody's home... If... if this was a home. Maybe it's something else.

Larry tried climbing into what looked like a chair, but it was too far off the ground. There were tables whose tops were too tall for him to see what was resting on them. From the sparse decor, he noted that everything looked space-age and ultra-modern. However, there was a lot of writing on the walls. Much of it was over the doorways.

The language was more than foreign - it was alien. He'd never seen anything like it, but it had the familiar look of petroglyphs at the Heavener Runestone, with some [142]hieroglyphs thrown in.

"Now I know what Jack must have felt in Jack and the Beanstock," he said, giving up in his latest attempt to climb up on a piece of furniture.

Just as the walls and ground outside, there was no dust whatsoever on the inside. He wondered if the air was filtered, but he didn't see any vents. It didn't smell dank or musty either, despite being sealed away for thousands of years. In fact, the air was crisp, even ionized.

As he looked around, he realized that not a stich of wood could be seen. The furnishings were made of mostly metal or he assumed a hard plastic. Some alien fabric covered the furnishings, but furs of giant animals were scattered around the rooms as rugs or wall hangings, or laid across furniture.

A woman's touch? And how do thay keep that stuff from decomposing?

If there was a woman around, she was nowhere to be found. In fact, despite the home's neat appearance, there was no sign of life anywhere.

He'd wandered around for a long time, careful not to get lost. He stuck to the straight, main hallway that appeared to run the length of the vast Chamber even though he knew it would limit his exploration. Balls of string would've been useful to avoid getting lost like those [143]spelunkers who explored caves. He'd have to remember that next time.

That thought reminded him of his Electro-Magnetic Meter. He pulled it out. It was pegged. He hit the side of it with his palm to make sure it wasn't broken. The needle bounced, but again went past the red line.

Fishing into his pocket, he brought out his Swiss Army Knife. He walked up close to the honed wall, held the knife six inches from it and let go. Like a fisherman reeling in a catch, an invisible hook latched onto the knife and yanked it the six inches to the wall, slapping it against the stone where it stayed.

Taylor scratched his chin and pulled the knife off the wall. He let it go and again it slapped against the stone and stuck.

Just as I thought. The whole place is magnetized. That would explain why my head has been swimming since I got here.

Larry crossed his arms and put his hand to his chin.

But that doesn't make sense. The iron in sand and dust is drawn to magnets. Yet, this place doesn't have any dust. That would mean this place didn't have iron anywhere around or... this wasn't magnetism like we understand it.

He took his cap off and scratched his head. More questions than answers...

Because his watch stopped working, he had no idea what time it was. However, his internal clock said it was maybe nine. He'd been walking for a long time now. Taylor knew he'd soon have to start heading back.

At the back of the long hallway, a taller, wider tunnel opened up "There's no end to this place!"

Doors similar to the front door, but narrower, divided the tunnel from what he assumed were rooms. The same strange language was written on the side of the doors.

He knew he was running out of time, so rather than going through all of the doors, he walked the fifty yards of passageway and came to a door.

A door identical to The Chamber's front door slid open silently when he touched it. As it did, his eyes glowed with excitement and he whistled.

The whistle came back to him in a long echo, because on the other side of that door was a cavernous tunnel that appeared to be part of a transport system.

"Well, I'll be..."

The tunnel was wide enough for two human trucks and tall enough so that even a semi would have clearance. The same sconces lit the tunnel every few feet.

225

As he craned his neck out the door in both directions, all he could see was the road disappearing deep inside the mountain.

Heavener! That's where those tunnels came from. I wonder if anyone who started there, ended up here? I doubt it, he thought, answering his own question. This place looks untouched, but...

He remembered the reason why those Heavener tunnels were dynamited.

People had gone down into them and had never come out!

The authorities at the time said that they were closing them off for public safety. But what if something else happened? What if they ran into whoever built this place?

Larry's excitement vaporized at the thought and he unconsciously checked his broken watch again.

With an empty feeling in the pit of this stomach, he said, "I think I need to wrap up this little excursion."

He was halfway down the tunnel that led to the hall when his curiosity got the better of him.

"Just one more room?" He checked his broken watch again, "Ahhhh!"

He was tired and thirsty, and he justified his curiosity, telling himself that if he found some water, it would make his trip back easier.

But it wasn't just one room he opened. He opened a few, only stopping at the threshold of each and not going in. He found what were obviously storage areas for strange things that his human mind failed to classify. Just like in the other rooms he couldn't see on top of the huge furniture. One of the rooms had smaller furniture that, if he had time to try, he could probably even climb up on. He guessed it was a child's room.

Okay... last door and you're out of here!

He touched the strange metal and the door slid open.

Before him were the occupants of The Chamber.

TWENTY-SEVEN

<u>Behind Enemy Lines – Present Day</u>

The men jogged in the opposite direction of the jihadists, their eyes shifting back and forth, looking for threats. They didn't talk, but questions burned in Zac's mind.

When they were a safe distance and under cover, in harsh whispered tones, Zac fired, "You want to tell me what just happened? What was that light? How did you know where to find me? And most importantly, why are you taking me this way? My objective is that way!" he pointed.

Bryce shared a look with his uncle and nodded.

Joe was Zechariah's friend. It only made sense for the explanation to come from him. He let out a long breath and spoke slowly, "Zac, you're not going to understand everything I'm about to tell you. There are," he glanced at Bryce, "supernatural events larger than ourselves taking place."

"Supernatural events? What are you talking about? This is war…"

Joe held up his hand and waited. Zac went quiet.

The elder Montanan continued, "I tell you these things because of where we need to go."

Zac's face pinched in confusion, "Go?! I'm not going anywhere! I have a mission to complete and…"

Bryce interrupted, "We know about your mission to find the Beast."

With narrowed eyes, Zac asked, "How did you know that?! That's code word. Eyes only!"

227

Bryce shook his head, "It doesn't matter. But the point is that you are hunting for the Beast in the wrong place. He isn't here."

Zac's jaw was tight and his head tilted, "Not here?"

"Look," Joe said, "You have to trust us. Bryce is right. You're hunting in the wrong place."

It was Zac's turn to let out a long breath and he threw up his hands, "Alright, I'll bite. If my Target is not here, where is he?"

Bryce's hazel eyes locked on him, "Canada."

Zac started, "Canada? He was just here three days ago. There's a war going on. Airspace is closed. He could not have escaped to Canada!"

"He didn't escape. He simply flew... and I'm sure he intends on coming back," Bryce said matter-of-factly.

"Flew? But..."

"Look," Joe interrupted, "if you're going to question everything we're telling you, this'll take a long time," he looked at Bryce. "Why don't we just show him?"

"Show me?"

"There you go again," Joe smirked.

Bryce pointed at Zechariah, "I'll make you a deal. We'll take you to where he is. If you don't think our information is absolutely credible, we'll turn right around and bring you back here. How does that sound?"

Zac laughed sarcastically, "That sounds terrible," he started counting off his fingers, "First, it will take time to get out of country. Then, I will need to verify your information. And then, WHEN YOU'RE WRONG," he looked back at Joe, "there's all the time to get back here. I will have wasted more than a week and my chance will be gone. I will have failed."

Joe chuckled and placed a hand on Zechariah's shoulder, "Son, what if I told you that you'll be convinced just by our means of travel alone?"

Zac pinched his forehead in his fingers, "Josiah, you're not making sense! And I am wasting time!"

Bryce held out five fingers, "Five more minutes and you'll see. If you're not convinced within those five minutes, we will leave you to your work. Deal?"

Zac's piercing, dark eyes bored into Bryce. After a moment he held out his open hand, "Five minutes. That's it!"

Joe slapped him on the back, "Glad to have ya on board!"

"I did not say I was on board. I simply said I would give you five minutes."

"Same diff," Joe said, "You'll see."

"Is this all of your stuff?" Bryce asked.

"Yes."

"Okay, let me think."

"You do know how to do this, right?" Joe asked his nephew.

"Well, to tell you the truth, Pop, I've never did it myself. I was with Gabe or I had the Garments on, or the LHC was running, or..."

"Okay, okay, I get it. You've never done it this way. So why do ya think you can do it now?"

"I..."

Zac interrupted them, "You are down to four minutes and who is this Gabe person?"

Bryce waved the question off. Looking at Joe, he said, "Gabe said something about the portals being unlocked."

"How?" Joe asked.

"Don't know, just doing what I was told."

"Three minutes," an impatient Zac said.

With a flurry of a hand, Cooper said, "All will be revealed."

"What-r-ya," Joe asked, "Ali Baba?"

Zac looked at the two Americans bantering, "This isn't funny! Two minutes!"

Bryce looked at Joe, "I hope this works..."

MT. GRAHAM OBSERVATORY, TUCSON, ARIZONA – PRESENT DAY

So many things make sense now, the Professor thought. [144]The solar anomalies with sightings of strange craft, the fact that no one ever saw those craft coming toward earth from a great distance...

"What is it, Professor?" Juni asked.

Pulled from his thoughts, Alvaro said, "Juni, you wouldn't believe it if I told you. In fact, I hardly believe it." He turned to Father Joshua, "I must speak to His Holiness, immediately."

Joshua's ears turned red and he adjusted his sleeve cuffs under his black clerics outfit, "I'm sorry, señor, it is not possible."

"What do you mean, not possible? I'm sure he will see me."

"I am sure he would, but he is no longer here."

Mora's voice raised an octave, "What do you mean he's not here? I just spoke to him a little while ago!"

"Yes, of course. After lunch, he had a series of meetings, gave us final instructions and left to catch his plane. He has an urgent conference. He asked me to tell you goodbye and let you know how pleased he was to see you. He also said he wished things could be different."

"He flew on an airplane? Doesn't he know there's a war..." Dr. Mora realized what he was just told. "Hold on, what do you mean he gave you final instructions?"

"Ah, yes. Well..." Joshua walked over and turned off the computer, "I believe your tour is over."

A side door opened and four large men came in and – they weren't priests.

"Angelo and his friends will show you to your quarters."

"Our quarters?!" The Professor looked at a wide-eyed Juni, "We have no intentions of staying the night."

"But I'm afraid," the Jesuit's face hardened, "I will have to insist." He nodded and the men surrounded The Professor and Juni.

The Professor pursed his lips, "I see... Now that we know

what's going on, you can't let us leave."

Joshua sneered, "It is only temporary. Soon it will not matter. You will be free to go tomorrow. But for tonight, you are our guests. You will find the accommodations very comfortable."

"Comfortable?" Juni said indignantly, "As comfortable as a prison!"

Alvaro took the Filipino's arm and led him to the door, "Not now..."

CAMP FINAL VICTORY, SOUTHERN CANADA – PRESENT DAY

They looked like regular soldiers coming in for a resupply, so getting on base was easy.

"This place has built up since I last saw it," Anya said quietly, as they walked casually through the base. They stayed away from other people so they didn't have to speak to anyone.

Danny did a double take. Through gritted teeth, he asked, "When was the last time you saw it?"

Anya pursed her lips, "Ahhh... six months ago, I guess. It was only bare land with..."

"Six months ago!" Goose blurted.

Danny nudged him hard on the arm, "Keep your voice down, Yankee!"

Duckett's eyes turned back to Anya and burned, "How are you supposed to know where anything is, much less this general?!"

She flicked her wrist, "Have no fear, dear Goose. We will do what any advance team does. We will recon."

"But we aren't an advance team," Goose rumbled, "We aren't even military. I'm a simple ranch hand!"

"Well," Danny said quietly, making a mental note of everything he was looking at, "we're in the military now, like it or not. There's no one else to save us. And if what Anya says is true, even allies have stabbed us in the back," he said distractedly. "Hey, what's that over there? That area looks like a compound within the compound. And it's smack-dab in the middle of the base."

"Ah, yes, good eye, Daniel," Anya cooed, "Those guards? They're Spetsnaz," she said, nodding at a group of hardened soldiers, "And those others in plain clothes are [145]GRU."

"GRU?" Goose asked.

"Glavnoye Razvedyvatel'noye – GRU. It is what replaced the KGB," she looked at Goose, "Different letters, same ugly mission. Spetsnaz and the GRU often work together. You can be sure that if they are guarding that area, the general is there."

The area was a fortress surrounded by a twelve-foot, chain-link fence, topped with constantine wire, at least two guard towers that could be seen, and stretched for a long way. Numerous Spetsnaz were guarding it and who knew how many were on the inside.

"What did you say the name of this place was?" Goose asked.

"Lager' Okonchatel'noy Pobedy," she said in Russian, "Camp Final Victory."

"Why final victory?"

She pursed her lips, "Most Americans never understood that the Cold War had never ended. It only transformed into another kind of subtle aggression. They... ah, we have been undermining your country for decades. Did you really think people would stop wanting what you had? In fact, I think there was a [146]KGB defector that told you this very thing. But your leaders didn't listen."

"Maybe they didn't want to listen. Maybe they weren't supposed to listen..." Danny thought aloud.

"What? You think this whole thing was planned? Like... like a conspiracy theory or something?" Goose asked.

Danny glanced sideways at him without turning his head, "A conspiracy theory is only a conspiracy theory [147]until it's proven.

Then it just becomes fact," he pointed his chin at the fortified complex, "Does that look like enough proof for you?"

Anya continued, "I don't remember very much from my childhood, but I do remember my father's brother, my uncle. He was a high-ranking military officer. He used to tell my father that someday we would live in America and that everything that America once had would be Russia's."

"What???" Goose exclaimed.

"They said that a Plan was in place to take over the country and that all we needed to do was to be patient."

"What did your father say?" Danny asked.

Anya lowered her head and her jaw tightened. She spoke in a low and deliberate tone, laced with bitterness, "He would say that he didn't want anything to do with a plan like that. He said that the American people were probably just like everyone else, that they just wanted to live their lives. He said they were no threat to Russia and that they should be left alone. This was an argument that the two of them had often.

"It was my uncle who ah... encouraged our immigration to Canada. It was also he who saw my potential as a spy. I cannot be sure, but I think it was," she stifled a sob, "he who took me from my parents."

Danny put a hand on her shoulder.

After a moment, she continued, "Anyway, as I was saying, your downfall has been planned for many years."

She paused, cleared her throat and said in a stronger voice, "We have to find a place where we can watch that front entrance without being seen. If those soldiers think we are loitering, they will come talk to us." She started heading toward an area full of barrels, boxes and equipment. It had direct line-of-sight on the entrance and was concealed enough for them not to be noticed.

Goose and Danny walked side by side behind her as Duckett bemoaned, "I just don't understand. How could our leaders let this happen?"

"You mean our politicians... the Republicans and Democrats? Those leaders?" Danny spat.

"Well... yeah."

"Goose, you just don't get it. The America we knew was gone a long time ago. Heck, just a few years ago, the Democrats wanted to [148]throw God out of the party. All the things that we believed in... all the things that we valued, Republican or Democrat, those so-called leaders couldn't have cared less about. It was all about them getting elected and lining their pockets. They sold us out. If this isn't proof, just take a look at what's going on down south.

"Just think about it," Danny said, "the people didn't do anything when the [149]President started making his own laws via," he made quote marks with his fingers, "Executive Action. He kicked Congress to the curb and [150]they didn't even fight him. He continued to ignore the Constitution and he even dropped our defense of the [151]southern border. Yet, no one lifted a finger. And then, when he changed the law and gave himself a [152]third term, people, as bad as he was, just let it go."

The trio casually made their way behind some equipment and settled in.

Squatting next to Anya, Goose asked, "Just how do you know that this general is in there?"

"Trust me. I know him well. He is in there," Anya said with finality.

Danny pulled the field glasses from his eyes, "He's right. This could all be for nothing. Just how DO you know?"

Her head drooped for a moment as she stared at the dirt. When she looked up again, she swallowed hard. Finally, in a voice just above a whisper, she said, "Because, the general is my uncle."

Twenty-Eight

"**W**hy are they holding us prisoner?" Juni asked the Professor.

With his hands behind his back, Dr. Mora paced the width of the locked guest quarters.

What was it that the priest said? "Soon it would not matter."

He stopped pacing and asked the volcanologist, "Juni, why do you think Joshua said that it would not matter if we left later?"

The Filipino thought for a moment and said, "Because something will happen and people will already know?"

"Know what?"

"Professor, I'm just a lava-and-rock guy. I don't really understand all of this. But if I were to take a guess, I'd say it would have to do with what you saw on the computer screen."

Dr. Mora had a toothy smile, "You may be a rock guy, but your head is not filled with rocks. Exactamente a la derecha! (Exactly right!)"

"What do you mean?"

"Those craft on the computer screen were due to arrive at any time. If so, when we get out of here no one will care what we say - because Disclosure will have already happened."

"Disclosure?"

"Disclosure is what UFO groups call the informing of the public about UFOs by the government."

"Informing? People know about UFO's already. I told you, I see them going in and out of volcanoes all the time."

"Ah yes... they are already here, so why would the Vatican care if we told people about them?" the Professor started pacing again.

Juni had his arms crossed, staring down at the floor, "I guess it has to do with who makes the announcement more than anything else."

Mora abruptly stopped pacing, "Juni, you are a genius. That is exactly the reason! Let's suppose that they, the Vatican, wanted to shape the announcement for consumption by the public."

"Shape?"

"Si. Remember, this whole edifice," he lifted his arms, palms up, "is designed to find evidence of ETs. Very powerful people in the Catholic Church, including the Pope, have made statements about aliens. Such a discovery would change the 153paradigm of the whole world!"

"And change the relationship of the Church to the world," Juni added quickly.

"That's right. People would fall away from the faith. That would mean..."

"Loss of influence. Loss of power. Loss of revenue."

"Right again."

"So they have been preparing for this, this announcement... Disclosure?"

"Si, on their terms. They believe that such an occurrence is inevitable. So if it has to come out, they want it done in a way that would enable them to continue their influence... maybe even increase it."

"Increase it? How?"

"Maybe to redefine the very tenants of the Church."

"Redefine? What do you mean?"

"Have you ever heard the phrase, Panspermia?"

"No, don't think so."

"It has to do with the idea that humans were not created by God, or even evolved on earth from the primordial soup."

"What else is there, then?"

"Ah... that is the question. Panspermia says that human DNA was placed here by... aliens."

Juni looked dumbfounded, "Huh?"

"That's right, my friend. Some people believe that the human race has come from extraterrestrials."

"But that's crazy!"

"Maybe, but I know at least one powerful person who would gladly promote the idea."

PERUVIAN DESERT – MANY YEARS AGO

Alvaro and Emo were young adventurers and the older and more independent they got, the farther they strayed from the rain forests of Costa Rica and Emo's local 154Atacama Desert.

Both young men knew that adult life would soon be pulling them away from their summer hobbies of deep sea fishing, nature walks and exploring archeological sites. This time next year Emo would be headed off to seminary and Alvaro to college. Since this was likely the last summer that they'd spend exploring together, they decided to drive deep into the desert of Peru for some camping.

As he often did, Emo disappeared from the camp site, telling Alvaro that he wanted to go for a walk in the cool of the day.

"Don't go far! You'll get lost! And take a flashlight in case it's dark when you come back. I'll leave the fire burning." the young Mora cautioned.

By early evening, the sun was dipping down behind the mountains and the heat of the desert began to bleed off. Emo had been gone a long time. Soon it would get very cold. With a frustrated sigh, Alvaro put down his book about the gas giant star in our solar system, stoked the fire and went looking for him.

Mora had a compass and he knew which direction Emmanuel had gone. As he searched in the fading light, he called, "Emo!

Emo! Come on, quit messing around! It's getting dark! Emo!"

After searching for ten minutes, he stumbled upon a sheer rock formation. He followed its hard surface straight up with his eyes. It was so tall that he couldn't see the top from his angle. He walked closer to the rock and noticed that new dirt and rocks were piled high around the base of the formation.

"What?"

Alvaro climbed up the pile until he saw where the loose material met the solid rock. He realized that this pile of new dirt and rock was the collapse of a cave entrance.

"My God! Emo! Emo!" he yelled frantically, "Are you in there?! Can you hear me?!"

He knew his friend's propensity to find a solitary place. Emo was missing. This was a cave. The cave-in was fresh. He began to dig.

Soon he realized that digging was pointless. He didn't know how far back the cave was, but it would take hours to dig even with equipment. There had to be another entrance.

With dusk quickly turning to night, Alvaro circumvented the rock formation's perimeter and then he began to climb.

On the backside of the formation, the ground slope was not so steep; he could hike up its back. Although he slipped several times in near darkness, banging his knees, he finally reached the top of the formation.

He could see the desert floor from here and make out their camp site not too far in the distance, with the fire still burning.

There has to be another way in!

Darkness had fully engulfed the desert. As he desperately searched for an opening, he tripped and fell, barely able to get his hands in front of him before smashing his face into the ground.

Sitting on his butt, in the dirt, he felt wetness on his hands and saw with the flashlight, dark blood trickling from his palms. Flicking his light to his pant legs, he also saw holes in the cloth at his knees and more blood.

His lips trembled and a silent tear rolled down his cheek. He whimpered, "Please God... Help me find him. I know he's in there."

Wiping his bloody hands on his dirty pants, he was about to get up when he felt a cool breeze blow on his face from under a rock on the ground.

"Qué es esto ?"

He put his hand above the stream of air.

Back pressure?

Alvaro muscled the large stone out of the way and a stream of cool air blew into his face. He laughed! "Gracias Padre!"

Adrenaline pumped through his veins as he used his torn hands to claw away the rock and sand from around the eight-inch hole.

"Emo!" he yelled, "Are you down there?!"

Finally able to make the hole big enough for his lanky body, he yelled, "Emo! Hold on! I'm coming for you."

If he's there, why isn't he calling back to me? He must be hurt!

"Emo!!!" he yelled again.

He wiggled through the hole that led into a larger tunnel, big enough for him to walk upright. Glowing walls immediately caught his attention.

He ran his hand across the grayish-white light and brought it to his nose.

Alvaro jerked his head back and scrunched his face, "Zinc Sulfide..."

In their adventures, the boys learned about minerals, chemicals and rocks. Zinc Sulfide was a luminescent material that was found in nature, but it needed an activator to glow. For it to glow on its own was highly unusual. It meant that someone had to have placed the activator on the walls where they knew the Zinc Sulfide was... "Who would do that?"

Alvaro, pulled himself from his musings and remembered why he was here, "Emo! Emo! Are you in here?!"

As he walked deeper into the cave, the light of the walls

became bright and he turned off his flashlight, "Emo!" he cried.

Drawings on the walls caused him to stop. They were hieroglyphics laced together with some strange writing. He'd seen cave paintings before, but not like this.

Beings were depicted with elongated heads and wings on their backs. Other pictures showed some kind of machines, some of which were flying. A few of the drawings showed the big-headed creatures sitting on what looked to be thrones. Other pictures showed some kind of machines, some of which were flying. A few of the drawings showed the big-headed creatures sitting on what looked to be thrones.

"Were they kings? And why were their heads that way?"

Subservient-looking smaller beings were gathered around the larger ones, almost like they were worshiping them.

"What?"

Mora shook off his confusion and continued into the cave. As he rounded a bending curve, the hair on the back of his neck and arms stood on end and he shivered. He stopped and looked around. Nothing had changed, but he felt... fear.

This place... something is here... something evil.

Now wide-eyed, with a new sense of urgency, he yelled, "Emo! You better tell me where you are or I'm not going to talk to you ever again! Emo! Quit messing around!"

The glow intensified ahead and he quickened. Although the wall drawings became more numerous, he ignored them, quick-walking around a bend and stopped abruptly.

Instead of lines and patches of Zinc Sulfide like in the tunnel, he was at the mouth of a large cavern whose walls were covered with the eerie glow.

Ancient furnishings, artifacts, gold and jewels lay scattered around the remnant of a throne.

This must be a burial chamber...

He cautiously rounded a mound of artifacts when he saw them.

A line of [155]giant skeletons lay side by side and they had the same elongated heads as in the cave drawings.

His friend, Emo, lay prostrate at the feet of the skeletons. His hands were clasped as if he were praying and his face was buried in the dirt.

"Emo?" Alvaro said incredulously, "Are you alright? Didn't you hear me calling you?"

His friend didn't answer.

Mora knelt beside him and shook him, "Emo! Are you hurt?"

Still the young Argentinian didn't respond.

"Emo!" he shook him even harder and rolled him over.

Still no answer.

The teen's eyes were open, but they were glazed over as if he were in a trance.

Mora slapped him in the face a few times, "Emo! Wake up!"

Slowly, life came back to Emo's eyes and his vision sharpened.

"Alvalito? Is that you?"

"Yes, my friend, are you alright?"

Ignoring his question, Emo slowly sat up.

"You... you should have seen it... you should have seen them! One moment I was here, and the next... Can you hear them? I can still hear them."

He must have gotten hit in the head during the cave-in. Hallucinations? He must have a concussion.

"Hear what, hermano (brother)?"

"The voices... the voices of these beings. They... they call to us. They say that they were first... and they left us..."

"I don't hear anything. Come now, let's get you back to camp so you can warm yourself by the fire."

"When... when I was there, they were telling me that they will come back for us. They told me that I should be ready..."

He's delirious.

Supporting his weak friend, Alvaro helped Emo back the way he had come. But aside from mentioning the cave and the giants, his friend never said anything else about what he'd seen or heard.

MT. GRAHAM OBSERVATORY, TUCSON, ARIZONA – PRESENT DAY

"I always thought he hit his head..." The Professor said aloud.

"Thought who hit their head?" Juni asked.

Alvaro had a distant look in his eyes, "He said they left us here... said they would come back. Could that cave have been a portal?"

"What cave, Professor?"

Alvaro remembered Juni was with him and his eyes cleared. He looked at the volcanologist and said, "I always thought he meant they went away. Now I'm thinking that he meant they planted us here. That's got to be what this is about! It's what he's been preparing for! All the work with the Church... the disclosures, this observatory!"

"Professor, you're not making sense."

"I'm sorry. I'm just remembering something that Em... I mean, Pope Peter told me a long time ago. If I'm right, it would explain what's happening and why they've locked us up."

"What is it?"

The Professor put his hand on Juni's shoulder, "He said that they told him to be ready. That's what all of this is about - final instructions! Being ready. But he's only expecting them to come from one direction. If I'm right about the portals, we may have an invasion on our hands."

"Invasion?"

"Yes, and it's not just little green men that will be coming. God, help us.

TWENTY-NINE

CAMP FINAL VICTORY, SOUTHERN CANADA – PRESENT DAY

"That's your big plan?!" Goose hissed. "You intend to stroll up there and tell them you're here to see your uncle?! Are you crazy?!"

"Anya, why didn't you tell us before that the general was your uncle?" Danny asked.

"It is not so hard to guess," replied Anya, "If you knew, would you have agreed to help me?"

Danny and Goose shared a look. "She's got a point," the smaller man said.

"Yeah, I guess. But it's still crazy!

"What do you think..."

A sleek, black Lincoln eased up to the gate, interrupting their conversation. The windows weren't tinted so they could see into the backseat.

"Hold on..." Danny said with the binoculars to his eyes, "You're not going to believe this! That's the Pope!"

"What? Let me see!" Goose yanked the field glasses from his hands. "Well, I'm not Catholic, but does a bear..."

"Let me see!" Anya said, shoving Goose and snatching the glasses from him. "Now isn't that strange..." she said as she lowered the binoculars.

"What's Pope Peter doing here?" Danny asked.

Anya shook her head, "I have no idea. If anything, you would think that the leader of the Russian Orthodox Church might make an appearance. But the Catholic Church? It

243

makes no sense."

Mendez had a feeling that things were going to get very interesting.

Large Hadron Collider, Geneva, Switzerland – Present Day

The star-fish disk spit a line of blue plasma into the dark, clouded sky. The laser's angle placed its focus directly above the LHC.

Even with fifteen miles of space between them and the dish, Durand and his crew felt the vibration in their chests.

The dish bellowed like a giant race car hitting second gear. The thundering decibels shattered windows within a twenty-square-mile radius.

A translucent wave of energy shot out into space, peeled away from the blue beam and rolled across the earth and its atmosphere in every direction.

The earth itself groaned as the wave tore through time and space. flipping open the locked [156]portals all over the world.

Earth and its physical reality was changed forever.

Jerusalem, Mossad Safe House – Present Day

Diggs was up at 5:30 am, even without the aid of an alarm clock.

He'd stayed up well past midnight talking to Stephanie. Although they hadn't known each other very long, they had a lot in common.

Normally, he found it hard to talk to women. She was the exception. He could have talked to her all night and into the morning. But both of them thought their conversation could wait. Who knew what the war might bring and they needed to be rested and alert.

As they retired to their own rooms, Diggs wondered if this

was the woman that he'd been waiting for his whole life.

He lazily stretched at the kitchen table just as Percy strolled through the door with a knowing smile.

"Up early as usual, cousin?" Percy asked.

"Old habits, I guess."

"Quite. I was wondering..."

A roar in the sky shook the windows.

"What was..."

Dishes in the cabinets banged against each other and the ground shook.

"Ouch! Hey..." Percy said.

Something akin to static electricity zapped both men. It wasn't enough to bite, but it gave them an odd tingling feeling all over their bodies.

"What was that?" Percy yelped.

"I don't know... I've never felt anything like it. I'd say it was just a small tremor, but did you feel that tingle?"

"I did, indeed. Did you hear that sound?"

"I did," Diggs got up and flicked the lights on and off. They worked fine. He checked the phone and it still worked. He looked at his watch and it was still ticking.

"That was weird," he said.

"Huh," was all that Percy said and then changed the subject, "So how long do you think we'll be cooped up here anyway..."

BENEATH THE OKLAHOMA MOUNTAIN GATEWAY – PRESENT DAY

Unlike the rest of The Chamber, this room was much cooler, even refrigerated.

Looking at the eyes that were looking back at him, Larry understood why.

"My God..."

A laboratory with furnishings and equipment befitting

giants gleamed under the artificial light. Macabre instruments, sickles, hammers and a host of other strange alien equipment hung on the wall, or sat on the cold counters.

Six beings stood entombed within odd encasements.

Hoses and strange umbilicals dangled from vertical standing, coffin-like metal containments. Glazed, unseeing eyes were the only thing visible through a plate of clear glass.

Larry rubbed the back of his neck. "[157]Suspended animation?" he questioned aloud as he walked up to the tubes. "Must be."

The giant-size tubes were at least twenty-five feet tall and Larry couldn't see through the glass when standing at the foot of them.

Taylor searched the room for smaller things he could stack up and stand on. He found a few boxes and other pieces of furniture and piled them up carefully.

By the time he was done, he was drenched in sweat and breathing heavy. Catching his wind, he drug his sleeve across his forehead and started climbing the rickety steps.

"Come on Taylor, don't break your neck before you get to the top!" he chided himself.

At the top of his pile, he was only chest high to the titans, but at least now he could see into the glass.

Dull, lifeless, lizard-eyes with vertical pupils stared straight ahead.

He reached up and rapped on the glass. *Nothin!*

"The lights are on, but nobody's home!"

Balancing on his toes and craning his neck, he saw that the skin around the eyes was pale green and pithy. The bridge of the nose looked human enough, but that's all that was uncovered.

"Who are you?"

He set back on his heels as his homemade ladder began to shake and he grabbed for the giant's capsule to steady himself.

He felt a prickly sensation traverse his body and then the shaking stopped.

"What the...?"

Earthquake? Naw... That was weird!

He realized he was still hugging the capsule and let go. Like a kid on a skateboard, he shifted his weight back and forth, testing the heap's stability under his feet.

Maybe I outta get down before I fall...

The monster in the tube jerked.

"Huh?"

Then the giant's eyes blinked and cleared.

Lizard-eyes shifted down to Larry.

"My Go..." Taylor jerked back and the mountain of junk beneath his feet collapsed. "Ah, ahh, ahhh!" he screamed, tumbling the five feet to the floor, smacked the back of his head on the hard ground.

"Ohhhh," he moaned and grabbed his head. Dizzy, he waited for the stars to go away.

He propped up on an elbow, "What in the blazes is going on?!"

In answer to his question, a hose that ran to the tube popped off with a hiss. Then another and another.

Larry was already on his feet.

The tubes started clanking and hissing and he knew the giants... were coming back to life.

He bolted for the door, stealing a look over his shoulder before he rounded the corner.

The lizard-eyes were tracking him and they were angry.

MT. GRAHAM OBSERVATORY, TUCSON, ARIZONA – PRESENT DAY

"What comes after?" Juni asked with a furrowed brow.

The Professor was pacing again, "I'm afraid if I told you, you..."

What sounded like a scream sounded from outside.

Pictures on the walls started rattling and the floor shook.

"Earthquake!" Juni said in a higher pitched voice than normal.

Both men shivered involuntarily.

"Did you feel that?" The Professor asked.

"Did you hear that scream? After that everything shook."

"Si but did you feel that tingling?"

Juni looked around, "Well, yes. But I thought it was just me."

"No, my friend. I felt it too."

Juni brought his hand to his mouth, "So it wasn't an earthquake?"

"I grew up in Costa Rica. We had lots of earthquakes. That felt more like..."

"Like what?"

Alvaro was heading toward the window, "Like it was in the air or the sky."

"A [158]skyquake?"

"I don't know about a [159]skyquake, but..." The Professor walked over to their second-story window and looked out. Forgetting the shaking for the moment, he tried to open it, "They're nailed shut."

"What did you mean when you said that that quake felt like it was coming from the sky?"

"I don't really know... It just didn't feel ri..."

White, silvery blotches far above the observatory dome caused The Professor to stop in mid-sentence. "Whatttt?"

"What is it?"

"I... I don't really know."

Juni popped up from his chair and rushed to the window.

The men gasped as a square of shimmering luminescence opened above the observatory's dome. It's shape blurred and rolled as it vibrated, as if trying to solidify.

Once stable, a bright light came out of the opening, then another, and another. These disc-shaped objects were followed by other strange craft and dark vapors which were much smaller. Like a floodgate that was left open, the objects poured out of the opening, one by one, until the sky around the observatory dome was filled with them.

An ashen-faced Professor turned to Juni, "We're too late."

Camp Final Victory, Southern Canada – Present Day

The sun had set, but the front of the compound was well-lit. As they knelt and peered around the containers, the ground began to move.

"What's happening?" Anya asked.

"Earthquake?" Goose guessed.

A roar came and went.

The air shimmered and each of them felt prickly tingles on their skin.

As quickly as it started, it stopped.

"What was that?" Danny asked.

"Not an earthquake?" Anya ventured.

"I don't remember earthquakes in this part of the country, but did you feel that shock?"

"Not really a shock, but a tingling on my skin you mean?"

"Yeah, that's it. I've never..."

"Look," Goose said from behind the field glasses, "Talk about strange."

A limo bearing a Chinese flag had just rolled up to the gate and then a German flagged vehicle drove to the barrier.

"Must be a meeting," Goose said.

Soon the Supreme Leader of the Iranians showed up, followed by the North Korean President. Lastly, a car pulled up to the gate with a flag that no one recognized. It reminded Danny of the jihadists banners he'd seen on the news before.

"Must be a meeting," Danny said. "Do you remember hearing about a meeting?"

Anya thought for a second and then said, "Not exactly. But remember I told you that a coalition was plotting against America."

The group was quiet for a moment until Danny broke the silence, "I guess they're here to discuss breaking up our land," he said through gritted teeth.

"Well, boys, we can sit here, or we can go find out," Anya said, "Time to get answers and find my uncle." She came out from behind the barricade and strode purposefully toward the compound's gate.

"She's gonna get us killed," Goose grumbled.

"Maybe," Danny said, "But at least we'll die trying," he slapped Goose in the arm. "C'mon! Let's go!" and he took off.

"Oh man..." Goose got to his feet, straightened his shirt and groused, "I swear if I ever get out of this, I'll never listen to another woman again!"

- Part Four -
Discerned
Subterfuge

THIRTY

L arry Taylor ran all the way back. His heart was pounding and he was drenched with sweat when he emerged from the fissure in the earth.

It was dark out and clear skies revealed, to his astonishment, a [160]blood moon in the sky.

I didn't know there was supposed to be a blood moon, he thought as he tried to catch his breath. *That can't be a good thing.*

What was it that the Prophet Joel said: "The sun will be turned into darkness and the moon into blood before the great and awesome day of the LORD comes."

I wonder if this is just the [161]beginning of sorrows.

His breathing was returning to normal and he looked over at the hole in the earth again. He wondered if the giant would follow him, but realized after he just came out of stasis, he'd have other things on his mind. That didn't mean that he wouldn't wander out later.

"Best fill in that hole."

But I'm gonna need a backhoe or something. That won't be until tomorrow at least. Only one thing to do:

Father, I ask that you would set your angels around this hole as guards. God, I pray that you would not let anything out of this hole that would seek to harm me or anyone else. I plead the Blood of the Lamb over this area and ask that you cover this mountain with your protection. And I ask all of these things in the mighty name of Yeshua HaMashiach, amen.

"That outta do it. Now, I just have to see if I can sleep in my cracked-up cab…"

But before he could finish his sentence, Larry Taylor vanished.

253

Between The Veil – Present Day

"Did you feel that?" Joe asked Bryce.

"I sure did."

Zac waved his hand, "Earthquakes are nothing new here. We have them from time to time."

"That didn't feel like an earthquake. It felt like the atmosphere shook. Did you feel that tingle?" he asked Joe.

"Yeah, not quite a shock, but I felt it."

"Alright, enough. You are out of time. Either give me good reason to go with you or I'm heading back right now," Zac said sternly.

"Alright. Ready?" Bryce asked.

Joe nodded, but Zac asked, "Ready for what?"

"This," Cooper said.

He closed his eyes, uttering a silent prayer. When he opened them, he emitted a strange series of tones.

A thunderclap boomed out of nowhere and six feet from where they stood a long, white crack of light appeared.

"Adoni…" Zac whispered.

Bryce pulled and pushed on the crack like he'd seen Gabe do, until it was big enough for a man to walk through.

"Wha, what is this?!" Zac's lips trembled.

"This is our poof," Bryce said.

"Prepare to be convinced," Joe added.

Bryce slid into the crack first, followed by Joe and with great hesitance, Zac went through.

As he did, he looked over his shoulder into the physical dimension of Assyria that they had just left. His teeth clenched when he saw ugly, dark wisps of vapor emerging from what looked like holes on the ground and in the air. Evil had just been unleashed on a country that had embraced evil. Despite his mission, he was glad he wasn't there any longer.

Bryce saw him looking and said, "Don't worry. They can't come in here." Then he took his hand and wiped the crack closed. "Come on, we have to hurry."

"Adoni!" Zac groaned, as his eyes shifted back and forth. "What the… is this place?"

Cooper kept walking and spoke without looking back, "This is the space between dimensions. The proof that I promised."

Zechariah's face was tight with confusion, "Josiah, do you know what's going on?"

Joe smirked, "Son, I'm just along for the ride like you. Just 'cus I look like I know what I'm doing, doesn't' mean I have a clue. This is only my second trip in this here wormhole. I don't know what Bryce has planned or where we're going. But I can tell you a couple of things."

"What are they?"

Joe pointed to the leading physicist, "Bryce disappeared from the Holy of Holies to enter into this area. How or why, I don't know. He prayed for me and my wounds from that chemical attack were healed."

Zac only grunted in response.

"It's okay, guys," Bryce said from the front, "I don't know what I'm supposed to do or what we'll find. All I know is the next place to go. Now you know what I know."

"I find that hard to believe," Zac said. "You got us in here."

Bryce thought back to the conversation with the Companion:

> "These things are necessary. You cannot stop what is coming.
> But you will be used to bring about the fulfillment of what the
> prophets warned about for centuries."

Bryce considered this for a moment, "That's the thing. Something's changed. Humans don't have access to these portals. Our fundamental physical laws have been broken. Something big has happened, and that something can't be good. That's why we have to hurry. I think time is running out."

"Running out?" Joe asked from the back.

"Yeah. I was told that time is at an end and the Great Deception is coming."

"What's the Great Deception?" Zac asked.

"It has to do something with the Others, the Fallen and The Group all teaming up together to draw mankind away from God."

Zac scoffed, "You mean that man from Nazareth…"

255

Bryce abruptly stopped, "Despite what you think, we're really on the same side!"

With that, Cooper spun around and led them off in silence to The Things Unseen.

THIRTY-ONE

The Other Place – Present Day

One moment Larry Taylor was standing in his dog pen, and the next, he was here. He'd been physically snatched away before, so this wasn't the first time.

Like many Believers he'd had spiritual dreams that were so vivid that he felt like he was there. He knew that God had given them to him for a reason. He'd also had visions. In an open vision, he was awake and his body remained where it was. But his spirit was taken to the supernatural realm where he saw things.

This was neither of those two experiences. There was no doubt; he was physically in The Other Place. But, somehow, this time was different.

He'd seen the war in heaven before. It was frightening and brutal. Like now, words defied explanation for the crossing of angelic swords and the crushing of supernatural beings.

Those experiences had given him great respect for The Things Unseen, but nothing could have prepared him for this.

Holes had appeared all around the place he was looking at. From those holes the black, angry, ugly, winged, bat-like beasts poured out.

The holes must be portals that were opened.

As monsters swooped in, entering the battle, they shouted in unison, *"[162]As above, so below!"*

As above, so below? What does that mean? Below what? No answer. He continued to watch.

He had no idea how long he'd been watching the battle when he saw the translucent wave roll into his peripheral vision. Focusing on the wave, he didn't know if it had just appeared or if it had been there all along. Then it struck him. He'd seen it before, just from a different angle – from the inside.

It was the space between dimensions - where God's elect walked Between The Veil.

Taylor had walked that very passageway himself, traveling along its simmering route.

Just then, movement within the wave caught his eye. He strained to look harder.

The three men had been moving quickly in silence. With Bryce in the lead, they were nearing their exit when Cooper saw an area on the right side of the corridor. A spot on the wall started thinning and he could see motion on the other side.

Cooper held up his hand for Joe and Zac to stop and walked over to the opening, looking out.

"What is it?" Uncle Joe asked.

"Don't know," Bryce said, "I've never seen a window in here before."

"A window?"

It was a full length fuzzy, translucent, opening.

Cooper's breath caught in his throat and his hand went to his mouth, "My God…"

"What is it?" Joe asked coming up beside him.

"That's happening right on the other side of this, this wall," Bryce said, "Anyone of those creatures could slice us to bits."

Joe swallowed hard, "Or worse."

Zac didn't look out. His head was already spinning.

"I knew there was war in the heavenlies," Bryce said, "But this is beyond comprehension. And look there," he pointed in the distance, "those dark creatures just keep coming! They're outnumbering the white beings."

Turning back to the window, one particular illuminated being caught his eye. He was huge and had a blinding brilliance. All the other times that Bryce had seen the being, the gleaming giant had worn a white robe and was barefoot. Now he was dressed in full armor which shown like the sun. His sword was pure light and the hilt of it was solid gold. His feet were no longer bare, but were clad with sandals that were laced up his massive calves. His immense muscles ripped as his sword swiped back and forth, slicing through the dark figures, one by one.

After he struck down the last of the attackers, the huge being looked at Bryce and lifted his sword in salute.

Cooper had never even seen the giant raise his sword in anger. As he acknowledged the physicist's presence, Bryce was again glad that Gabe was on his side.

Gabe lowered his sword and his eyes shifted over to his right. Bryce followed where he was looking.

Standing there in his street clothes was the portal keeper, Larry Taylor.

"How did..." Cooper started to say.

A blur of action pulled his eyes back to Gabe. He was once again surrounded by the ugly, black bats and continued to fight.

"Adoni, please give him strength," Bryce prayed, as he shifted his eyes back to Larry.

———————————————————

Taylor had been watching the battle and praying when he

noticed the thinning wall of the wave. To his surprise, he saw Dr. Bryce Cooper.

The two men looked at each other for a moment.

After a few beats, Larry gestured to the battle before him and mouthed:

"It has begun."

———————————————————————

"It has begun," Bryce said, reading Taylor's lips.

"What has begun? What's going on?" Zac asked.

Cooper stepped back, "Come on! We got to go. One more stop to make," and he took off in a dead run.

Bryce's heart was thumping in his chest.

Time was almost up.

Thirty-Two

M ost of the craft that came through the wormhole scattered. However, a few settled over the top of the observatory's glistening, white dome. The Professor and Juni watched as the Director, Father Joshua and other staff went out to greet the Visitors.

When they could no longer see what was going on, the Professor plopped down in a chair and Juni sat across from him.

"Now what are we going to do?" Juni asked.

Alvaro didn't answer him. Instead, he sat with his lower lip sticking out, staring at the far wall. "Well, you heard the man. He said he would let us out tomorrow."

"But tomorrow will be too late."

Dr. Mora sighed, "It may already be too late."

Juni slapped the top of his knees and bounced to his feet, "I can't believe that! Why would Dr. Bryce put us together in this place, only to fail?!"

"Of course you are right," Alvaro admitted, "but I don't know the answer." He looked to the ceiling, "Padre, you know. Please help."

"What did Father Joshua mean about those things," he pointed his chin to the window, "needed to help us with that Hercolubus."

The Professor was leaning forward in his chair, "Oh that. How much do you know about the Bible, Juni?"

Juni shuffled his feet, "Just what I remembered from when I was a kid."

"In Matthew 24 and Mark 13, Jesus gives us a sketch of things that will happen at the end of the age. The volcanoes, the earthquakes, the tsunamis, the wars, the sickness, etcetera, are all leading up to a time called the great tribulation. That is a time of hatred and bloodshed like the world has never seen. But after that, Christ comes back for His Bride. Then [163]Armageddon takes place. I'm sure you've heard of it."

Juni nodded, "I seem to remember something about that."

"But people don't really talk about how the earth will be destroyed by fire."

"Fire?!"

"Yes. And I think I may have found the source of that fire."

Juni swallowed hard. "You have?"

"Yes. In my observations of the sun, I've seen numerous anomalies. Some of these could be explained away, but others remain a mystery. Just a few days ago, I connected the dots to an Interloper within our solar system which is causing a perturbation of the planets."

"Perturbation?"

"Yes, it means to disrupt."

"Got it.

"When I thought I'd found the connection, believe it or not, someone had erased the data on the computer servers around the world and then tried to kill me."

"Kill you?" Juni asked in surprise, "Was that the plane crash you talked about?"

"The plane crash? No, then I was just in the wrong place at the wrong time. Before that, someone ran a semi-truck into me and tried to knock me over a cliff!"

"Oh my."

"Anyway, they failed, but things moved so fast that I forgot about what I saw around the sun."

"What did you see around the sun?"

"I saw what will cause the earth to be ripped from its current rotation and experience a polar shift. I saw what will cause the sun to belch out huge solar flares as it passes. When that happens, the earth will be..."

"Destroyed by fire. My God!" Juni said, sitting back down. "The Destroyer?"

"I'm afraid so."

A high-pitched squeal broke the silence between them and a crack of brilliant light appeared in the center of the room. Slowly it grew to over six feet tall and stabilized.

A hand came out of the crack, and then a head and the upper torso of a man

"Hey, you guys want a ride?" Bryce asked from the crack, "Let's get a move on, we've got places to go!"

Camp Final Victory, Southern Canada – Present Day

"Anya? What are you doing here?" the Spetsnaz gate-guard asked in Russian. "I thought you were in the field."

"It is good to see you too, Ivan," Anya said as she sauntered up to the guard. "We came for a resupply run. I need to speak with my uncle."

"It is not a good time, Anya," the guard narrowed his eyes and looked around. "The General is about to go into a meeting. Security is very tight. I can't…"

"Ivan, don't tell me you can't. Do you forget that you owe me? I can make your life very miserable, or short lived, should I say."

The elite soldier scowled and lowered his voice, "I told you the last time. I paid you back over and over. You said you wouldn't mention these things to anyone aga…"

Just then, Danny and Goose hustled up to join Anya.

The soldier's scowl deepened and he raised his rifle, "Halt. What is your business?"

Danny and Goose raised their hands.

Anya pushed the barrel of the gun down, "Relax. They're with me. We are tired, dirty and hungry. I just need to speak with my Uncle quickly and we'll be on our way."

On cue, Danny scrunched his face and said to Goose, ""Ty pakhnesh', kak vam nuzhno prinyat' dush!"

With an embarrassed look Goose nodded, "Daaa. I vodka."

The Spetsnaz soldier shook his head in disgust at the regular army troops.

"I told you I…"

Another limo came around the bend, headed for the soldier's gate. He looked around quickly, "Okay, okay. Go, go! But I didn't let you in! Do you understand?!"

"Da, da," she said and told her companions to follow.

When the three entered the gate, they didn't look back. If they had, they would have seen the Banker arriving.

THIRTY-THREE

"**I** can't believe that worked!" Danny said.

"I told you," Anya quipped, "People know me."

Goose grinned, "I don't speak Russian, but that sounded like blackmail."

A sly smile spread across Anya's lips, "A girl's gotta do, what a girl's gotta do."

Goose thumped Danny's arm, "I'm glad she's on our side."

Danny ignored him, "Okay, what now?"

"Now? Now we get as close to this meeting as possible and wait for our chance to snatch the general."

With searching eyes, Goose said, "Lady, I don't know if you noticed this, but we're in the securest place on this base. How do you suppose we snatch your uncle without getting shot?"

"Are you not listening? I told you, I know things. Lots of things. I can tell my uncle that I'm going to disclose some very damaging information if he doesn't come with us."

Goose's face tightened, "That simple, huh?"

Danny said, "At least it's a start. We couldn't have gotten here without her help."

Goose breathed out a long breath, "Well, it's not like we have another play."

"Good," Anya said coyly, "Let's go find this meeting," she looked at Danny and smiled. Then she got up and walked off.

"I see that look on your face," Goose said to Danny.

He had a grin, "Can't help it. I'm beginning to like this girl."

Goose shoved him, "Keep your head in the game, cowboy, or you might get it blowed off."

"Right," Danny said as he and Goose got up and followed her.

————————————————————————

The Man With The Book's car was the last to arrive. As he stepped out into the night air, something felt different to him; the air felt heavy. A thin smile creased his lips.

A brave new world.

With his copy of A Post American World tucked tightly under his arm, he strode toward the meeting room.

BETWEEN THE VEIL – PRESENT DAY

"Alright, Professor, how did your mission go?" Bryce asked over his shoulder while the group walked onward.

"Our mission," the Professor frowned, "was too late. They've opened the portals and there's an armada of ships headed our way."

After a few steps, Cooper said, "Dr. Mora, you were never supposed to stop the wormholes from opening. You couldn't. But because of your close association with the Pope, we were hoping that you could tell us of their plans."

Juni was third in line, "Plans? You mean like locking us up?"

"You know the Pope?" Zac asked from the rear.

Bryce stopped and turned to face the group, "Look, everybody. There have been things put into motion that we cannot, must not, change, as painful as that is. These things must take place because they were written a long time ago. They have to be fulfilled."

Cooper spun around and continued walking, "So Professor, what else did you find?"

"Well, my suspicions about an Interloper were confirmed and not only is the Vatican aware of it, they are tracking it."

"That doesn't surprise me," Bryce said. "What else? Juni, did you discover anything?"

"Funny of you to ask. Remember you asked me about how the volcano in Mexico City seemed to attract UFOs?"

"Yeah."

"I know it sounds crazy, but I think that volcanoes are doorways for them."

"That's not crazy," the Professor added, "I also think the sun is being used as a giant portal. Those ships have been able to pop in and out of our dimension using it."

"Bryce," Joe asked, "So what does all of this mean? What good is this information if we can't stop anything?"

Cooper puffed out his cheeks and blew out a long breath, "I don't rightly know, Pop. But I get the feeling that we'll find out part of the answer at our next stop. So let's get going."

I just hope that we don't make things worse.

Camp Final Victory, Southern Canada – Present Day

"Alright," Anya said, "we obviously can't get into that meeting room."

The group found a strategic spot where they could recon without being seen. Danny stared at the two, heavily-armed, Spetsnaz soldiers at the door. "You got that right," he said, "we wouldn't get ten feet from the general."

Goose added, "There's no telling what other guns they have in the room."

Anya had her finger to her lips, "I don't know about that. Remember, they're winning. They're confident about their security. How many people have we seen walking into the place? It looks like principals and I don't see translators."

"Humm, I think you're right," Danny agreed, "That tells us something."

"Like what?" Goose asked.

"That they will limit their conversation to one language, probably English. Secondly, because they aren't allowing any other ears to overhear the conversation, it's a highly secretive meeting."

"I'd agree. But what is the topic?" Anya pondered.

"The invasion?" Goose guessed.

"Has to be the invasion, but what about it?" Danny asked. "For all intents and purposes, the war is won."

"Maybe to divide the spoils of war?" Anya ventured.

In answer to the question, a final figure strode up to the meeting room doors. He had on business attire and held a hardcover book under his arm. His was the blue-and-white airplane that the trio saw landing when they were coming into town.

He was the President of the United States.

THIRTY-FOUR

Amerca's first black president, Baquir Hasim Imad, was Indonesian by heritage and despite his political claims of being a Christian, he was distinctively Muslim.

In defiance of the country's misgivings, Imad miraculously won a third term as U.S. President, thus sealing the fate of America.

"I apologize for my tardiness," he said entering the room, "My plane had difficulty circumventing the thermal flows and updrafts created by the, ah, nuclear weapons used throughout the country."

"It is of no consequence," the seated General said, in heavily accented English, "You are here now. Please have a seat."

Imad walked up to Abdullah Abbas Tabak, Caliph of the ISNW. "Your Excellency," The President shook his hand, kissed his ring and bowed his head, "it is good to finally see you in your rightful place."

Tabak's eyes burned red for a moment and then shifted back to their normal dark pools of nothingness. "I appreciate your service," he said in nearly perfect English.

With all eyes on the entering American, Pope Peter curled his toes in his shoes and subtly covered his mouth to hide his disdain. Such a greeting would normally be given to a man in his position. No more, I suppose, he privately thought.

As The President rounded the table, he walked by The Banker and nodded. The American, and everyone else in the room, knew that it was this man who was responsible for the Plan that brought the actions of the last few days. He was the lone representative of The Group and while he appeared to be a quiet spectator, everyone took their cues from him.

As Imad took his seat, he cleared his throat and asked, "I trust all is going well, General?"

General Igor Alexei Zolnerowich's eyes danced with blood-thirsty delight as he said, "Da, better than expected. The EMP from the bombs, and the EMP weapons themselves, have totally disabled all electronics in the country. There has been little resistance because the attack was centered on your military complex. Their mere rifles were no match for our fully functional equipment."

The General was known for his ruthless reputation which was the main reason for his appointment as the Russian North American Commander.

"Yes," Chinese President Liu Qiang said, "You have done well to prepare for our [164]reimbursement of U.S. Debt. Because our countries," he looked around the conference table, "had agreed to use primarily Neutron bombs in the attack, the radioactive effects of the tritium will dissipate in roughly two-and-a-half decades. According to our calculations, China's resources and farming should support us until then. Like everyone else here, we intend to move into those areas assigned to China as soon as possible."

"So," Imad said with a thin smile, "Our debt is paid?"

"Of course, we have much work to do, but yes, your deliverance of the land is sufficient. You will be highly rewarded for your work."

Imad nodded graciously.

"Mr. President," the Iranian Supreme Leader asked the Chinese man with alarm, "We are all interested in the," he cleared his throat, "inheritance we will receive from the Great Satan," his eyes flicked to Tabak and back, "but as far as your resources go, with the culling of our populations, there should be plenty left for the remaining chosen. So, are we to assume that you are not paring down the number of your citizens?"

The Chinese President's eyes flared, "Supreme Leader," he spat, "of course we are taking the steps we've agreed upon. We have, in fact, been doing this for years. What do you think our 'One-Child-Only' policy was about? 165Although we have stopped it, we have shown more interest than most," his nostrils flared, "to reduce our population. And because ours is a captive population, we have been eradicating whole villages. After we evacuated the elect out of the cities, we too used those very same bombs on those population centers," he looked to Imad and back, "and blamed the Americans. So, do not question me about what our responsibilities are!"

"Gentlemen, please!" the General said, "We have pressing issues to discuss and this meeting is not a forum to air concerns. Before I turn this meeting over to The Banker, "I regret to inform you that the President of Russia will not be attending. His plane was unable to circumvent the wall of radiation along the west coast. However, I am well versed on all matters and will represent the people of Russia. Now, Mr. Banker, will you please?"

"Thank you, General," the Banker said with an air of authority and eloquence. "All of your respective countries have done well and The Group is pleased. We will now move into the final phase of The Plan.

"This final phase has two parts to its implementation. It is not to be mistaken with the transference of land and natural resources," he looked at the Chinese and Iranians. "Rather, the first part of the transition is the world's transcendence to a new governing body."

"Transcendence to a new governing body?" the German Chancellor asked as she looked around the table in surprise. The other leaders looked just as confused.

"Yes, the first part of the final phase is this: henceforth, your countries will no longer be sovereign, but rather a State of a larger [166]New World Government."

A collective gasp was heard around the table.

"What is the meaning of this!" the little leader from North Korea shouted and slapped the table. "We did not agree to such a demand!"

Anarchy erupted as thunderous shouting from the world's leaders bounced off the walls of the small room. They pounded the table with their fists and pointed their fingers at The Banker and each other as they leveled accusations. Although The Banker raised his voice to regain order, no one was listening. He looked over at Tabak, who nodded.

The Caliph got up from his chair and walked to the other side of the Chinese President where the North Korean was standing with his arms flailing. Tabak's eyes flared and he touched the shoulder of the little man.

His tirade was silenced as a puff of smoke appeared all around him.

Then his uniform flared with smoldering fire. His skin and clothes turned to dark gray ash and for a moment, he looked like a still shadow on the wall. The room gawked as the form of a human stood before them and then disintegrated to dust on the floor.

The room was silenced.

––––––––––––––––––––––––––––––––

"The President? It can't be!" Goose said with narrowed eyes and tight jaw.

"Unmistakable," Danny said, "Sold us out!"

"I tried to tell you," Anya said with a pale, haunting look, "This has all been planned for a very long time. They had to have inside help."

"What now?" Goose asked.

"We wait," Danny said through gritted teeth. "We are going to grab that general and take him with us if it's the last thing we do!"

It might be the last thing we do, Goose thought, but he didn't voice his opinion. Instead he asked, "So how are we going to play it?"

After a moment's thought, Danny said, "Okay, Anya, since you are so good at being a distraction, you're gonna..."

After their plan was formulated, the three lay in wait for the opportunity to snatch the general and turn the tide.

But they would never get the chance.

THIRTY-FIVE

CAMP FINAL VICTORY, SOUTHERN CANADA – PRESENT DAY

Two ramrod, straight guards stood post outside the building where the meeting was taking place. Every ten minutes, in a stiff choreographed dance, they would slowly march at right angles away from the building, spin and march back.

Already the trio had seen the maneuver dozens of times. The constant crouching in their hide left their legs stiff and tired.

"I have to pee," Anya said.

Goose made a show of looking around, "Don't see a restroom. Could always squat in a corner," he said with a grin.

"What? And give our position away with my scent? What kind of spy are you?"

"The stiff kind," Duckett said.

"It might be a good idea to rotate out and take a break, one at a time. No telling how long they'll be in there," Danny said.

"That could be dangerous," Anya said, "What if someone tries to speak to you..."

Before she finished the sentence, the dark sky was lit up with a shimmering light, high above the building they were watching. It developed into a [167]spiral which grew a long tail. The undulant circle spun clockwise, growing larger and more luminous.

273

It stabilized high in the sky, making night turn to day.

"Wha, what is that?" Anya asked.

Danny's eyebrows were raised and his face paled, "I've never seen anything like that!"

Everyone on the base turned their eyes to the sky and all activity stopped.

The stoic guards from the front of the building abandoned their routine, and stood slack-jawed at the edge of their route, staring at the sky.

As they watched, the clear middle of the spiral began to show a reflection of the spiral itself.

"What in the world..." Danny whispered.

"I don't like this," Anya said.

An aide came through the front doors of the building and looked to the sky, mouth open. After gazing at the spiral for a moment, he tore his eyes from the sight and rushed back into the building.

"There will be no further discussion," The Banker hissed, "your countries will be consolidated into a one world government. Those who do not comply," he looked at the vacant chair full of ash where the North Korean leader sat, "will be convinced."

The Banker was quiet for a moment, letting the new reality sink in.

It was the General who broke the silence, "Who, may I ask, will be the leader of this new world government?"

Considering the question for a moment, The Banker's eyes narrowed and then shifted to Tabak. The General stiffened.

"It will, of course, be," The Banker said, "His Excellency."

Murmurs of begrudged support were heard from around the table.

The aide slid through the door and quietly walked to the General's side, not waiting to be acknowledged. He bent over and cupped his hand in front of the General's ear, whispering.

The General's head jerked back as if he'd been bit, "Here?! Now?!"

"Yes, sir," the pale aide said and backed away.

"My friends," the General said with his hands spread out on the table, "Apparently there is something going on outside that you probably want to see."

"And that," The Banker said as he looked at the Pope and then around the table, "Is the second part of the final phase."

"Please follow me," the General said, as he quickly made his way to the door.

The leaders joined him.

Walking out single file, they tilted their heads to the sky with stunned expressions.

None of them spoke, except for a jubilant Pope Peter, "My God, they are finally here!" His hands were raised and he moved his finger tips to his lips and back out like he was blowing kisses. "Welcome, welcome!"

The Banker walked to the side of The Assyrian and they spoke in hushed tones, unfazed by the display in the sky.

"There! They came out of the building," Anya said, pulling her eyes from the sky.

"Now's our chance," Danny said, "while everyone is distracted."

"Alright," Anya said, preparing to stand.

A light flashed in the center of the spiral and Anya stopped moving.

From the flash, a UFO popped through the hole, appearing to stretch until it came through. When it did, it moved slowly off to the side.

The crowd on the ground gasped.

"What???" Danny said

Then another craft came through, and another and another.

Ships of various shapes and sizes continued to pour out of the portal until the skies above the building were filled with layer upon layer of the alien vessels.

The last ship to come through the opening was gleaming white and shaped like a long cigar. It drifted down and hovered ten feet off the ground.

As the leaders watched, a slit opened on the lower side of the craft and a long ramp telescoped out of the ship, angled down. It came to rest directly in front of the world leaders.

With all eyes glued to the UFO, no one saw the crack of light that appeared just above the ground, a few feet away from where the leaders stood.

THIRTY-SIX

"**B**e ready for anything," Bryce told the small group as he once again sounded the tones.

—————————————————————————

Cooper's eyes drifted in the direction everyone was looking. His face was pinched tight with confusion. A long, tube-like ship sat hovering off the ground. He tilted his head skyward and saw a fleet of UFOs that filled the air.

The Professor asked, "Are we back at the observatory?"

"No, I don't think so. These are the coordinates that Gabe gave..."

Zac's Mossad training kicked in and he made a quick threat assessment. His eyes scanned the sky and the dream he had on the plane while jumping into Assyria immediately came back to him. "This is impossible," he said.

"No," Joe said, standing next to him, "I'm seeing 'em too."

Next, Zac's eyes dropped down to ground level, looking for hostiles. Although he saw many, they were too distracted to see him. No one had noticed the group emerge from the portal.

Already his rifle was up and tracking targets. One man, talking quietly to another in a business suit caught his attention. It was his Target, code named: The Beast.

He set his sights on The Assyrian and was about to squeeze the trigger when a familiar-sounding puff of air came from the long tubular ship. His rifle still raised, he turned his head toward the noise.

Just like in his dream, a seam appeared on the ship's side and a door opened.

His head started spinning when a tall, regal being dressed in white began to descend the ramp.

"It can't be!" Zac said aloud.

It was Dormin from his dream.

"Noooo!" He wrenched his eyes away from the illusion and fixed them back on his Target.

He lined up his shot and squeezed the trigger.

The rifle bellowed a single crack and Abdullah Abbas Tabak's head exploded. The Assyrian slumped to the ground with [168]a mortal head wound.

People were watching Dormin walk down the ramp and didn't realize what had happened until they heard The Banker shouting for a doctor.

That was when all hell broke loose.

Danny heard the shot and tracked its source back with his eyes, "Boss?!" he said to himself in confusion.

The other leaders snapped out of their revere and looked down to the New World President. "What has happened?" the Iranian asked The Banker.

With anger blazing in his eyes, The Banker said, "The Caliph is dead!"

Goose shouted, "Follow me!"

He jumped to his feet like a spring uncoiled and raced headlong in the direction of the world leaders. Danny and Anya were right behind him.

The bearded man crossed the divide in less than three seconds.

The General was standing farthest away, on the outskirts of the group, with his back to the onrushing Duckett.

Goose hit the general with his lowered shoulder and kept on going, dragging the Russian by his shirt collar.

Bryce heard the shot and knew that Zac was responsible. It was time to bug out. He already had the portal open and ready.

Turning his head, he saw Goose running in his direction while dragging a man in uniform. Then he saw Danny on his heels, followed by a petite young woman also in a uniform. "Goose? Danny? What are..."

"Boss!" Danny said. "How did you get here?! You got a car?!"

Gunfire erupted from behind them. Ducking, Bryce said, "No time to explain! Get in!!!"

A wide-eyed Goose was the first through the portal entrance and then Mendez and Anya. Joe followed them without being told.

Zac was already laying down cover fire.

One of the guards from the front of the building raised his rifle.

Not more than forty feet in front of him stood the Professor. The guard pulled the trigger.

"Noooo!" Juni yelled, and he lunged at Dr. Mora, knocking him to the ground. Juni's body spasmed as it was riddled with bullets.

"God no!" the Professor yelled to his friend. He reached over and grabbed the Filipino's wrist and drug him the few feet to the wormhole.

Cooper went in next.

Zac was backing in, still laying down fire until they could clear the area.

Before he backed into the entrance, his body was hammered with several rounds hitting directly in his center mass. He fell backward to the ground.

Bryce stepped out of the portal and grabbed Zac by his shoulders, pulling him in. Then Cooper quickly wiped the crack closed.

Breathing hard, Cooper looked down at Zac. His eyes were clouding over, but his lips were moving.

Bryce lowered his ear to the Israeli's mouth as he strained to hear.

"I believe…" the Mossad agent said and then he was gone.

"No!" Joe said, and ripped Zac's shirt open. The agent's bulletproof vest had taken several armor piercing rounds in the chest. The massive hole and hemorrhaging was evidence enough that nothing more could be done.

Bryce's face fell and he stood up. When he looked over at the Professor he saw tears in the scientist's eyes. He was kneeled over Juni's lifeless body.

"He, he saved me. He sacrificed himself for me."

Moaning and crying drew his eyes away from the Professor. He saw the young woman in the uniform, sitting on the ground, barely conscious and bleeding profusely from a shoulder wound. Danny was desperately trying to stop the bleeding. Bryce noted that she didn't look as if she was going to make it.

Danny was tying off a tourniquet and was drenched with the girl's blood, "Boss?! Where did you come from?! What is this place?! How did you get here?"

Ignoring the questions, Cooper looked at a Russian general, laying prone on the ground and unconscious with Goose sitting next to him. "Who's that?" he asked a breathless Goose.

"Ah," Goose said, trying to catch his breath, "Russian general. Danny's idea," he pointed to Mendez, "Supposed to deliver him to your wife for interrogation. I had to knock him out to keep him from struggling."

Cooper surveyed the carnage around him.

Suddenly he was very tired.

"Come on," he said, "Let's go home."

EPILOGUE

"In related news, Abdullah Abbas Tabak, the leader of the ISNW, has made a full recovery from his mortal head wound after Dormin, the leader of the Visitors, came down from their spaceship and healed him. The Assyrian stated that this miraculous event has given him a new perspective on his role in the world's peace process. Countries around the globe have unanimously voted Tabak in as the Chancellor of the New World Government. The new government will encompass all formally sovereign countries of the world. These one-time countries will be given statehood in this new union.

"The Visitors have insisted that all hostilities around the world cease. While most of the pre-hostility State lines have been reestablished, the United States remains divided and an occupied territory. Justification for her division was made by the Visitors themselves, who said that the debt America owed to the world must be paid.

"The human race is hardly in the mood to argue with the benevolent beings. They have provided the world with many gifts. Free and clean energy has been made available to everyone. Incredible medicines capable of extending human life indefinitely have also been provided. And scientists have been given the technology to raise enough crops to feed the entire world, thus

281

eliminating starvation.

"The Visitors confirmed Pope Peter's assertion that life on planet earth was started by them. Panspermia is now being taught as the only viable explanation of how mankind came into existence. While some evolutionists have gladly embraced this new revelation, staunch creationists are insisting that an all-powerful god is responsible for the creation of mankind. Current laws do not prohibit such teaching; however, a counter to the religious zealots is already being established with [169]Earth Universal Church. This organization is favored by the Visitors and will encompass all the great religions in the world. The headquarters for the new organization will be the new Third Temple on the Temple Mount in Jerusalem. Heading the new religion will be Emmanuel Jesus Bianachi himself who will receive the new title of [170]Prophet Peter.

"Because it is the headquarters for the new one-world religion, Jerusalem, and all of Israel, has been granted solitary statehood, completely separate from the unified world government. In a show of good faith, Chancellor Tabak has signed a seven-year peace treaty with the nation.

"In unrelated news, the Visitors have discussed with Chancellor Tabak and the world's leaders about an Interloper within our own solar system. With their technology and human ingenuity, both parties believe that the people of earth will be able to find a solution before the Interloper poses a significant threat to our planet.

"You are listening to Free American Radio, behind occupied territory via short-wave..."

Bryce reached over and turned off the radio.

"Yo Dad!" eight-year-old Little Joe called as he rounded the corner of the radio room.

"Shhhh…" Bryce said with his finger to his lips, "Your little brother's sleeping." He gestured down with his chin to the days-old infant in his arms.

"Oh, sorry," LJ whispered, "It sure is good to have you home, Dad."

"It's good to be home, son. Where's your sister?"

"She's out helping the women in the main cave."

"Such a big girl," he said with a smile. "Both of you grew up so much when I was gone."

"Yeah, I know and," Gabby walked into the room with two coffee cups in hand.

"LJ, I thought I told you to go wash that grubby face of yours and get changed into some clean clothes for dinner.

"Ah ma, we live in a cave. Everything's dirty. Why do I gotta…"

"Enough!" Gabby said, with a wave of her hand. "Go do what I ask or you're in big trouble."

"Ooookayyyy," Little Joe said with a pout, as he trounced off.

Bryce chuckled, "Boy, I guess what they're saying is true."

Gabrielle looked sideways at her husband and sat in the sofa bench beside him, "What are they saying?"

"That you've turned into a general," he smirked. "You really do make them shake when you're around."

"I did what I had to do. I'd rather just be a mom," she stroked her sleeping baby's hair. "I am so glad you made it home. I don't know what I would have done without you."

"I am too," he said quietly and lapsed into silence while shaking his head.

"What?" she asked concerned, "You're not happy to be home?"

"No, I mean, yes. I'm happy to be home. It's just that…" he was quiet again.

"It's just that what?"

> *"These things are necessary. You cannot stop what is coming. But you will be used to bring about the fulfillment of what the prophets warned about for centuries."*

"I don't understand any of this. Why was I involved if I couldn't change the outcome?"

"But we're okay for now," she objected.

"Sure, but what were we warned about: '[171]Peace, peace and then destruction will come upon you?' Besides, all of the stuff that's happening: Tabak coming back to life, the Pope desecrating the Temple. We were told about all of it and yet, because the Visitors gave us free energy, people are just falling in line."

"You know something else that's strange," Gabby asked with a faraway look.

"What?"

"Dormin."

"Well, he's supposedly from outer space. That's pretty strange."

"No, I don't mean that."

"What then?"

"Dormin. Dormin spelled backward is [172]Nimrod."

"Ha, I hadn't thought of that."

She nudged him with her elbow, "It's okay. I'm the general, remember. I have to look out for all of you little people," she said with a chuckle.

Bryce laughed, leaned over and kissed her on the head.

Gabby looked deeply into her husband's eyes, "Seriously, for now, we have you and we're safe."

Changing the subject, Bryce asked, "Speaking of safe, how's everyone holding up?"

She sat back, considering the question. "I'd say that we're doing better than most people."

"Whad-a-ya mean?"

"I heard a report on the radio that three-billion people died as a result of those wars."

Bryce whistled, "That's hard to believe."

"I wish it weren't true. Who knows how many more will die of radiation poisoning. Plus you wouldn't believe how much land was ruined for decades and some for thousands of years."

"Do I want to know how much?"

She looked at him with a pained expression, "At least a third of all land, they're saying."

Bryce winched, "Wow."

"And none of that takes into consideration the damage done by the natural disasters. Those tsunami's in the Pacific spread Fukushima's radiation throughout that whole ocean. It's totally ruined."

"A third of the world's oceans," Bryce mused.

"At least the Russians stopped killing people per the Visitor's orders. But they're not giving anyone back their land. And a lot of our people have left to find life outside of the cave."

"You think they'll tell anyone we're here?"

"I don't think so. They are like-minded, and we did save their lives. In fact, many of them are already reporting back to us about what's going on out there."

"But how are they going to live? I heard that the Visitors are embedding a capsule thing under the skin of everyone who wants one. Supposed to help them fight off diseases like Ebola and stuff. I also heard that it's tied to the new money system. Credits instead of money. If you don't have one, you can't buy or sell?"

"The [173]mark of the beast you mean?"

"Maybe. But what-da-I-know? I never thought things would play out like this. All I know is that WE aren't getting one."

"I guess they'll have to see for themselves."

After a couple of beats Bryce asked, "What about the general? Are they still looking for him?"

"You bet they are. But they have no idea he's here."

"Is he talking?"

"Some… with Anya's persuasion."

"Persuasion, huh?"

Gabby smiled with a twinkle in her eye, "She is quite the woman. We are very fortunate to have her around."

"Sure, and I know Danny's happy."

"Ohhh, that reminds me," she said giddily, "did you hear? He asked her to marry him!"

"No, he didn't."

"Yes, he did."

"But, they haven't known each other that long."

"He said, when you know, you just know."

"How 'bout that? Mendez is getting married. Will wonders never cease?"

"Gives you hope that we'll have a regular life again someday, doesn't it?"

Bryce looked down at his newborn son and stroked his cheek, "At least for [174]three-and-a-half more years anyway."

He let out a long breath, "I'm going to go out and get some air. Here ya go." He gently laid the baby in her arms.

"The guards outside have reported activity far to the west," she said, "but right outside should be clear."

He shook his head, "Always the general."

"Of course," she said with a smirk, "be careful."

"Of course," he said and gave her a peck.

As he exited the cave, well-wishers told him how glad they were to see him. Still, he hadn't gotten used to the idea of living in a cave with strangers. He needed the sunlight and fresh air to clear his head.

Careful to look around before he came out from behind the bushes concealing the cave's entrance, he moved slowly into the sunlight.

He peeled off the top of a piece of long grass and put it in his mouth and plopped down on a big rock. He breathed in deeply with his eyes closed and sat that way for a long time. Thinking of all the things that had happened in the last week, he was grateful to be alive, but he wondered what the future would bring.

"Well, hello, Dr. Cooper!"

A familiar baritone voice with a thick Russian accent startled him and he opened his eyes.

It was the personage of Dr. Yuri Mikhail Zaslavsky from the HAARP complex, before the Reset.

A slack-jawed and pale Bryce said, "It can't be!"

"Why cannot it be?" The Russian teased, "You thought that I would..."

The Russian's bloated body began to bounce and vibrate until it shrunk into a much smaller man in a tailored Italian suit.

"…always be stuck in the Abyss?" the man with the gravelly, Italian accent asked.

It was Giovanni of the CERN Board, also before the Reset.

"You forget…"

His body started shaking again, but his time it turned black and grew to nearly twenty-feet tall. The bat-like creature had sprouted wings and had massive muscles. Its eyes were blood-red and its face was contorted with rage.

"…the portals around the world have been opened. That includes the ones to the Abyss. Are you not surprised?" the monster asked.

Bryce just sat on the rock with his arms crossed and he looked around.

"Oh, you cannot depend on yourrr friend, Gabe," the creature said sarcastically, "He is rather busy with my brothers. As I said before, I am rather disappointed in you."

"Well, I'll be," Cooper said, "I didn't see that coming."

"You don't look surprised, huuuman. Nor do you look scared. Do you not understand what I am about to do to you?!"

Bryce spit the straw out of his mouth and stood up with his hands on his hips. "You know, Yuri or Giovanni or whatever your name is… you know what your problem is?"

The monster took a menacing step toward Cooper. The Montanan held his ground.

"Why don't you tell me, human, before I rip you apart?"

"You guys actually think you can win. But here's the problem."

The monster took another step.

"I've read the end of the book and I know how the story ends."

"Is that so?" the drooling monster said, now towering over Cooper with his stench-filled sulfury breath spewing into Bryce's face.

"Yep," Bryce stood on his toes and stuck his finger in the monster's face, "Now in the mighty name of Yeshua HaMashiach and by the [175]Blood…"

The creature stumbled back, holding his ears, "Nooooooo! Sssstoppp! Noooo!" he screamed.

"…of the Lamb. Get out of my face and leave us alone!"

The monster vaporized into thin air.

Cooper pushed the cowboy hat back on his head, "Amateurs!"

He breathed in the Montana Big Sky air and wondered what life will be like walking in occupied territory.

Living in a cave, dodging Russians, watching to see if the Visitors and fulfill their promises, a new one-world government and an alien religion based in Jerusalem, he shook his head.

As Bryce headed back into the cave, he said, "Ya know Lord. Seems to me that it was a whole lot easier just walking - **Between The Veil.**"

INTERNET REFERENCES

The following is a brief internet list of items discussed in the book. Simply type the link into the address bar of your computer's browser. It is not the author's intent to make it exhaustive. Rather, it should be used as a jumping off point for further research. In addition, the writer does not necessarily endorse or condone the topics contained herein. He has simply used these points as a means to weave a story. You are encouraged use discretion when studying these topics and come to your own conclusions.

1.   *Stargates & The Tower of Babel* –
http://www.islandmix.com/backchat/f6/stargates-tower-babel-stan-deyo-full-length-242083/

2.   *Large Hadron Collider* –
http://home.web.cern.ch/topics/large-hadron-collider

3.   *Ed Dames & The Kill Shot* –
https://www.youtube. com/watch?v=mDc4AcnXm8Q

4.   *Sea of Aden Stargate* –
http://www.utaot.com/ 2013/01/21/an-interdimensional-vortex-in-the-gulf-of-aden/

5.   *Underground Bases* –
https://www.youtube.com/ watch?v=Xj3jXpm5uLk

6.   *Denver International Airport* -
http://vigilantcitizen.com/sinistersites/sinister-sites-the-denver-international-airport/

7.   *U.S. Largest Oil Producer* -

http://www.bloomberg.com/news/2014-07-04/u-s-seen-as-biggest-oil-producer-after-overtaking-saudi.html

8. *The Reading of "A Post American World"* - http://www.truthorfiction.com/rumors/p/post-american-world.htm#.VAPtSU0g9xA

9. *The Nephilim (L.A. Marzulli)* - http://extraordinaryintelligence.com/beyond-extraordinary-ep-25-l-a-marzulli/

10. *HAARP* – http://www.bariumblues.com/haarp1.htm

11. *Parallel Universes* - http://leminuteur.free.fr/Universes.htm

12. *Angels* - http://www.youtube.com/watch?v=LT_eXHtKW-Q

13. *Chemtrails* - https://www.youtube.com/watch?v=72rOaPeTCVI

14. *Caliphate Declared* - http://www.theguardian.com/world/middle-east-live/2014/jun/30/isis-declares-caliphate-in-iraq-and-syria-live-updates

15. *Black Stone* - http://angels.about.com/od/AngelsReligiousTexts/f/What-Is-The-Black-Stone-Of-Kaaba.htm

16. *Cigar Shaped UFO* - https://www.youtube.com/watch?v=XG76xkW5adI

17. *Variety of UFOs* - https://www.youtube.com/watch?v=t2cDBjDaAR8

18. *Snake UFO* - https://www.youtube.com/watch?v=E2SIshZhDc4

19. *Tall White Aliens* - https://www.youtube.com/watch?v=J_-HFAiNRTM

20. *IDF Special Forces* - http://en.wikipedia.org/wiki/Sayeret_Matkal

21. *Pop Volcano Cylinder UFO (Oct 2012)* –
https://www.youtube.com/watch?v=MjLwWVRkxG4

22. *Pop Volcano UFO (May 2013)* –
https://www.youtube.com/watch?v=cZdP_49FlIQ

23. *The Coming Civil War* –
http://www.thecommonsenseshow.com/2014/05/01/the-reason-why-there-will-be-a-second-american-civil-war/

24. *EMP Threat* –
http://vimeo.com/98832883

25. *Russian Troops in America* –
https://www.youtube.com/watch?v=CMNuEhDFj9M

26. *A Crack In Time* –
http://www.coasttocoastam.com/photo/view/a_crack_in_time/50710

27. *Muslims Want Jerusalem* –
http://english.alarabiya.net/articles/2012/06/07/219272.html

28. *Shapeshifter* – http://www.youtube.com/watch?v=RPBa0JVi0iM

29. *The People Saw Thunder* –
http://prodigalministries.wordpress.com/2014/09/29/torah-tidbit-pentecost/

30. *Tearing SpaceTime* –
http://beforeitsnews.com/prophecy/2014/01/urgent-warning-the-bottomless-pit-is-being-opened-for-end-times-hell-every-nation-is-contributing-financially-to-make-this-happen-must-see-videos-2457616.html

31. *Invasion By Foreign Troops* –
http://www.thecommonsenseshow.com/2014/01/17/enemies-both-foreign-and-domestic-prepare-to-invade-america/

32. *First Jesuit Pope* –
http://www.newswithviews.com/Horn/thomas201.htm

33.   *The Final Pope -*
http://www.newswithviews.com/Horn/thomas167.htm

34.   *The Pope On Trial -*
http://itccs.org/category/video/

35.   *Zombies -* http://www.stevequayle.com/pdf/zombie_pt1.pdf

36.   *Protection of Southern U.S. Border -*
http://www.thepoliticalinsider.com/proof-the-obama-administration-ignored-the-border-crisis-for-political-reasons/

37.   *Drug Cartels in U.S. -*
http://www.thenewamerican.com/usnews/crime/item/18349-cartel-style-billboards-hanged-mannequins-shock-el-paso-citizens

38.   *ISIS Coming Over Border -*
http://www.youtube.com/watch?v=S_RHJgVapGQ

39.   *Muslims Beheading People -*
http://www.ijreview.com/2014/09/181797-8-chilling-facts-oklahoma-beheading-suspects-alleged-facebook-page-reveal-true-motives/?utm_source=dailynewsletter
&utm_medium=email&utm_campaign=%7BCAMPAIGN_ID%7D

40.   *Ebola on Border -*
http://www.infowars.com/ebola-case-in-texas-validates-concerns-over-open-border/

41.   *Tachyons -*
http://en.wikipedia.org/wiki/Tachyon

42.   *Faulty Element -*
http://www.symmetrymagazine.org/article/march-2013/opera-snags-third-tau-neutrino

43.   *OPERA -* http://www.symmetrymagazine.org/article/march-2013/opera-snags-third-tau-neutrino

44.   *LHC Portal -*
http://www.theregister.co.uk/2011/02/01/lhc_upgrade_shutdown_post

poned/

45. *Acoustic Resonance -*
http://en.wikipedia.org/wiki/Acoustic_resonance

46. *Breakdown of Civilization -*
http://www.ipsnews.net/2013/01/experts-fear-collapse-of-global-civilisation/

47. *America To Be Hit With Nuclear Missiles -*
http://www.youtube.com/watch?v=6fGq279mE3Y

48. *Chinese Submarines Off SoCal -*
http://www.infowars.com/wayne-madsen-china-fired-missile-seen-in-southern-california/

49. *Tokyo Evacuated -*
http://enenews.com/japan-doctor-tokyo-longer-be-inhabited-everyone-living-victim-fukushima-disaster-began-notice-childrens-blood-test-results-around-mid-2013-time-running-short-physicians-save-citizens-future-g

50. *Lucifer Device -*
http://www.newswithviews.com/Horn/thomas186.htm

51. *Vatican Observatory -*
http://www.omegashock.com/2014/03/27/alien-deception-vatican-searches-for-alien-god/

52. *UFO at ISS -* http://www.youtube.com/watch?v=pAsxflfMXtg

53. *Who Are They? -*
http://www.newswithviews.com/Horn/thomas187.htm

54. *Jerusalem -* http://www.letusreason.org/Biblexp194.htm

55. *Jews as God's People -*
http://Bible.knowing-jesus.com/topics/Jews-As-God~s-Chosen-People

56. *The NWO -*
http://www.threeworldwars.com/new-world-order.htm

57. *Weird Clouds -*

https://www.youtube.com/watch?v=MjUDGtAzN8w

58. *Electromagnetism* -
http://rsta.royalsocietypublishing.org/content/372/2023/20130292.abstract

59. *Wormholes* -
http://www.youtube.com/watch?v=WHRtdyW9ong

60. *Georgia Guidestones* -
http://vigilantcitizen.com/sinistersites/sinister-sites-the-georgia-guidestones/#!prettyPhoto

61. *Transhumanism* -
http://www.youtube.com/watch?v=v_zICXzhXkQ

62. *The Veil* -
http://the-tabernacle-place.com/articles/what_is_the_tabernacle/tabernacle_holy_of_holies

63. *Ark of the Covenant* -
http://www.jewishvirtuallibrary.org/jsource/Judaism/ark.html

64. *Urimm and Thummim* -
http://www.jewishencyclopedia.com/articles/14609-urim-and-thummim

65. *The Third Jewish Temple* -
http://www.timesofisrael.com/want-mideast-peace-build-the-3rd-temple/

66. *Spring Equinox* - http://www.itv.com/news/west/story/2013-03-20/spring-solstice-at-stonehenge/

67. *Planet X* - http://www.youtube.com/watch?v=qS3JoVkh3Hg

68. *Disclosure* -
http://www.youtube.com/watch?v=WOHGeZZ8JZA

69. *Orbital Perturbations* - http://beforeitsnews.com/watercooler-topics/2014/01/nibiru-position-01-22-2014-armageddon-collision-horizon-ii-iii-2435938.html

70. *Earth Wobbling* -

http://www.youtube.com/watch?v=ohDPoIhA8nA

71. *Weather Changes -*
https://www.youtube.com/watch?v=qm_zTxOXFsE&list=UU6Ck6N7gR
st7qwkXdapbLaQ

72. *Wandering North Pole -*
https://www.youtube.com/watch?v=2MP45u4yyIE

73. *The Flood -*
http://www.apologeticspress.org/apcontent.aspx?category=9&article=64

74. *The Nephilim Corruption -*
http://www.apologeticspress.org/apcontent.aspx?category=9&article=64

75. *The Messiah -*
http://www.drwatchman.com/12/post/2013/12/the-incarnation-of-
dna.html

76. *Corrupting Man's DNA -*
http://www.youtube.com/watch?v=cCTuiugo7mU

77. *Homosapiens 2.0 -* http://www.92y.org/Event/Homosapiens-2-
0-Future-of-Humanity.aspx

78. *Neutron Bombs -* http://en.wikipedia.org/wiki/Neutron_bomb

79. *Tritium -*
http://chemistry.about.com/od/chemistryfaqs/f/neutronbomb.htm

80. *Culling of Man -*
http://thenewalexandrialibrary.com/depopulation.html

81. *Alex Jones -*
http://www.infowars.com/

82. *Matt Drudge -*
http://drudgereport.com/

83. *Exit Plan -*
http://www.shtfplan.com/headline-news/matt-drudge-issues-warning-
have-an-exit-plan_01272014

84.   *PRISM* - http://www.infoplease.com/news/2013/edward-snowden-leaks.html

85.   *Weather Modification* -
http://www.geoengineeringwatch.org/global-weather-modification-assault-causing-climate-chaos-and-environmental-catastrophe-2/

86.   *HAARP Theories* -
http://www.activistpost.com/2014/05/conspiracy-theorists-vindicated-haarp.html

87.   *Lasers For WM* -
http://rt.com/news/dressed-lasers-weather-rain-548/

88.   *Food Riots* -
http://thewatchers.adorraeli.com/2014/06/23/food-prices-are-rising-in-america-researchers-predict-food-shortages-followed-by-mass-riots/

89.   *Gold Ring* -
http://thelastgreatstand.com/lgs/2014/08/23/obamas-ring-there-is-no-god-but-allah/

90.   *Airborne Ebola* -
http://www.cnn.com/2014/09/12/health/ebola-airborne/

91.   *Useless Eaters* -
http://beforeitsnews.com/prophecy/2014/10/had-enough-happening-now-extinction-of-useless-eaters-globalists-have-begun-implementation-of-their-plan-to-kill-90-of-the-population-a-stunning-revelation-2464540.html

92.   *Geomagnetic Currents* -
http://www.sciencedaily.com/releases/2012/07/ 120729142156.htm

93.   *Pole Shift* - http://www.youtube.com/watch?v=m2o1IB9VMUA

94.   *EM & Electronics* -
http://www.newton.dep.anl.gov/askasci/phy00/phy00209.htm

95.   *Ball Lightning* - http://www.youtube.com/watch?v=D62KzIc-R-4

96. *Heavener Runestone -*
http://heavener-runestone.com/

97. *Christians Beheaded -*
http://www.politifact.com/texas/statements/2014/sep/05/ted-cruz/ted-cruz-says-isis-crucifying-christians-iraq-nail/

98. *Demanding Allegiance -*
http://www.thedailybeast.com/articles/2014/10/07/isis-s-gruesome-muslim-death-toll.html

99. *Little Girl Chained To Fence -*
http://www.homelandsecurityus.com/archives/8770

100. *China Facts -*
http://www.echinacities.com/china-media/16-Shocking-Facts-about-Chineses-Economy-Production-and-Natural-Resources

101. *Chinese Economy Crash -*
http://seekingalpha.com/article/2224063-7-signs-chinas-economy-is-headed-for-collapse

102. *Chinese Buying Gold -*
http://www.offthegridnews.com/2014/07/09/what-does-china-know-country-rushes-to-buy-up-worlds-gold/

103. *The Mahdi -*
http://en.wikipedia.org/wiki/Mahdi

104. *The Coming of the Mahdi -*
http://www.inter-islam.org/faith/mahdi1.htm

105. *Caliphate -*
http://www.bbc.com/news/world-middle-east-28849919

106. *Red Headed Giants -*
http://www.youtube.com/watch?v=94iLFmylVO0

107. *Nephilim Today -*
http://www.fallenangels-ckquarterman.com/nephilim-seen-alive/

108. *Nephilim & UFOs* -
http://www.youtube.com/watch?v=1IKlvCbyPx8

109. *HAARP & Time* -
http://beforeitsnews.com/science-and-technology/2012/05/physicist-haarp-manipulates-time-2167703.html

110. *Super Lasers* -
http://rt.com/news/dressed-lasers-weather-rain-548/

111. *HALPS* - http://www.dailymail.co.uk/sciencetech/article-2552589/The-real-life-DEATH-STAR-US-researchers-developing-laser-powerful-Earths-power-stations-combined.html

112. *Harvesting Energy* - http://www.nuenergy.org/nikola-tesla-radiant-energy-system/

113. *Illuminati Plans* -
http://www.youtube.com/watch?v=3szaF5R3wsc

114. *Panspermia Theory* -
http://www.panspermia-theory.com/

115. *ET Is My Brother* -
http://exopolitics.blogs.com/exopolitics/2013/04/the-extraterrestrial-is-my-brother-father-funes-argentinian-jesuit-director-of-vatican-observatory-r.html

116. *The Rapture* - http://www.newwine.org/Articles/PreTrib.htm

117. *Pre-Trib Problems* -
http://www.newwine.org/Articles/PreTrib.htm

118. *Rapture Origin* -
http://www.Bibleanswerstand.org/nuggets_12.htm

119. *Crystal Cave* -
http://www.youtube.com/watch?v=0OLdSJmvcUs

120. *Big Bertha* -
http://en.wikipedia.org/wiki/Bertha_(tunnel_boring_machine)

121.   *Hercolubus -*
http://beforeitsnews.com/space/2013/10/hercolubus-is-coming-warns-top-astronomer-fascinating-video-2467638.html

122.   *Planet X -*
http://www.americaspace.com/?p=62547

123.   *Nibiru Confirmation -*
http://www.youtube.com/watch?v=CV2isidnaYc

124.   *Blue Star Kachina -*
http://www.youtube.com/watch?v=CfQ9nc0aUes

125.   *The Destroyer -*
http://www.youtube.com/watch?v=qzdonWLdESE

126.   *Wormwood -*
https://www.Biblegateway.com/passage/?search=Revelation+8%3A10-11&version=NIV

127.   *Nemesis -*
http://www.youtube.com/watch?v=e5wA-DF_9sI

128.   *The Anunnaki -*
http://www.ufoevidence.org/documents/doc147.htm

129.   *Disclosure -*
http://www.collective-evolution.com/2014/01/15/obama-appoints-ufo-disclosure-advocate-into-administration/

130.   *The Flyby -*
http://www.collective-evolution.com/2014/01/15/obama-appoints-ufo-disclosure-advocate-into-administration/

131.   *Pluto Demoted -*
http://www.space.com/2791-pluto-demoted-longer-planet-highly-controversial-definition.html

132.   *Brown Dwarf -* http://en.wikipedia.org/wiki/Brown_dwarf

133.   *Zecharia Sitchin -*

http://www.mars-earth.com/sitchin.htm

134. *Advanced Aircraft -*
https://www.youtube.com/watch?v=nAnaOXiQO5w

135. *The Illuminati -* http://www.youtube.com/watch?v=YE-Hvo0hSr0

136. *Royal Bloodlines -*
http://www.mindserpent.com/American_History/organization/illuminati/blood11.html

137. *Who Built The Pyramids -*
http://www.youtube.com/watch?v=sXk9d3GZaxk

138. *Nephilim Technology -*
http://beforeitsnews.com/prophecy/2014/02/impossible-3000-year-old-heiroglyphics-depict-modern-day-technology-markings-of-the-fallen-angels-shocking-video-and-pictures-2458842.html

139. *Embedded Nephilim -*
http://socioecohistory.wordpress.com/2014/03/08/karen-hudes-exposes-the-global-puppet-masters-illuminati-the-biblical-nephilim-seed-of-the-serpent-at-the-core-of-the-illuminati/

140. *Fallen Angels & Demons -*
http://www.youtube.com/watch?v=2ti9HGEftmE

141. *Spetsnaz -*
http://en.wikipedia.org/wiki/Spetsnaz

142. *Petroglyphs vs. Hieroglyphs -*
http://www.archaeologywordsmith.com/lookup.php?terms=glyph

143. *Splunkers -*
http://members.socket.net/~joschaper/wspelunk.html

144. *Sun as a Portal -*
http://www.youtube.com/watch?v=2ykXPoCQ9YM

145. *The GRU -*

http://simple.wikipedia.org/wiki/GRU

146. *KGB Defector Warns* -
http://www.youtube.com/watch?v=bX3EZCVj2XA

147. *Proven Conspiracies* - http://www.infowars.com/33-conspiracy-theories-that-turned-out-to-be-true-what-every-person-should-know/

148. *Vote To Throw God Out* -
http://www.youtube.com/watch?v=eUJE9YfsbNQ

149. *President Making Own Laws* -
http://nypost.com/2014/02/15/barack-obama-makes-up-his-own-rules/

150. *Congress Afraid* - http://dailycaller.com/2014/07/15/why-are-boehner-and-the-house-gop-afraid-of-impeaching-obama/

151. *Border Defense Dropped* -
http://www.wnd.com/2014/06/shocking-hidden-agenda-behind-border-crisis/

152. *Third Term* - http://www.youtube.com/watch?v=LAyfJZTd3bs

153. *After Disclosure* -
http://www.youtube.com/watch?v=IMylY_8k02c

154. *Atacama Humanoid* -
http://www.youtube.com/watch?v=xcg3l7VOgZY

155. *Peru Giants* -
http://www.infowars.com/dna-results-for-the-nephilim-skulls-in-peru-are-in-and-the-results-are-absolutely-shocking/

156. *Portals Opening* - http://www.danielholdings.com/pertinent-articles/all-of-these-things-info-in-work/stargates-wormholes-portals/

157. *Suspended Animation* -
http://survincity.com/2012/06/somatic-keep-humanity/

158. *Skyquake* -
http://survincity.com/2012/06/somatic-keep-humanity/

159. *Strange Sounds -*

http://www.youtube.com/watch?v=IZQwyV7wHzM

160. *Blood Moons -*

http://www.elshaddaiministries.us/topics/eclipses.html

161. *Beginning of Sorrows -*

http://www.youtube.com/watch?v=k_C5OnOZfp4

162. *As Above, So Below -*

http://www.godlikeproductions.com/forum1/message1886711/pg1

163. *Prep for Armageddon -*

http://www.youtube.com/watch?v=XW6HXPjQAL8

164. *Land For Debt -*

http://www.thecommonsenseshow.com/2014/01/23/american-citizens-are-one-step-away-from-being-chinese-slaves/

165. *China One Child Policy -*

http://www.businessweek.com/articles/2014-08-01/with-end-of-chinas-one-child-policy-there-hasnt-been-a-baby-boom

166. *One World Government -*

http://www.youtube.com/watch?v=CfJYNiMT7ZU

167. *Spiral in the Sky -*

http://www.youtube.com/watch?v=1hrWjkn_DHs

168. *Mortal Head Wound -*

https://www.Biblegateway.com/passage/?search=rev+13%3A3&version=NASB

169. *One World Religion -* http://www.infowars.com/pope-francis-and-the-emerging-one-world-religion/

170. *False Prophet -* http://www.endtimeupdates.com/pope-francis-may-be-the-false-prophet-of-revelation-according-to-prophecy-says-catholic-theologian/

171. *Peace & Safety -* http://www.youtube.com/watch?v=-

hl3jcNKies

172. *Nimrod -* http://www.youtube.com/watch?v=mYFaVKnlPn4

173. *Mark of the Beast -*
http://www.cbn.com/cbnnews/healthscience/2014/April/RFID-Tech-
Opening-Doors-for-Revelation-Fulfillment/

174. *False Peace -*
http://www.youtube.com/watch?v=TwBBV2zmZqQ

175. *The Blood of the Lamb -*
https://www.Biblegateway.com/passage/?search=rev+12%3A11&version
=NASB

ABOUT THE AUTHOR

Daniel Holdings jokes that he stumbled into being an author. Before he started writing, he'd already been a Christian for a number of years. Through some eye-opening changes in his personal and professional life, he started seeing the world differently. With this paradigm shift, the Bible came alive and sprung off the page. He began to understand "spiritual" things were something much more. Like a thirsty man walking through the desert, he explored the arena of science, specifically physics, to help color the supernatural things that were found in scripture. It was during that same time that he began to discern how many social, political and economic issues of the day were falsely tailored for the public's consumption. The combination of world events seemingly rushing to a conclusion and a public that had been lulled to sleep, disturbed him greatly. That's why he started writing: to warn people. While his books are not designed to be religious or faith based, his stories are shaped by his longtime relationship with Yeshua, Jesus. His first novel "Three Days in the Belly of the Beast" was miraculously found in the Ancient Torah Code. Unbelievably, it also seemed to predict the discovery of the God Particle by CERN the following year. In his second novel, "As The Darkness Falls", he took a hard look at the world's condition. He wrote about the rise of a brutal Islamic State with a Caliph. In early 2014 the real-world ISIS came on to the scene – People were stunned. The author is adamant when he says he is a simple storyteller, inspired by God to speak the truth to a world that would rather stay asleep. Yet, his books continue to captivate with their facsimile to real life. Between The Veil is Mr. Holdings' third novel in The Cooper Chronicles. Daniel is a former businessman and award winning public speaker. The native Californian and veteran, has been married for over thirty years to his wife Vickie and they have a beautiful teenage daughter named Sarrah. The family currently lives in rural America where he is working on several projects. He's host to Hebrew Nation Radio's Prepare The Way and Co-Host To the Monday Morning Show there, The Remnant Road, as well as guests on several shows throughout the year and lectures publically whenever invited. Daniel's website is www.danielholdings.com and be sure to follow him on facebook.